GUARDIAN ANGEL

BY ERIC H. BOWEN

Celesta
Press
Houston

Celesta Press LLC
11200 Fuqua St., STE 100 PMB 155
Houston, Texas 77089
https://www.celestapress.com

This is a work of fiction. The events described here are imaginary. The settings are either entirely fictitious or, when inspired by real-world locations, heavily fictionalized and not intended to represent actual locations or firms. All characters described are fictitious and not intended to represent any specific living persons, whether human, demonic, or divine.

Book Design: Mark Kartischko
Cover Art and Design: Steve Merryman
Editor: Imogen Howson
Illustrations: Warren Muzak

Typeset in TeX Gyre Pagella 11 point.
Display Text: Brilon Regular.

ISBN 979-8-9895129-1-1
Library of Congress Control Number: 2023923777

Other Versions:
Hardcover Library Edition [POD]: ISBN: 979-8-9895129-0-4
e-Book (ePub): ISBN 979-8-9895129-2-8
Softcover Large Type Edition [POD]: 979-8-9895129-3-5

Country of first publication: United States of America

No AI: No Artificial Intelligence was used in the writing, illustration, or cover design of this novel.

For

Clive Staples Lewis

and

The Reverend Billy Graham, Jr.

who lit the fire.

Guardian Angel

CONTENTS

Preface

Those who know me best will agree that I am willing to entertain concepts which push the bounds of orthodoxy to the breaking point and beyond. But, through the years, I have become even more firmly convinced that the sixty-six books of canonical Scripture are in fact divinely inspired and preserved, that every word as originally penned is exactly what God intended to say to men at that point in time, and that the picture of God which it paints is both accurate and authoritative. It truly is living, and powerful, and sharper than any two-edged sword. Take it to heart.

But the genesis of this story comes from two classic Christian authors. First, when I was twelve years old Dr. Billy Graham published his work, *Angels: God's Secret Agents,* which I quickly devoured; it led me to begin studying and thinking about these mysterious messengers. Secondly, in the Preface to "Screwtape

Proposes a Toast" in the Collier Books paperback edition of *The Screwtape Letters*, C. S. Lewis laments that,

> *I had, moreover, a sort of grudge against my book for not being a different book which no one could write. Ideally, Screwtape's advice to Wormwood should have been balanced by archangel advice to the patient's guardian angel. Without this the picture of human life is lopsided. But who could supply the deficiency? Even if a man—and he would have to be a far better man than I—could scale the spiritual heights required, what "answerable style" could he use? For the style would really be part of the content. Mere advice would be no good; every sentence would have to smell of Heaven....*

I TOOK THAT AS A challenge. I began to think, seriously, on what an angel might say when dealing with us fallen humans. A few ideas came to mind. And those drops became a trickle, and the trickle eventually became a steady stream. What you are about to read is the result. Enjoy.

Prologue

The following account was originally written purely for internal distribution. Rather as a lark, I requested permission for a special communication. To my great surprise it was granted, with the proviso that everything be handled on a strictly unofficial basis. Accordingly, names, dates, and places have been changed to protect the innocent on the one hand while shielding those so obviously ridden with guilt from embarrassment on the other. Likewise, information which must regrettably remain confidential for the present has been deleted, but by way of compensation I have included additional material in this edition which may help you to better understand our world and our interactions with yours.

You will note many events which occurred at times or in places where I was not present to observe directly. In reconstructing those events I rely upon material gleaned from other observers or, in some cases, from the interrogation of prisoners. This latter source of information is notoriously unreliable and I utilize it with a great deal of trepidation. I urge you to take accounts which so originate with rather a large grain of salt.

I would also encourage you not to rely too strongly upon my little asides and observations. While I do believe they have validity, my own understanding is still very far from perfect. There are many underlying details which remain secret, even to me. If you wish to have truly reliable information as regards the spiritual realm, I would encourage you to turn to the sixty-six official communications we have made over the past four millennia, which are available in a conveniently compiled format…better known as your Bible.

—Ariel

Chapter One

Introduction

There are good days and there are bad days. But for every day since Michael was conceived, on that late winter night thirty-plus years ago, there has been a letter. Sometimes short and sweet, sometimes long and detailed. Altogether they comprise a comprehensive diary of his life, filling several large mailbags. Dawn treasures them (as do I!) and we look forward to the day we can finally deliver them to him in person, hopefully as souvenirs of a life well lived.

From a good day:

> *Dear Michael: You rode a bicycle today, all by yourself! That's wonderful!*

From a not-so-good day:

> *Dear Michael: You can blame me for calling your mom's attention to you in the store. You know better than to try to sneak candy*

like that! It's stealing! What's worse, it gives the other side another piece of evidence to use against you. I can only plead childish innocence for so long before it starts to ring hollow, even to me!

From another pretty good day:

Dear Michael: I hope that you had a blast at Astroworld! You and your dad rode five roller coasters! I hope you don't mind but Ariel and I reached through and copied your lunch in Western Junction. Just for a taste, you know! The barbecue sandwich wasn't bad but I personally preferred that stuffed baked potato your Dad ordered. I know it's a long shot but someday I'd like the chance to visit that park with you.

From another not-so-good day seven years later:

Dear Michael: So Astroworld closed today, forever. I thought perhaps it might be sold to some other company, but it's being torn down and demolished. Sic transit gloria.

And, from a really bad day a couple of years before that:

Dear Michael: I don't exactly know how to say this to you….

*   *   *

WHILE THERE IS A PAIR of eyes on every one of you every single minute, it may not always be exactly the same pair of eyes. We do like to take the occasional break, after all…talk with friends, relax, sing a bit, recharge batteries…but then it's back out to the Border. We have a pitch staked out there which is close enough for a good view but far enough back to keep from sparking any confrontations with the enemy—well, for the most part.

And so it was that I returned from a quick trip Home one quiet night to find Dawn in an uncharacteristically silent mood, watching Michael through the portal as he slept. A quill was in her right hand and she was tapping it nervously. "Writer's block?" I ventured.

"No, I'm finished," she absently replied.

I haven't been a Counselor for nearly a thousand years for nothing. "Dawn, we've been best friends since before there was a before," I said. "It's not like you to be this quiet."

"Just…thinking."

"About what?"

"You know."

"The big day?"

"Yeah."

"Do you know when it's going to be?

"Ariel, I don't *want* to know. I want to be as surprised as he is!"

"Then what's the problem?"

"It's just…we're so *different!*"

"Sometimes that can be a very good thing!"

"But what is he going to think? I mean, when he knows?

I laughed, and transitioned into something closer to what you might call Full Dress Uniform. It's impressive. "Dawn, I understand that humans tend to be very

Dawn writes a letter.

positively affected when they meet us for the first time. I doubt that you have anything to worry about!"

"Ariel, please! Yes, I know how to put on a show! But what happens when the show's over? What happens when he gets to know *me*, for who I am, not just what I am?" There was a pause, and then she asked, "Do you think he'll like me?"

I chose my words carefully. "Well, if he doesn't, I think he needs more help than this Counselor knows how to offer."

"I wish I knew."

A brief silence; then she added, "Fifteen minutes."

"What?"

"I just wish that I could cross into his world for just fifteen minutes. Not to do anything 'special', not really. Just to get to know him, and give him a chance to know me."

"Oh, nothing 'special'?" I replied with raised eyebrow. "You want to break protocol, cross the Border, possibly touch off a major interdimensional incident, for a spot of tea and a chitchat?"

"I know, I know," she sighed.

"I do admire your spirit. But we both know you wouldn't be satisfied with fifteen minutes. Next there would be fifteen more, then an hour, then a night, then pretty soon you'd be *living* there. Just wait. You'll meet him soon enough."

"Yes. You're right."

Guardian Angel

I turned away, thinking my work was done. Then I heard her mutter, "Even so…it'd be a nice start."

I still can't say exactly when it all started. But, if I had to lay a wager—I'd choose that very moment.

Chapter Two

It Was a Dark and Stormy Night...

Or perhaps not. It could have begun far, far earlier. I'm sure that I could write volumes about the thousands of years of praying, petitioning, practicing, training, learning and serving which it takes to be selected as a Guardian, and perhaps someday I shall. But the young boy whom Dawn had been given to shepherd thirty-plus years back (with my eager assistance!) has now grown into a fine, albeit somewhat nondescript, young man. He lives near his widowed mother in the Eastwood subdivision in Houston's East End, where he grew up after his Green Beret father Samuel Lane Wilson never came home from Iraq. Oh, we were certainly there to welcome Sam Home with us for all time…but it was so hard on the two other members of his family, which

Dawn acknowledged in the somber letter she wrote that night.

Michael Glenn Wilson is a graduate of Austin High School, receiving his diploma in December of 2007, and a Navy veteran having enlisted immediately upon graduation. At first a Machinist's Mate (and still quite handy with tools), upon making petty officer second class with a clean record he transitioned to Master At Arms, the Navy's shipboard police force. His best friend and youthful partner in mischief, Rick Smith, who was a bit of a hellion—what am I saying, Rick *is* a bit of a hellion!—graduated a year and a half ahead of him, joined the Houston Police Department after two years of college and began working his way up the ladder.

Mike re-enlisted, was promoted to first class—and then was let go during a reduction in force. Coming home to Houston with Rick as a reference, Mike applied for a position with the police department, was accepted, and trained in their academy. He graduated and did his time as a rookie officer. Then, through devious channels involving an uncle on his mother's side, he was approached by the local office of the Kansas, Pacific & Gulf Railway. They were looking to add a position for a railroad police officer. Would he be interested? He was.

Railroad police officers in the States have a rather unique status. They are employed by private companies, yes, but they are fully commissioned peace officers with jurisdiction recognized by both state and federal law. Their delegated authority varies from state to state, but at least in Texas they have the full power to conduct investigations and make arrests so long as they are acting to protect railroad property, equipment, employees, freight, or passengers. They do not, however, make traffic stops!

And so it came to pass that on one cold rainy night in late January Michael was walking his beat, which has been aptly described as "100 feet wide and 10,000 miles long." Of course, nobody expected him to walk the full ten thousand miles. As it was, there had been reports of tampering and vandalism in the area. Mike was inconspicuously inspecting the tracks, looking for any evidence of criminal mischief and hoping for the potential lucky break of catching someone in the act. Then Dawn goosed him.

He would have noted it himself, most likely; he is an observant sort. But the all of us working together make a good team. There had been suspicious activity in this area which he remembered from his time as a rookie officer, but nothing had ever come of it. Tonight, something would.

A windowless cargo van with plain white sides pulled up in the driveway of a run-down home in a run-down neighborhood. Two men got out, carrying an ice chest. They brought it to a back door, where they exchanged it for yet another ice chest. This one they carried back to the van, slammed the door, and drove away. Time elapsed: under two minutes.

This activity was, technically, outside of his jurisdiction. But Michael is a peace officer, and his childhood best friend is now a lieutenant in the Narcotics Division of HPD. And he had a pair of binoculars in his raincoat pocket. Along with a notebook.

They really should have run the risk of driving without a license plate.

*　　*　　*

THE WHEELS SOMETIMES GRIND SLOWLY, but at least in this case they ground exceedingly fine. Surveillance was set up in the area, and Michael's initial tip was confirmed. The license plate did turn out to be stolen—fancy that—but they left it on the van; they did not exchange it during the period of observation. A pattern of regular activity was noted and several other potential hot zones were identified. The force did not intend to sit on this one long; opportunities such as this can be very ephemeral. But when the white van was found stripped and abandoned on the far side of town the Narcotics Department was motivated to action. And so it was that just over three weeks after his tip Michael answered a call from his best friend.

"Rick? Hey, what's going on?"

"Michael. Are you alone?"

"Yeah, I'm the only one in the office. Something going on?"

"Can't say. But do you think that you could meet me and a few friends two blocks south of that tip you called in last month at a convenient time? Say, two in the morning, day after tomorrow?"

"I…yes, I can do that."

Rick didn't have to say anything more, but he did. "Oh, by the way, bring your gear—all of it. And keep a low profile."

"Got it!"

*　　*　　*

It Was a Dark and Stormy Night...

SWAT TEAMS DO NOT SPECIALIZE in being discreet. However, in a neighborhood which is filled with bars and houses of ill repute it is important to keep from letting the local yokels know too much too soon about what is going down. There were no obvious congregations of squad cars, although as Mike was driving through the area—in his personal truck, a white Ram, not the Jeep marked "RAILROAD POLICE" with the light bar and the company name and logo—he noted a cruiser on every corner. When he did reach the meeting point, even without specific directions, it was obvious to him; twelve men wearing black windbreakers and with military-style haircuts all waiting quietly in a parking lot, far from any bar or other open business. Four of them were Narcotics; the other eight were SWAT. A similar number, Mike was sure, were waiting a couple blocks north of his tip.

Upon pulling into the lot, Mike was challenged by an officer who showed his badge. "This lot is private property, and it's being used for training tonight."

Mike showed his own badge and ID. "I was asked to come here tonight and meet Lieutenant Rick Smith."

"Rick?" the SWAT officer asked over his shoulder.

"It's OK," Rick said as he stepped towards the pickup. "He's the reason we're here tonight. It was his tip."

"I take it you know to stay in the background?" the SWAT officer asked.

"I'm just here to watch," Mike answered. Then he parked the truck and stepped out.

"We move in exactly seventeen minutes," Rick told him privately. "SWAT will start filtering in a few minutes early. Once we have men on foot surrounding the house, the vehicles move in."

Mike, by now, has grown into a blue-eyed young man of medium height with a medium build; quite unremarkable but we think he looks good. His most notable feature is his shock of thick black hair which tends towards the unkempt. Well, it's thick at the present, but Dawn and I know his genes. Most of that hair is not long for this world; it may not be apparent yet but the countdown has begun. Rick, on the other hand, is a couple inches taller and lanky with green eyes and a notable chin which the ladies swoon over, and very athletic. Mike doesn't exactly skimp on the physical fitness training needed to stay in good standing with his department, but he's not a nut about the subject as Rick is. Rick's sandy hair is also thick and full, but—do I detect traces of Rogaine when I look at him closely? Possibly so.

Time wound down and the officers set out on foot towards their destination two blocks away, two by two. Mike trailed the last pair by a few yards. Dawn and I, of course, were eager to see what was going on. Neither of us were surprised that we couldn't "see" much at all. There are Barriers, you should know. However, the barriers cut both ways. And, when we saw a couple of our colleagues in deep concealment working to keep the waters muddied—and who flashed us a "thumbs-up"— we knew that our request made through Nathan, our current regional commander, the day before was being acted on.

We had asked him—and, by extension, the hierarchy—to "keep it honest." The humans had achieved this much by human effort alone; the last thing we wanted at this point was supernatural interference from the other side.

* * *

DRAGORA WAS BORED.

Of course, when your other realistic option is being the main course on the banquet table in Hell—thank you very much for that image, Mister Clive Staples Lewis—you tend not to protest too much. She could, it is true, hope for promotion...by plotting the downfall of someone in the hierarchy above her. She considered the risk/reward calculation of doing so for a few minutes, looked at the barely competent "help" which surrounded her, and sighed.

Dragora was bored.

At least she had moved up from safeguarding a pusher. This was a fairly successful crack house; in fact, a distribution center. She discouraged selling to retail customers; she had raked one of her associates over the coals two weeks ago for allowing one of the humans to do so. She preferred that they cater to neighborhood pushers...known quantities; much more reliable. The last thing she wanted was to hear a knock on the door at two in the morning.

The knock, in fact, came at two twenty-three.

* * *

THE BUST HAD BEEN WELL-CHOREOGRAPHED. Michael followed the last wave of officers on foot. Behind him, police cruisers set up to protect against exit from the area by car. But they did leave one gap.

Lights are on, Michael noted. As had every other officer on the team. *Someone's awake.* One officer, in full ballistic gear and clutching a warrant, came to the door of the shabby little house. They had tried, but failed, to obtain a true no-knock warrant; thousands of dollars' worth of cocaine can be sent down the johnnyflusher in mere seconds. The judge had stated specifically that the officers had to allow at least fifteen seconds for the occupants to answer the door. The process was being videoed to document compliance. The clock started with the first knock on the door.

"Open up! Police! We have a warrant!" came the voice over the megaphone. Then, again, in Spanish.

Two of the men inside had been up drinking beer and watching a forgettable movie. "You've got the wrong house! Go away!" one called. Neither one thought of acting to destroy the contraband. Our enemies aren't the only ones who know how to use the weapon of confusion.

The door flew open. A rather large armored tank followed behind it.

* * *

ON THE HUMAN SIDE OF the Border, Mike was staying in the background like a good boy. On our side—well, let's just say that Dawn didn't get general's stars by being a good girl.

Oh, yes, my best friend is a Warrior. Well, was a Warrior. No, make that is a…never mind. Suffice it to say that feminine Warriors are unusual among our ranks, but hardly unprecedented; while most of we girls gravitate to the Counselor and Teacher roles we do always leave doors open for exceptional individuals. Dawn actually went high up the ranks, very high. In fact, she was our regional commander in this very same city for the fifty or so years prior to her current assignment. She was at the time on the cusp of yet another promotion; I waxed nostalgic at the thought of my best friend working alongside and advising the archangels before the notice came in that she had a choice; she was at long last being considered as a candidate Guardian. There are two human words which most concisely define the period of deliberation which she required to consider that dilemma. I believe that they are "Planck time."

So spiritual conflict was old hat to Dawn, but she knew better than to interfere. She had been out of the command loop for three decades; away from field operations even longer than that, and she would never disrupt the operation of a well-drilled team. Still, she knew all the tricks—and she was watching.

You normally know within seconds whether you have a fight on your hands or whether the enemy is just going to turn tail and run. In this case, it was the latter. Enemy spirits started to slip away almost immediately.

"Hold! Hold your position! Hold!" Dragora called in a vain attempt to rally her troops. It was no use. While I can't say that any of them had studied calculus—we have—they were all able to integrate the possibilities of them personally escaping a literal fate worse than death in the very near future and every one of them came up with the same answer, slim and none—and Slim just left town. Several of them shot us silent, pleading looks begging us to take them prisoner. It did no good; there have to be *very* special circumstances before we risk taking rebels into the realms under Heaven's jurisdiction, even as prisoners. Their chances were better on the lam…so they lammed.

It did not take long before Ms. Dragora was the only unholy spiritual presence in the room. We were still unlikely to take her prisoner—I think she knew that—but we did intend to ask her a few questions. Not that we expected any honest answers!…but sometimes you can piece together valuable information even from the lies. Anyhow, with only one of her side and three full squads from our side, I have to admit that we let our guard down a bit.

Big mistake.

Without any warning Dragora lunged out at the angel closest to her. You need to understand, when I talk of weapons such as swords and arrows and such, it's not the physical forms which are of concern. We are spirits, and the only thing which can really harm an angel is…another angel. The sword or other weapon simply represents an extension of our own being. Which means that it's difficult to disarm another angel, as well; you can never know what he or she may be concealing. One second Dragora was standing there just minding her own business; the next she was all teeth and claws and who knows what else, tearing into the unfortunate being of poor Gregory.

She had, surreptitiously, engaged a time slope to slow our responses while speeding up her own actions, and now proceeded to eviscerate him spiritually and physically. While the physical damage could be healed, there was so much of it in so little of a time that the reflex action of his spirit to heal his body drained him of the energy he needed to remain conscious and functioning. We were slow to react—and, before we did, she was all

It Was a Dark and Stormy Night...

Dragora

back to Little Miss Innocent with the grin of a Cheshire Cat on her face. We froze. "Turn the other cheek," and all that rot. Sometimes, to be perfectly frank, I'd like to take a few of them into a dark alley and just leave no traces. But yes, I know better than that.

Dragora egged us on, fully aware of the conundrum we faced. "Go ahead," she taunted. " Do unto others'… isn't that right?" Then, when no one took the bait, she stretched indolently and disappeared.

We rushed to Gregory; Dawn was there first. "I can feel him," she called. "He's hurt…hurt bad…but we still have contact." We are immortal, true, but it's possible to so bleed and/or drain one of us that we lose contact with this reality altogether and vanish into infernal realms unknown. Presumably God still knows where we are—but, under the limitations imposed by current agreements, He must remain neutral. And, if WE don't know where we are—it's rather difficult to get back. I'll leave the details of being trapped in the deepest levels of Hell with no way out to your own imagination. But there was still a tenuous contact with Gregory's soul. It would be possible to heal him…best done back Home, we all knew.

Three of his squad mates extended themselves to completely surround his being. Then they opened a portal and carried him back to a safe zone well behind our side of the Border. Philip, Nathan's second in command, looked at the rest of us with a grave reminder.

"Let that be a lesson," he said. "Don't *ever* trust them. Not ever."

Chapter Three

AFTER ACTION REVIEWS

AFTER A NIGHT—OR MORNING—LIKE THAT, nobody gets any sleep. There is evidence to collect and catalog, reports to write, time sheets to fill out…Mike would record his as "HPD Liaison Activity." There were prisoners to book into the local lockup, not to mention CPS to call for the children…three of them, all trained to tell anyone asking that anything questionable belonged to Uncle Frank who was just visiting for the week. A transparent ruse, but I suppose it must have worked at least once—a long time ago in a galaxy far, far away.

But there is a camaraderie among law enforcers. After a successful bust such as this with perpetrators apprehended and evidence seized in full compliance with your rather Byzantine and arcane legal code, making criminal punishment virtually certain to follow, and with—very important!—no human on either side of the law injured or even seriously threatened, there was quite a bit of jubilation and back-slapping. Oh, and on your side, as well.

"What'd we get?" Rick asked one of his detectives who was leaving the house.

"Found a full key of coke…plus a little bit more, about half…but there's over a quarter million in cash all packed and ready to go. We must have just missed another delivery. Too bad, but a good bust. Really good bust!"

Rick turned to slap Mike on the back. "My man! Nice work, for a rent-a-cop!" Yes, Rick knows better than that. But he's that type of personality who pushes things just about as far as he can, all the time. Amy, bless her heart, has done magnificent work keeping him from taking that last step too far. More on that later.

Michael, for his part, gave an exasperated sigh. "Rick, I am not a rent-a-cop!"

Rick gave that haw-haw laugh that Mike hates so much. How their friendship has endured…? Anyway.

Now that Gregory was well taken care of and recovering, we were celebrating amongst ourselves as well. Dawn turned to Nathan. "Thanks for letting me lead in. Like old times!"

"Oh, yes," he replied. "Still the cowboy, I see."

"Cow…*boy?*" She laughed, then pulled a Western hat out of nowhere and clapped it on her head. "Pardner, I was a cowboy before we knew what a cowboy was!"

"I think someone's been working Texas too long," I observed.

"Excuse me, Miss Brit? And just how long did it take you to pick up that accent?"

Really, now! So I worked behind the scenes in Merrie Olde England for nearly nine hundred years before being detached to my present assignment...I *define* the King's English! Quite literally, if you must know. "I do *not* have an accent! You, now, have an accent one could cut with a knife!"

"Ladies!" Nathan interjected.

"Well, she does!"

*   *   *

MIKE COULDN'T HANG AROUND THE scene for very long. He came over to where Rick was still in conversation with his detectives. "Rick? Thanks for letting me watch, but I really need to get back on patrol. This is my scheduled shift."

"Yeah, I understand that," Rick answered. "I'll be busy here another couple of hours. Do the robber barons give you a lunch break?"

"I usually break about five, five thirty or so when I work this shift. Feel like grabbing an early breakfast? Or just a cup of coffee?"

"Yeah, that sounds good! What works for you?"

"How about the Denny's at Gulfgate?"

"Denny's. Gulfgate. Five a.m. I'll be there!"

Mike exchanged his "RAILROAD POLICE" ID vest for his plain black windbreaker on top. "See you!"

*   *   *

On the far side of the Border, there was an After Action Review being conducted as well.

After escaping from us—that's how it felt to her—Dragora was at a loss. Her "command", such as it was, was now gone. Her underlings had fled, but if anyone was going to be tracked down and punished for this failure, it was her. How best to ditch a tail and try to find a new hierarchy where she could start over as an unknown?

She needn't have bothered. She was already being watched. She began to become aware of that fact. Running, now, would most decidedly not be in her best interest. Perhaps she could find a way to make common cause with her observer. "Hello, Dravang."

The subject in question emerged from a few dimensional layers' worth of concealment. He was good at that; more on that later. He was followed by a few of his personal retainers; icy, emotionless enforcers. They were loyal; I can't question that…he held leverage on every single one of them. In a thugocracy the nastiest thugs are the ones who rise to the top.

Not that Dravang *looked* like evil incarnate; oh no no no. He was actually rather handsome, at least to some eyes, with his angular features, black hair and goatee, and steel-blue eyes; he affected a cool, suave, debonair albeit icy exterior. And Dragora herself was not unattractive in a feminine manner…I speak as an expert. Why, it was a match made in…certainly not Heaven!

"My dear Dragora," Dravang spoke. There was a pause as he materialized a kind of podium and began taking notes. "Well?"

"They were on us so quickly!" Dragora pleaded. "We never had a chance!"

"Oh, come now. Your perimeter guards should have spotted that tank miles away! Where were they stationed?"

Ms. Dragora looked very, very uncomfortable.

"I thought so. 'Failure to maintain a proper perimeter.' And what is this that my sources tell me? The police captured *written records?*"

"A notebook. The idiot kept a notebook! I tried to at least get him to put it in code...."

"But you failed. What does that tell me about your abilities?"

"I use what I have to work with! I've got these mindless street hoods, not rocket scientists!"

"So. You admit that you are not competent to recruit a higher caliber of pawn. This is very interesting. And you let every one of them be captured? You couldn't arrange to have even one of them escape when you saw the enemy approaching? Oh, I forgot. You didn't see the enemy approaching. Tell me, how much of a fight did you put up when the situation came to a head? Enemy casualties? Prisoners taken?"

At this, Dragora brightened up. "I got one of them good!"

"One," Dravang responded patronizingly. Dragora looked utterly defeated.

"Well," he continued, "this is going to be an interesting report. I think I can guarantee that, when our prince sees this, you will find yourself reassigned to one of the...lower levels."

"We used to be friends," Dragora muttered.

"Don't be ridiculous. You used me, and I used you. Now I am on the way up, and you, my dear Dragora, are on the way down." He tucked his notes inside a red folder, which he then slipped away into a storage dimension. He turned back to Dragora. "Come with me. We have an appointment."

Through the viewing warp, there was a sudden surge of activity. A couple of the police officers raced from the bust house to their cruisers and roared away.

"What's that?" Dravang wondered aloud. Dragora had the same question, but she kept it to herself.

*　　*　　*

Mike was trudging the two and a half blocks back to his truck as the two of us followed. Give credit where credit is due. Of the three of us, he saw it first.

What's a plumbing truck doing on this street at three in the morning?

*　　*　　*

"Almost there, Leroy."

"'Bout friendly time!" the black man in the passenger seat responded. "God-blessed flat tire!" Actually, he was using much stronger language than that, but an angel needs to be careful about what she puts in a missive intended for public consumption.

At that point a bell began ringing and a pair of red lights ahead of them began flashing. The driver took the Lord's name in vain. I really don't see why; it was just a train. He gunned the accelerator, trying to beat the crossing arms. He failed. At least he had enough sense

28

not to try to drive through them; if he had, this story would be ending right here. The train was moving at a pretty fair clip.

"Friendly (ahem!) train," Leroy muttered. "Diego, I need a smoke!"

"We're almost there. Can't you wait five minutes?"

"No!"

* * *

MIKE OBSERVED THE RAILROAD CROSSING up ahead with professional interest. He saw the light of a train approaching, but it was still out of the block and the signals had not yet activated. He crossed the tracks on foot just as the engineer began his whistle sequence.

At first he thought that the van was going to run the crossing, and prepared to note its license plate thinking that he might have to write a citation. Then he saw how close the train was, and how quickly it was moving, and thought that he might instead be placing a call for an ambulance. Or a coroner.

* * *

"I NEED A SMOKE *NOW*, amigo!"

"Stuff! All right, at least roll down the molly-farewell window!

* * *

TO MIKE'S RELIEF, THE VAN screeched to a stop just clear of the crossing arm. It was over the white line and he could still have written a citation had he chose, but he was willing enough to let the matter drop. Then he studied the van more closely. Brown, with faded white markings reading "Lopez Plumbing." No plumbing license, though; he could see where the license numbers had been removed. No pipe or ladders in the ladder rack. And two men, inside. At three in the morning?

* * *

"YOU OUGHTA TRY ONE TOO, amigo!"

"I ain't gonna touch the stuff. I want to die an old man!"

Leroy flipped his Bic and took a deep, long drag of the cigarette. "Aaaah!"

* * *

THE PASSENGER SIDE WINDOW OF the van rolled down. The flare of the cigarette lighter was just as good as a flashbulb...even better, actually; it lasted longer. Mike got a good look at both driver and passenger through the open window.

It was the same two men he had seen through binoculars the night he first reported the tip on the crack house, three weeks ago.

* * *

WHAT'S THAT MAN IN THE black windbreaker doing standing by this railroad track at three in the morning? Diego asked himself. Then he saw the man pull out a portable radio and speak into it. *Cop!*

* * *

MIKE'S PORTABLE RADIO WAS A railroad walkie-talkie; he did not have direct communications with HPD dispatch. He relayed his message through the railroad dispatcher, asking her to pass it on to local law enforcement. He stressed the urgency.

* * *

IT WAS NOT A LONG train. It passed, still doing every bit of the legally allowed thirty miles an hour—and then some, truth be told—and the tracks were soon clear again. But, while waiting for the crossing arms to go back up, Diego looked ahead in the distance. In the treetops, a couple of blocks away, he saw reflected flashing red and blue lights in the direction of his intended destination. *Shellfish!*

He made an illegal U-turn right on the railroad crossing and floored the accelerator. The nerve of some people!

* * *

THERE WAS THE USUAL CHATTER back and forth on the police radios in the early morning hours. Rick and the others at the crack house let it filter in one ear and out the other. Then came a call which diverted their attention completely.

"Attention all units East End area: Be On the Look Out for brown Chevy cargo van, marked 'Lopez Plumbing,' reported as headed east on Leeland at Cullen at high speed. Suspects associated with drug activity at..."

"That's here!" one of the detectives cried. Others started running to their squad cars, precipitating the activity which Mr. Dravang and Ms. Dragora noted above.

Rick grabbed his radio. "This is Lieutenant Rick Smith, Narcotics. Source of that last report?"

"It was relayed by K. P. & G. railroad dispatch; special agent in area."

"Son of a bitch!" Rick exclaimed, pardon my French. "He did it again!"

*   *   *

THE VAN BLEW THROUGH A stop light at Ernestine. Diego figured that the cops would expect him to head for the freeway, so he headed away from it, making a hard left turn at Lockwood. He slowed down and began to drive almost legally as he figured out his next move. He knew that twenty years of his life was waiting in the cargo bay. At least he knew the neighborhood.

*   *   *

PATROL OFFICER THUY NGUYEN AND her partner Alberto Reyes were cruising their beat in the East End when they heard the radio call about the fleeing van. Thuy turned right from Park Drive onto Lockwood to head south towards the freeway.

Then she saw the van.

*   *   *

DIEGO SAW THE SUDDEN U-TURN and then red and blue flashing lights in the rearview mirror and knew that the jig was up. He floored the accelerator and blew through another stop light, heading northbound. There was another golly-dashed railroad crossing up ahead… at least this one was clear. He ran another red light at Harrisburg. His luck would only hold so long….

*   *   *

"Do you have the camera running?" Thuy called to Alberto.

"Si, Señora!" he answered.

* * *

THERE HAD ONCE BEEN YET another railway line through this neighborhood. Now it was a bicycle and pedestrian trail. Diego swerved left, jumped the median, turned onto it and gunned the accelerator yet again.

If he thought this would shake his pursuer, he was wrong.

* * *

"SUSPECTS ARE HEADED NORTH ON Harrisburg Hike & Bike Trail!" Alberto called out.

"We have backup units en route," the dispatcher promised.

* * *

"WHEN I STOP, YOU JUMP out and *run!*" Diego called. "And don't you dare follow me!"

"You ain't gotta tell me twice!" Leroy replied.

* * *

THE VAN SKIDDED TO A stop on the soft grass. The two men jumped out. "Police! Freeze!" Alberto called over the squad car's bullhorn.

I suppose they couldn't hear. Diego ran one way, Leroy the other. Officers Nguyen and Reyes faced a conundrum. There was no backup in the area yet; it was dark; it was a residential area—and these two were not suspected of anything violent beyond reckless driving. It was not worth pursuing them on foot. "Let's secure the van. Check the tape," Thuy finally said to her partner.

The video showed the van skidding to a stop, the doors opening, the suspects fleeing, but….

"Can't see their faces," Alberto sighed.

Chapter Four

MEETINGS

THE PLANT WAS OLD, VERY old. At least by Colonial standards; where I've spent most of the past thousand years, a residence this old is just getting well broken in. But the original building had been erected in 1913 in order to build Model T automobiles for Henry Ford. Shortly after the successful conclusion of your second World War it was purchased by General Foods and re-purposed into the definitive center for roasting and preparing coffee for consumer consumption. It had grown like Topsy over the decades as wings were added and renovations made, eventually becoming at over a million square feet the largest such enterprise under one roof on your planet. A giant animated neon coffee cup at the top of the seventeen-story decaffeinating tower proclaimed, "Good to the last drip!" for many decades.

But the glory of your earth passes away. Over the years and in the course of several mergers, buyouts, and restructurings the parent corporation transitioned from a producing company to a branding and marketing concern. The production facilities, including this one, were divested and sold off to boost stock prices. The new owners milked what profit they could from the old facility, investing as little in it as possible, and succeeded in running it into the ground. It had roasted its last coffee bean only two years or so previously.

There was speculation that the plant might be purchased by yet another food production operator, or that the whole lot might be razed for condominiums. But no, it was picked up by a private concern in an all-cash deal and re-purposed again. Its new role: paint mixing and fertilizer production.

At least, that's what everyone thought.

*   *   *

THE DELIVERY WINDOW CLOSED AT four in the morning. Odd hours, but the manager had explained that they wanted to have the chemicals unloaded before the regular shift workers arrived at seven. And the customer was always right. They were going to make it, but they had to hustle.

The switch engine crew stopped on the far side of the Milby Street grade crossing after pulling through far enough to deactivate the crossing signals. They came up to the guard shack and knocked on the window.

The security guard was in a sour mood. "You're almost late!"

"I like to think of it as, 'on time,'" the train guard—excuse me; on this side of the pond it's "conductor"—replied. "Got two loads today."

"All right. I'll radio Receiving."

The large, powered, sliding perimeter gate slowly slid open. Originally a simple industrial chain-link fence, it had been reinforced with heavy steel beams all the way around. A logical precaution in these days of terrorism and truck bombs, no? A flagman approached to walk the cars into the building. When the big metal roll-up door was all the way open, he waved a "come ahead" signal to the railroad crew in the locomotive.

The two tank cars were slowly pushed onto the spur track and through the gate. On the side of the car one could read the legend, MAGNESIUM HYDROXIDE and, below that, PRODUCTO DE MÉXICO. The cars made a safety stop beside the old and now unused steam boiler. Then, at another command, they were actually pushed inside the building.

The train crew set the hand brakes on the two cars, then uncoupled the locomotive and withdrew it to beside the boiler. The Receiving crew immediately closed the big roll-up door, securing the cars inside. Their foreman, a scowl on his face, walked up to close out the waybills.

The conductor answered his scowl with a broad smile; the customer is always right! "Sign here, please," he said cheerfully. Inside, though, he was thinking, *Jesus, what a bunch of Grinches. What happened to this place?* He had been with the railroad for thirty years and remembered coming through this very same gate with hopper cars full of rice for Uncle Benji's. It had been friendly and welcoming then. Now…anything but. "Okay. You have twenty-four hours before we start charging demurrage…."

"We know, we know," the foreman spat. "We'll have them unloaded by six tonight."

"See you later!" the conductor called. *Let's get out of here, now!*

They backed the locomotive out of the gate, which slid shut behind them. As they did, they felt a sensation as of almost a weight lifting from them as they left the property.

"Always feels good to get out of this place," the engineer commented.

* * *

Inside the building, barrier screens were unfolded and erected. They bore signs, "HAZARDOUS CHEMICALS – AUTHORIZED PERSONNEL ONLY." I don't see why; magnesium hydroxide slurry is not particularly hazardous; it's the major component of "Milk of Magnesia." It just happens to be quite heavy… almost twice as dense as water…and rather effective at absorbing X-rays.

Not that this was likely to pose a problem; the real owners of the concern had matters choreographed like a ballet. The "special" cars crossed the border only on days when a certain somewhat compromised customs agent was on duty. Plausible deniability and all, you understand. Security guards took station outside of the barrier screens; they were armed. I think you will find that they were not licensed by the State of Texas, however.

Behind the screen, the door to a large freight elevator opened. Inside were six pallets, all filled with large portable totes. A man with a pallet jack began taking them out and lining them up on the loading dock.

From an overhead walkway, a man with a wrench and a measuring stick stepped down onto the car top of the first tank car. He loosened the bolts on the hatch, and then opened the lid. He dropped the measuring stick into the thick, soupy liquid and took a reading. "Eight-six and a half!"

He looked around, carefully. It was not beyond the realm of possibility for a health and safety or environmental inspector to be present watching, although a signal system was in place. Beside the tracks there was a "TRAIN MOVING" sign with a flashing red light which was supposed to be illuminated if special caution was called for. It was dark. He reached his measuring stick into the depths of the slurry again.

It had a hook screwed into its tip.

*   *   *

THE PRECEDING ACTIVITY WAS TAKING place in Building 10. Elsewhere on the property, Building 13 held the office complex. It was a four-story brick building, but only the first and fourth floors were officially in use. The first floor held security posts, safety offices, training rooms, that sort of thing. The fourth floor held the plant manager, personnel, official bookkeeping, and so forth. The second and third floors were no longer occupied. Oh, they had file rooms, dead storage, abandoned offices....

As well as the true management headquarters.

Enrique did *not* appreciate being awakened at four in the morning, especially to hear the news that he had just lost a quarter-million dollars' worth of cash and the equivalent wholesale amount of cocaine. The good news was that his operation was quite compartmentalized. No one in the crack house knew exactly where their source of supply was, and the drugs which came in through this plant were "laundered" through two layers of legitimate business activities before being delivered for wholesale distribution. The van had been bought from a retiring independent plumber for cash but never registered in the name of its new owner; it was untraceable. And Diego had sworn up and down that he and Leroy had observed all of Enrique's security precautions....

The loss of the cash and the drugs was grating, but there was more where they came from. As long as he staunched the damage here and now. "Get them out of the country, right away," he ordered an associate. The associate picked up a mobile "burner" phone to call Diego and then Leroy. They would be on a private jet departing Hobby Airport for a friendly unofficial port of entry in Mexico before sunrise.

*   *   *

THE BAGS HELD FIVE KILOS each. They were weighted, of course, to keep them deep in the soup. The man up top fished for the lines, and then hauled them out one by one. God help him if he missed one.

The bags, dripping with slurry, were dropped into the totes. The totes were lifted with a pallet jack and pulled into Building 12, where a freight elevator lifted them to the third floor. There, they were transferred through a connecting passageway through building 15 into building 16.

The bags were removed from the totes and the traces of magnesium slurry were rinsed from them. Then, they were loaded into clean totes and lifted onto another pallet jack which was then moved into a different freight elevator into Building 20 to await...special handling.

*   *   *

OUR WORLD DOES NOT EXACTLY touch yours, at least not under normal circumstances, but it does overlap. And, especially when you are dealing with matters of concern in the human realm, it is helpful for a spirit to "anchor" his or her base of operations to a specific point in yours. And so it was that the *real* power behind the throne of Enrique's enterprise was just a couple of dimensions removed from…Enrique's office.

Fantar was even more displeased than his pawn Enrique. It takes effort, luck, and more than a little bit of plotting and backstabbing to rise to a position of power in the demonic realms. Fantar had experience with all of that, and then some. His territory of influence covered much of the continental United States, at least in some specialized aspects. He held little direct sway over, say, Hollywood and/or Washington—but when those hierarchies needed stimulants to motivate their creative juices or money to grease political palms, he was the go-to demon. And, in return, he extracted favors such as the shaping of a general *laissez-faire* public attitude about the subject and protection of his activities from the annoying interference of the Dudley Do-Rights of your realm. All in all, they kept each other in power… and in check. Couldn't possibly think of one of them rising high enough to challenge the real Mister Big, now, could we?

Fantar liked the trappings of power. His throne was ornate and ostentatious. Really, there is something to be said for elegance and understatement. He himself maintained a corpulent, bloated appearance which was intended to be intimidating but that I personally think looked rather ridiculous. Dravang approached the throne, bowing low.

"Most noble Fantar!"

"Approach us."

Dravang rose, approached, and knelt before the throne.

"Have you completed your investigation?" Fantar asked.

"Yes, my prince."

"Well?"

Dravang opened a portal and withdrew a blue folder. Not the same one which he had tucked away just over an hour earlier. Dragora, observing from the rear, noted the difference and silently observed the proceedings with increased interest.

"A well-planned enemy assault concealed the police activity," Dravang began. "Our commander attempted to defend our position, but was overwhelmed by superior force. This was a clear-cut case of totally unjustified enemy interference in our affairs. I think some retaliation is in order. I'm formulating a plan."

Fantar nodded, satisfied. "Very well. And what about her?"

"She was caught up in circumstances beyond her control. I recommend temporary demotion and reassignment to my detail for additional training."

"So be it."

Reaming Out

Dravang bowed his head again. "By your command, my prince." He respectfully backed away from the throne, then turned to leave. He grasped Dragora by the arm and drew her away. When they were in a position to communicate privately he said, "You owe me."

"I know."

* * *

MIKE ARRIVED AT DENNY'S JUST three minutes after five. There were two police vehicles in the parking lot but… not Rick. Inside four patrol officers were chatting and working on a hearty breakfast as they shared a booth. Mike nodded to them, then took a place at another booth nearby.

Rick was normally prompt. Mike waited ten minutes before figuring that something must have come up, whereupon he placed his order. Ten minutes later, shortly after his food had arrived, Rick walked in through the door.

"Sorry I'm late," Rick said. "But it's all your fault!"

"Uh-oh. What did I do?"

"You know what was in that van? *Twelve keys* of pure cocaine! Two ice chests full—the lab guys could hardly believe it!"

The four officers at the nearby table perked up immediately when they overheard this. Yes, cops do eavesdrop. So do others—visible and invisible.

"Did you catch the driver?"

Rick sighed. "No, the driver and passenger got away on foot. Patrol car took video, but it's not clear enough to ID a suspect. I've got detectives checking the van for physical evidence right now, but so far no leads. You're the only one who saw them." He paused. "How good a look did you get of them?"

"Pretty good."

"Good to know. We might need to have you come in; I'll keep that in mind. Really good bust tonight. Nice work, rent-a-cop!"

The police officers finishing up their meal at the next table laughed. Mike just sighed. Rick continued, "You could always rejoin the force, you know. We'd love to have you back!"

"Well, Rick, I kind of like working alone."

"It can get dangerous out there without someone to watch your back."

*   *   *

NOT BEING TIED TO A physical body means that nourishment is hardly a necessity for us, but being very much engaged with your world we do enjoy the occasional taste of a culinary delight. However, Denny's doesn't really appeal to me. Instead, I reached back Homeward and requisitioned a small sample from the King's table. Ah. Very satisfactory.

Dawn did likewise, although in accordance with her position as lead Guardian she copied a bit of Mike's breakfast and dutifully tasted it. Nothing spectacular, but nothing worth warning him about, either. The two of us reached out hoping to make contact with Amy, Rick's Guardian. Soon we succeeded.

With all of the dimensional layers and connections and barriers and whatnot it's not as simple for us to greet one another out here on the Border as it is back Home, or for you to greet a friend on a street corner for that matter, but it can be done—particularly if you already have a preexisting personal link. We suspected that Amy would welcome the companionship. We were correct.

"Good morning, Amy!" said Dawn after the link fully opened.

"Hi, Dawn. Hello, Ariel," she replied. She seemed dejected. Strange; Rick has wanted to be a law enforcement officer ever since boyhood and Amy latched on to that and did everything in her considerable power to assist him in that goal. I must modestly add that Dawn's seniority and connections were quite a bit of a help along the way once the two boys became best friends. The events of this morning should have been a triumph for her.

"Cheer up, Amy!" said Dawn. "I really don't think you're going to have to worry about your boy's annual evaluations this year!" Rick truly is a good officer, and an honest cop, but his personal life keeps him…shall we say, "on the edge?" More on that later.

"That's the least of my worries."

Her concern was genuine. I immediately shifted into full-blown Counselor mode. "Would you be willing to talk it out?"

"I thought I had contact with his soul. I thought I was finally in position to really work on him. But…."

She sighed. "He's dropped another layer. At least. I don't know how much deeper I can go. I'm not giving up yet. But I'm afraid…I'm going to lose him!"

Ouch. Nothing eats on a Guardian's heart more than that prospect. Nothing. Almost across the board, you'll find that Guardians would be willing to trade places with their charges if only that meant the humans could finally be rescued. Unfortunately, with the present state of affairs, it is more likely that both would be lost.

We trace our profession back to the years immediately following the Flood. In the antediluvian world, angels and humans interacted routinely. Who do you think coached Eve through her first pregnancy? But, once the realms were well and truly divided and the enemy was officially barred from directly entering yours, a question was raised by the other side. There were certain humans who were calling out for the enemy's involvement. Might they be allowed to assign demonic familiars to shadow humans in whom they had a particular interest and aid them in their activities? After some consideration the agreement was reached that, yes, this would be permitted provided that we ourselves were also able to assign Guardians to any humans in which *we* had a particular interest. We most carefully did not mention that we intended to take a "particular interest" in every single human being to walk the face of your planet.

"I keep second-guessing myself," Amy continued. "Maybe I should have *let* him get in trouble! Maybe I shouldn't have worked so hard to smooth things over with Internal Affairs! If he'd just had a run of bad luck, maybe he'd be more inclined to look for some help!"

"You mustn't blame yourself," I told Amy. I shot a warning look at Dawn. She misinterpreted it. Silence would have been best, just then. Sigh.

"You can't give up now," Dawn said encouragingly. "Not when you're this close!"

"Listen to her," Amy said bitterly. "She goes right out there, and she gets him. First time! Me, I've lost three. Going on four."

"Amy…."

"There won't be five. Once I'm done with Rick, one way or the other…I'm done. I just can't take it any more!"

When you do attain the status of Guardian, a Guardian you remain until you succeed in bringing a human Home from Earth. Unless, like Amy, you reach the point where the heartbreak grows too much to bear. There is still a role for you; experts with actual working knowledge of the human world have a place, always. But I don't know of a single ex-Guardian who wouldn't trade the status of an elder statesman for the joy of bringing a partner Home, even just one time.

*   *   *

"So, what's the report on Gregory?" Nathan asked.

"Not good," Philip replied. "It's not just the physical damage; there was trauma inflicted on multiple psychic levels."

"That quick? Vicious. Maybe we shouldn't have let her go, after all."

"We both know the Rules."

"Yeah. So, how long before he's fit to return to front-line duty?"

"The therapists are saying it could be six months!"

"Ouch. That leaves a hole on the team. Sorry to lose him, but we'll find him an opening in some other sector. Maybe your old neighborhood?"

"China? Could be, lots of potential openings there. I'll stay in touch with them."

"Right. Okay, who's available at the top of the waiting list?"

*   *   *

"I'M JUST ABOUT TO START my days off after I get off shift this morning," Mike told Rick.

"You know," Rick said, "a couple of the guys were going to join me and visit the club tonight. Why don't you come along?"

Mike hesitated a second before answering, "Nah. That's not me."

"Are you sure? I think you would enjoy some beautiful scenery!"

Mike set down his coffee cup. The nearby booths were now empty, but he kept his voice low. "Rick, for the life of me I don't understand how you made lieutenant when you keep hanging out in that place!"

"It's a perfectly legitimate topless joint. Business center and all. Never any vice activity as far back as we have records. I don't mix business and pleasure." He waited a second and then continued. "But maybe you should. Have you ever really had a girlfriend?"

That's a sore subject. "Not like you've had. Three, or is it four?"

"Looking for number five, actually. Number four…I found she swapped sugar pills for her birth control without telling me. Trying to get me hooked. I bailed just in time." (Girls, not entirely wise to attempt such subterfuge with a boyfriend who is also a narcotics detective…)

"Charming."

"You gotta look out for yourself; nobody else is! There's plenty of fish in the sea! Get in the swim!"

"Not like that."

"And why not? I guess all that Sunday School your parents dragged you to ruined you!"

"You might believe that. I don't."

"Seriously, Mike, why not?"

Mike sighed and took a sip of coffee. Rick was still looking the question at him. Mike sighed again. "All right. Yes, it was Sunday School. Just before Dad got his orders to Iraq, and we moved to Fort Campbell. December '02, I'd just turned twelve. My Sunday school teacher, Chuck Harrison, challenged us to trust God to find the right girl for us."

"Trust God?" Rick guffawed. "Mike, you kill me!"

"Seriously. Who else knows every single girl out there? He might have someone in mind I'd never find any other way!"

"Or he might not give a rat's ass one way or the other! Mike, you're thirty years old now! Thirty-one?

Thirty-two? I lose count. What happens when you're sixty years old and still single?"

"At least I won't be dealing with five exes!"

That brought Rick up short. "Mike, c'mon!" he finally said. "Take a walk on the wild side! That Sunday school teacher's probably dead by now!"

"He's not. I see him at church once in a while."

"So you still let him tell you what to do?"

"It's not just him. I asked my dad about it, just before he deployed. He told me it was a great idea and that he found my mom the same way. He was KIA not three months later. I'm doing it for him as well."

"Mike, you really want ghosts running your life? See how the other half lives! This place is great! And they like having cops there. Show your badge, and they waive the cover charge!"

Mike looked aghast. "I can't do that! K. P. & G. would have my hide!"

"You only have to do it once. Their maître d' has a good memory. Hey, you're a Navy man. I can't believe you'd ignore a target-rich environment!"

"Rick...look. I don't just want a girl, I want a girl *friend*. I want someone who's going to commit, to be with me for the long term. I'd rather do it right than do it over!"

Rick looked his best friend in the eye and said, "Friendship is overrated. Come with me tonight, and you'll meet all of the wild and luscious women you ever dared to dream about. If you want a friend"—he paused—"buy a dog!"

*   *   *

SHE'S VERY CUTE. SHE'S A Cocker-terrier mix. Mike named her Sassy.

Chapter Five

EXECUTIVE DECISIONS

THE EXECUTIVE CENTER REALLY IS one of the finer establishments of its type, I suppose. Slightly over twelve thousand square feet, if you include the kitchen and the performers' dressing rooms. Or undressing rooms. Whatever.

There is a business center with scanners, fax machines and color laser printers; they advertise the availability of the best wireless Internet in town. It's probably true. The kitchen, also, is one of the better-run such facilities in the city; at the very least it has never shown up on the nightly newscast's restaurant report. The bar is generously stocked; even their "well" liquors would appear on some of their competitors' premium lists. All in all, I could see reasons to frequent the concern even without the attractions of the main draw.

Those attractions are, of course, almost entirely feminine. Especially in the customer service positions. Oh, the maître d's are male, as are the bouncers and two of the bartenders but…that's about it. And the ladies employed there all must possess…let us say, cup sizes towards the starboard side of the alphabet. I mean, I appreciate an admiring glance as much as any other girl, but to carry such a display around *all the time*…! Thank you, but I'll pass.

Rick entered the doorway, followed by three other officers. For one, it was his first time. The maître d' greeted them warmly. "Welcome back, Mr. Smith!"

*　*　*

A very few levels distant, the welcome was not nearly so warm. "Oh, no. Not you. Not here!" the enforcer told Stephen.

The officer's Guardian had come too close to the Border. Other enforcers converged on the area. Legally we are supposed to have safe-conduct to remain with our partners, but that doesn't mean that we can't get dusted up now and again. As the saying goes, don't bring a knife to a gun fight. Trying to argue out of a law book is even worse. Stephen sighed and retreated.

The enforcer eyed the rest of the Guardians suspiciously. His next words were directed specifically at Amy. "You know the drill!"

"We know," she sighed. "We know." They retreated back a couple of levels. They could still watch, but if something happened….

Well, they could *watch*.

*　*　*

"And I see you've brought friends," the maître d' continued. "Mr. Hoth, Mr. Martin, good to see you again!" He began to open checks, placing an inconspicuous mark in a box at the lower right on each card. "And is this a new face?"

"Jim Thompson. He works with us."

"Oh, I'm very glad to hear that, Mr. Smith, but…."

Rick spoke to the newcomer in a low voice. "Show him, Jim. It's okay."

Somewhat embarrassed, the rookie officer opened his ID folder and showed his badge. The maître d' nodded and made the same inconspicuous check mark on Jim's order card. "This way, gentlemen. Would you like a table near the stage?"

*   *   *

Click.

Oh, no human camera recorded Officer Thompson flashing his badge in exchange for a gratuity. There was no physical evidence which Internal Affairs could ever subpoena. But in the library of dark secrets, the moment was recorded. If at any time in the future the enemy ever needed "leverage" on young Officer Thompson, it would come out.

Dravang looked satisfied. The complimentary cover charges had done more for him than any amount of leg-breaking had ever done for Prince Fantar. It wasn't just police officers who had swallowed the hook; he had a rather nice file of local politicians, also. Even a few judges…. Well.

Dragora was observing the showgirls dancing with a professional eye. They did have some talents aside from their large…personalities, yes. She turned back to Dravang. "My, my, my. Wouldn't our esteemed Prince Fantar just love to see you building your own little empire around here?

He gave her a deadly look. "Don't you even think about it. I have more on you than you'll ever have on me!"

She gave an uncomfortable laugh. As far as she knew, he was right. She changed the subject. "I'm surprised to see you in a place like this. I thought these 'physical indulgences' were beneath you!"

Dravang regarded her narrowly. "You always did have a penchant for living dangerously. It almost got you into real trouble, once before."

"That world belongs to *us*. Those people belong to *us*. At one time we weren't so inhibited in dealing with them!"

"And you were rather less inhibited than most, as I recall."

"Now, listen! I did not let things get out of control! I was not about to be saddled with some half-breed brat!"

"How fortunate. Otherwise you might have ended up locked away in irons like so many of the others these past five thousand years or so. But you do like to be involved. Directly. You can't be very happy with our current policy to stay under cover. Camouflage our activities. Never show our faces. Is that right?"

"Where are you going with this, Dravang?"

"Up, my dear Dragora. Up. Care to come along for the ride?"

*　*　*

Dravang

Earlier that same morning…

All-night twelve hour shifts are exhausting. And then there's turnover. Mike has been with K. P. & G. for just over a year and a half, now, but at least in the local office he's still "the new guy" and ends up with the schedules no one else wants. Officially he was relieved at ten a.m., but he didn't get out of the office until almost ten-thirty. Fortunately it was not a long drive home, and he had the next three days off.

But before heading home he took a short break for sightseeing. The local offices for the railroad are on floors six and seven of a forty-story office tower in downtown Houston. True, the police department office takes up only a few hundred square feet of the sixth floor but, things being what they are and what with being a peace officer and a friend of the building engineer who is also a Navy veteran, Michael has obtained a maintenance sub-master key which gives him access to most of the support areas of the building. Including the roof. It's a nice view, even from our perspective, and Mike finds his way upstairs to take it in several times a week. Especially at night; the city lights laid out like a carpet below are magical.

His mother still lives in the old family house in Eastwood. Mike is nearby, but he bought his own place with a VA loan shortly after graduating from the police academy. Older home, but nice; wood floors, very high ceilings. It doesn't look good to be living in your mother's basement when you're nearly thirty.

That also means that his mother is unavailable to clean for him. And that is a problem. Mike is not much of a bachelor housekeeper. To be perfectly frank, the place is a pig sty. Well, it was. A new puppy in the home didn't help matters; there was a puddle and a pile to deal with before putting her on the leash for a short walk around the block.

Returning, he looked around the living room, cluttered with thirty years' worth of mementos going back to baby pictures. Mike, bless him, is a sentimental type with a fondness for old music and functional antiques; in that home you'll find everything from a couple of his grandfather's old repair manuals and tool bags, reminding him of the teenage days Glenn spent showing him how to work on cars, and some memories from his parents which he rescued when his mother, ever the practical type, was going to throw them away. One of those is his father's military portrait and Purple Heart. He looked at it, closed his eyes, and sighed.

Dawn was there in an instant. He couldn't see her, of course, but as she protectively curled a wing about him he felt a touch of comfort and sensed the thought, *Remember the good times!*

It was at the Army base in Stuttgart. Mike was… what, three years old? Not yet four, I do believe; I can look through Dawn's letters to be sure. There was a pool party for Sam's company; Mike's parents brought him along. The young Michael was playing in the shallow end of the pool as his father talked.

"So, do you think it's going to be over soon?" Sam asked.

"I dunno. I can't see any end in sight," the other soldier replied with a sigh. "I just got back from the Middle East. It's a mess. You scheduled to deploy there any time soon?"

"Not that I know about," Sam answered. "I hope it'll be a while."

Mike wasn't listening to this conversation, of course. His attention was on the other side of the pool, on an eight-foot water slide. To the eyes of a three-year-old, it seemed absolutely huge. Other kids were playing on and around it, sliding down happily into the four-foot-deep water. Michael stood not quite three feet tall at the time. He was envious.

Sam noticed. Actually, I must say that Dawn "helped" him notice. Not that it required much of an effort. He spoke to his son. "Do you want to go down the slide?"

"Uh huh," Mike answered tentatively.

"Go ahead!"

"I can't swim!" young Mike cried.

Sam made his way over towards the foot of the slide, positioning himself near its end. "Don't be afraid!" he called. "I'll catch you!"

Mike was encouraged. He climbed the (seemingly!) towering ladder, all the way to the top, and uncertainly took his seat on the top of the slide. He looked downward, at his father waiting far below, and took courage. He pushed off.

Quickly he zipped down the slide and off its edge, hanging in midair for a heart-stopping fraction of a second. Then he plunged into the deep water and a wave of fear flashed over him. But an instant later he felt his father's strong arms wrapping around him and bringing him to the surface. He drew a breath of air, then laughed delightedly.

The flashback ends here. Special Agent Michael Wilson finished undressing, and then climbed into bed, little Sassy curled up beside him.

Chapter Six

REVENGE

THE SCENE NOW RETURNS TO the offices where the real decisions for this realm of the kingdom of darkness are made. Dravang, Dragora, and Fantar were watching Enrique talk on a mobile phone.

"Tony? Ricky. I want you to put your ear to the ground. Find out how the cops busted our guys last night. And when you do find out I may have a job for your boys. Got that?"

"Well? Satisfied?" Fantar asked Dravang who was kneeling before him.

"Quite so, my prince," he answered. "If you will excuse me?"

"You may go."

Dravang bowed obsequiously once again, then withdrew and took Dragora by the hand. They disappeared from the demon prince's lair.

They reappeared in Dravang's comfortable circumstances at the Executive Center. Dragora eyed Dravang suspiciously. "This is a very dangerous game you're playing."

"How so? I have already been authorized to take retaliatory measures. The murder of a detective qualifies quite nicely, I would think. It will anger the other police officers, true, but that's only to be expected, is it not?"

"But if Fantar finds out your real plan…."

"How is he to know?" His voice took on a harder edge. "And, if he does, it's simply your word against mine."

He paused to observe her, and then continued. "Our prince has committed a grave strategic error. Humans love to look for conspiracies, for links between our activities. *We* should be the conspiracy; invisible, untouchable, untraceable. Instead, he has woven his pawns into a net that other humans can unravel. It will cost him."

"And you might just 'help' with the unraveling?"

"The possibility exists. And when everything collapses around him, Fantar's influence will be gone. It will be time for a restructuring of our activities. The humans are ripe for a more direct approach. We have hidden long enough."

*   *   *

"Sir, I'm very happy to be here!"

"Glad to have you, Timothy," said Nathan as he shook hands. "Any prior experience?"

"Well, I've been fully trained," said the newcomer. "But…"

"…no previous field experience," finished Nathan. "Okay. We'll put you with a running mate for a month. Go everywhere he goes, watch everything he does. Just try not to be overly eager to 'help' until you get some experience, okay?"

"Okay!" Timothy agreed with an eager expression.

"Whose turn is it?" Nathan asked Philip.

"Hmm. Actually, it should be Greg's," Philip answered.

"Who's next on the list?"

"Well, that would be… Never mind. I'll take him myself!"

"Are you sure? Might be some action coming up!"

"I know. That's why."

The new recruit smiled.

*　　*　　*

RICK HAD HIT A DEAD end. The detectives searching the van had found no physical evidence which would be useful for identifying the suspects. They had worn disposable gloves and left no fingerprints; as far as DNA was concerned, one of Enrique's underlings had connections with some local barber shops and the lab technicians had thrown their hands up after finding more than twenty different and unrelated hair samples in the first few batches they had tested.

So Rick called K. P. & G. to request Michael's presence downtown in the main offices of HPD. There, he spent some time speaking with a sketch artist about the suspects he had seen. The composites would be fed into a facial recognition database; hopefully there would be a match which he could positively identify. Now Mike was headed to the cinema to enjoy the rest of his day off taking in a movie.

I suppose every peace officer has feet of clay in some area or other. In Michael's case, the most annoying from our perspective is related to his distaste for the use of restraining harnesses while in his personal vehicle.

"Michael," Dawn whispered. "Seat belts?"

His hand did drop to his side for an instant, but just then a gap in traffic opened up to his left and he quickly swerved to change lanes into it. An exasperated horn sounded.

Dawn gave a disgusted sigh. "Sometimes I don't know why I even try!"

I chuckled.

"You could at least turn on the radio," Dawn muttered.

It got through. Michael turned on the satellite radio, which was tuned to the oldies station. In what universe is a song written less than seventy years ago called an "oldie?"

But the tune which came forth from the speakers was one of our favorites. Once in a very great while, your song writers truly do hit the nail on the head. One such was recorded by The Association, namely "Cherish." Dawn heard it coming over the radio and sighed with wistful longing, as it so clearly described the feelings hiding within her own heart for Michael....

Just at that moment, the both of us heard a call. From headquarters.

"Ariel?"

"I'll take care of it," I replied. "Back in a bit."

* * *

By the time I returned, the movie had already commenced. The crowd was sparse, but everyone else was at least with a date. Michael was the only one there alone. If he was self-conscious about it, it didn't show.

Perhaps because, of course, he was not truly alone. Dawn was in the empty seat next to him, just as close to the Border as she could possibly come without setting off alarm bells. She reached through and copied a helping of his popcorn. The song "Cherish" was still running through her head.

Oh, Mike, you really don't know how many times I've wished that I could hold you, shape you, tell you how deeply you're loved. And if only you might someday come to feel the same way about me....

As I watched, he nonchalantly threw his arm around the empty seat to his right where Dawn nestled beside him. With a sigh, she laid her head next to his. I normally would never dream of disturbing such a touching picture, but this was important. "Dawn?"

She looked at me. "Well? What's up?"

"Possibly some rather disturbing news." But then, I looked around the theater with slightly more discerning eyes. Some shadowy forms were watching. Were they watching that closely? I knew that I could not hear them—but was it possible that they could hear us? Did I know their capabilities that well?

"Spill it!" Dawn commanded.

I made my decision. It could wait. "Not here; not now. Later."

"All right."

She resumed watching the movie, while I watched the two of them and wondered.

*　　*　　*

You must understand that the enemy kingdom is not a monolith.

And that's the way the management likes it. They enjoy playing factions off against each other, backstabbing here, undermining there. Survival of the fittest and all that, you know. The weak must deserve their fate.

But there are a few—a very few—of the weak who would like to change their fate. Actually, I'm sure that there are quite a number; but most of them simply don't believe that they would succeed even if they tried. Perhaps they are right. But a handful of them are desperate enough to try.

Please understand; I am not offering a "deal". I am not so authorized. Even if I were I would still hesitate; suppose that the other side were to offer a better one? We are not out to become the highest bidder, especially when the auction house is packed with shills. But I will state that, regardless of your present affiliation, if you wish to coöperate with us and offer us information without preconditions, we will accept it. We can promise you nothing in return; certainly nothing as generous as the offer of salvation by grace through faith which has been extended to human beings for the past two thousand years. But everything will eventually come out in the wash; that I do believe; and if you wish to try to throw in a little detergent—well, I'm confident that it won't hurt.

So it is that sometimes we develop inside intelligence from sometimes reliable sources. And sometimes those tidbits of information match. I'm certain that the Throne could confirm such bits and pieces without question, but He plays by the rules. Strictly. We angels must develop and evaluate the intelligence on our own. And this latest news was somewhat disturbing.

Or was it? It could be the very best thing that could possibly happen to both Michael and Dawn! I mean, Michael belongs to us, no question about that whatsoever. It's simply a matter of when. And if when is now, then why not? Mike has very few Earthly ties, no wife, no children. His mother is really his only close living relative—his uncle's family is in Topeka—and it wouldn't take much to bring her along as well in the very near future; the condition of her heart is questionable. He really doesn't have a lot of close friends who don't also belong to us.

Save one. And that one is important to him. In spite of his exasperating manner, Rick really is a true friend. And what of the world beyond our own tight little circle? Were there other lives which Mike would someday be in a position to touch? It was a thorny question. I prayed that Dawn would have the wisdom to know the correct answer.

Guardian Angel

Dawn

Right now she was preparing to write her nightly letter. Her desk materialized before her, and then she gestured and an inkwell appeared. She pulled a piece of parchment from thin air, and then plucked a feather from her own wing and dipped it in ink as she mused upon how to begin.

"Have you told her yet?" Nathan asked from beside me. I was startled.

"Told me what?" Dawn asked.

"Not yet," I said. "I was going to let her finish this."

"Tell me now!"

"Dawn, it's Michael. We think they might...." My voice trailed off.

Nathan was more forthright. "We've seen some disturbing enemy activity." He didn't speak about the intelligence; he didn't have to. "We think they might be planning an attack. Revenge for the other night. And we think the most likely target is...." He gestured at the sleeping Michael.

"Dawn," I said, "we think they're going to try to take him out."

I was concerned; I wasn't sure how she was going to take the news. I needn't have worried. She became calm; almost frighteningly calm. "When?"

"Soon. Very soon," I answered.

"Next couple of days, most likely," Nathan said.

"So. What do we do?" Dawn asked.

"It's up to you."

This surprised her. "What?"

"I've already checked. He's going to let you make the call." I hesitated a second. "We all know how much you've wanted to…."

I honestly wasn't expecting a laugh. "Ariel, I'm not ready to retire just yet!" Then she added, "I do think that after all these years a trained Counselor should know me better than that! Maybe that's the problem. You're a Counselor; when something goes wrong you say, 'Let's talk this out.' Me, I'm a Warrior. I want to go kill something!"

The mood was much lighter now. Nathan smiled. I chuckled and said, "So we fight."

"You better believe it." She turned to Nathan. "What can you give me for backup?"

Now it was Nathan's turn to look very uncomfortable.

"Nathan? I don't like that look, Nathan!"

"I'm stretched thin enough as it is. And we're really not sure about this. It could be a ruse; a deception meant to pull us off guard somewhere else." He hesitated, then added, "You could pull rank on me."

Dawn shook her head. "I wouldn't do that to you; I used to have your job. But, if we get in trouble, you will come, right?"

"Absolutely."

"Fair enough. See you later."

Chapter Seven

BREAKTHROUGH

THE NEXT FEW DAYS PASSED uneventfully. I honestly thought the window of opportunity had passed and that the reported threat really was a feint, after all. These things generally resolve themselves within three days; more on that later. Mike had three full days off, and then three more days on the twelve-hour night shift.

He was conducting a foot patrol through the Old South Yard, checking physical security of the boxcars and shipping containers. Just another routine night in the life of a railroad special agent. It was coming up on three of a quiet Sunday morning, and he needed a cup of coffee. There was a Thermos of it in his Jeep.

The Houston Police officers had noted his Jeep earlier while driving through the area patrolling their own beat, but a marked railroad police vehicle parked in a railroad yard is hardly suspicious. They saw Mike stepping out of the shadows and opening the passenger door to retrieve his coffee as they drove past again, and he saw them as well and toasted them with the Thermos. They waved back and continued on their way.

Mike refreshed himself with a sip of coffee, then called in to the railroad dispatcher making his hourly roll call report. He picked up his clipboard, locked the door of the Jeep, and headed out to check the last two tracks' worth of rail cars.

It was a fine night, clear and cold, and all the stars in the sky were out. But no moon. A "blue norther"—the local name for a winter cold front—had recently blown through town, and the temperature was just above freezing. All the rain had dried up, though, and you couldn't have asked for a prettier introduction to the wee hours of the day. I was looking up, actually, refreshing my acquaintance with your constellations as seen from the surface of this world. Vega and Arcturus were especially prominent. There really wasn't much else to look at other than old boxcars and hopper cars covered with graffiti.

Perhaps I should have been paying closer attention. Dawn was. "Ariel," she said presently, "do you sense anything?"

"Nothing, Chief."

"Too nothing. I think we're being blocked!"

Alarmed, I turned up my senses. I felt…it felt like mush! "You could be right," I reluctantly agreed.

"I know I'm right. Mike, get out of here!"

A hint of it got through. Mike froze, and looked around as though sensing something. But he only got the barest hint. When nothing was obvious to his own senses, and knowing that this boring task was nearly complete, he tapped his clipboard for a second and then resumed his walk to check car seals and integrity.

"That tears it. Ariel, get us some backup, now!"

I tried to call in some of our friends. Nothing! "I can't reach anybody!"

Dawn drew her sword. I hadn't seen it unsheathed for action in over a century. She looked around dangerously. "Go. Get help. Anyone you can find. Get back here, right away!"

"*What?*" I cried. "Leave you here by yourself?"

"Just do it!"

I know a military order when I hear one. But carrying it out wasn't quite so easy. This empty rail yard was *packed*, I realized as I tried to penetrate the enemy perimeter. Some of them converged on me. I'm no Warrior, but I do know a few moves myself. Dawn has trained me better than whoever was managing them. It took some doing, but I got through. And then I got away fast.

Unfortunately, now the other side knew that we knew. And numbers do count for something in combat. They pressed in around my solitary friend.

"I can't see!" she cried out as she attempted to fight her way through the static and keep watch on her charge.

*   *   *

There was motion down towards the end of the line of cars. With the slight hint of Dawn's warning still in the back of his mind, Mike unholstered his sidearm and approached quietly and carefully. It's a .45 caliber Colt M1911A1 Government Model semi-automatic which once belonged to his father—and his grandfather, and his great-grandfather to whom it was issued during World War II (Amazing, how such items tend to find their way home in duffel bags!). Then, as he came close enough to recognize the activity, he relaxed. Just a 'tagger'—a graffiti vandal with a spray can. He holstered his sidearm and exchanged it for his torch… er, flashlight. The flashlight came on.

The tagger froze. Mike could see him clearly now. It was a boy, maybe twelve years old. He acted positively terrified. Perhaps he was; it's not easy being bait. More on that later.

The body language was convincing, though. Mike relaxed. "I hope you're as handy with a bucket and sponge as you are with a spray can, son!" The kid dropped his spray can and looked petrified. Coming closer, Mike continued, "Do you know how much it costs us to keep these things clean? You need to try washing one of these…."

Dawn was still fighting her way through the static. But then she got a glimpse, only a glimpse, of what was hiding. "MICHAEL! DUCK!" she cried at the top of her voice.

Once again, only the barest hint of it got through. But enough to where Michael flinched. And the crowbar which swung down from between the boxcars caught him on the side of the head, instead of a crushing blow squarely on the skull.

I've mentioned previously that the rail yard was packed with demons. Now every one of them was on top of Dawn.

*   *   *

Except for the two which were pursuing me. But I shook them, after a bit of a merry chase, and then made contact with Nathan. His rapid response team was well trained; I must give them that. It was still short odds on our side, but they were up for a pitched battle no matter what.

*   *   *

In the interim, the twelve-year-old bait looked down at his catch with a swelling of pride. He was now "in", he knew!

"Nice work, Frankie," said the gang leader as he stepped out from between the boxcars.

"I think you got him," said another. "Yeah, let's get out of here," said the third.

But theirs were not the only voices. From the invisible audience, Dawn heard several more egging them on. Words such as "Kill the pig!" and "Get rid of him!" were prominent. The dominant theme was, "Finish him off!"

It had the desired effect. The gang leader told his motley crew, "Wait. Let's finish him off!"

He reached down and extracted Mike's sidearm from its holster. He started to take aim at Mike's bleeding form—then suddenly thought better of it. He handed the pistol to the young initiate. "Frankie, you do it!"

Once again, the young boy swelled with pride. Now he was a man!

*　*　*

THE ENEMY'S ATTENTION WAS FOCUSED on the drama taking place with the gang members. I can't say that we blindsided them, but we came close. But there were still more of them than there were of us. We had our hands full.

Below us, young Frankie was preparing to make his first kill. But the boy had absolutely no conception of how to handle a firearm! Events were proceeding as Dravang had hoped, but...it was quite possible that this young man would miss from only six feet away! He reached in through the intervening layers to steady the young boy's hand.

Nobody was trying to block Dawn's view any more. She saw it all clearly. She was being restrained, but she was no longer the prime object of their concern. That was a mistake on their part.

Warriors have moves. And they know how to execute them. Dawn broke free of her captors. But instead of escaping, as expected, she aimed herself squarely into the midst of the drama.

Her attention was focused on the weapon. Knock it away, deflect it, do something. Clear the immediate threat. Then, get the attention of the dispatcher. The police. Somebody. The medical facilities in general and the trauma centers in particular in this city were world-class; more on that later. If she could arrange to get him there with no further delay he stood a fighting chance.

*   *   *

AND SO TO EXPLAIN WHAT happened next requires a bit of amplification. You see, you are unitary beings. You are in one place and only one place at any given time. For us, not quite so. Now, we can't be *everywhere* at once—that is reserved for Deity—but we can so extend our beings as to be functionally present in quite a few different places at the same time.

Now it shouldn't be hard to grasp that, when we are so extended, our strength and power is stretched and divided as well. We have enough power and might— quite a bit, thank you very much!—that this seldom if ever becomes an issue. Except in combat.

One place that, virtually without exception, you will find us present at continually is around the Throne. Guardians, especially; we have a front row seat. Even as a lowly assistant, I am always welcomed to look upon the face of the Father. And when our being is stretched, there is a connection—think of it as a kind of a cord— between our various facets.

Again, so far so good. The fall down comes when we attempt to enter and engage directly in your world. The "cord" extending through the Border stands out like a neon beacon to the enemy. And so you will find that, whenever there is a credible story of we angels interacting in your world, either there is a pitched Mother Of All Battles going on behind the scenes or else, occasionally, it is the result of a negotiated settlement which usually (i.e., always!) means that the enemy benefits from a tit-for-tat in some other time or place. Either way the incursion does not last long, and then it's back to business as usual.

While theoretically it would be possible to penetrate the Border without such a "cord" behind us, no angel in his or her right mind would do so. That cord is our safety line, our recourse of last resort. Through it we always maintain a connection to Heaven; we can be retrieved with it in most cases or at the very least a specialized team of Warriors can trace it and follow it if we are unfortunate enough to be captured. Crossing the Border without that safety line would be as foolish as climbing a two-thousand-foot sheer rock wall without equivalent precautions. Even more so; no one seriously tries to shoot at climbers scaling El Capitán!

And so at this instant in space and time, a number of factors all converged at once. Dravang was reaching through the Border, steadying young Frankie's aim. It created a weak spot, and as he himself was making the penetration, the alarms which would normally alert those on the enemy's side were ignored. Dawn was focused completely on that very spot, as well. And I do mean completely. She poured every last bit of her being and her strength into that charge, forsaking even the barest hint of concern for her own safety and welfare. Everyone else around—and I must say that this includes me—was focused on the drama at hand; were we about to welcome a saint Home?

*　*　*

Young Frankie's finger tightened on the trigger.

Suddenly there was a flash! It was as much a surprise as if a grenade had gone off in his face…and it resembled that possibility by more than just a little bit!

The gang members were all knocked backwards by the force of the report. It caught them completely off guard. "What was that?" said one.

"The gun blew!" cried Frankie.

Really, now; is it very likely that a quality firearm which has been properly maintained and practiced with regularly will suddenly "just blow" when fired a single time? Looking back, I don't see how I didn't recognize that at the moment. But Frankie's conclusion made sense to me, and not only me but all the rest of the assembled audience, visible and invisible.

The youngsters were struck with confusion, abetted by the spiritual pressure our side was now exerting. "Let's get out of here," one cried. Now they were no longer a gang, but a bunch of frightened children. They turned tail and fled. With no human pawns left to manipulate, the enemy forces melted away just as quickly as Nathan and his troops roused themselves back into action.

"Keep them moving! Set up a perimeter! Everybody report in! Muster up! Do we have any casualties? Sweep the area; make sure it's clear!" A few seconds while he digested the reports of his teammates, and then he turned to me to report. "Area secure. We have them on the run. No serious casualties…wait! Dawn! Where's Dawn?"

I barely heard him. My attention was captivated by the underside of a boxcar. I must admit that rather a bit of a predatory gleam was coming across my face. Nathan turned to follow my gaze, and much the same look came across his face as well. "I don't believe it," he said in a hushed voice.

For from under the boxcar, there came a visible glow.

Chapter Eight

Encounter

Dawn shook her head, dazed. She was lying prone, wings half-spread to each side. She couldn't ever remember being this uncomfortable in her life, outside of training.

The Colt M1911A1 pistol was in her hand. *Mission accomplished,* she thought with relief. Or was it? She began to raise her head—and it smacked into something heavy and hard. *Ouch!*

It's not as if we don't have experience with bodies at all; as a matter of fact over the past two thousand years especially they've become quite the thing. But what all but a bare handful of us lack, though, is experience wearing a body in your world. Things back Home are quite real, of course, but they're all so energetic and alive that the experience is entirely different. The corner of that kitchen cabinet doesn't gently push your head away, for example, and the door doesn't close of its own accord to keep from barking your shin. Dawn felt real, physical pain. It was quite a strange sensation for her. She rubbed her head absently and began to take in her situation.

The space was cramped, very cramped. It would have been dark, save for the light of her own glory. There was metal above her head; metal strips to each side not quite five feet apart. She was lying on a surface which seemed to be alternating strips of wood and rock. The odor of creosote assaulted her nostrils—*that* was something novel!

Where am I?

She attempted to "feel" around, but there were no dimensional portals apparent to her augmented senses. As she continued to recover from her daze—this all happened in three seconds or so—the memories of recent events flooded back to her. *Michael! Where is Michael?*

Where was she? The last she remembered, she had been in combat just a few layers away from an Earthly railroad yard. So, most logically, she was….

At once she was fully alert. She plunged her hand into the crushed rock ballast of the railroad track beneath her, scooping up a handful of gravel. Wonderingly, she let it trickle through her fingers. *I'm in?* Then, triumphantly, she spoke aloud. "I'm IN!"

Hastily she crawled to her left, out from under the boxcar. Michael lay unconscious alongside the track, bleeding profusely. Heedless of the blood, she scooped his head up and held it in her lap. "Oh, Michael!"

I turned to Nathan and began barking orders. "I want a hard perimeter up at a quarter mile, and pickets out a half mile beyond that! Nothing gets through, do you hear? Nothing! Diversions—set up diversions to draw any roving patrols! I don't want them to have any idea of what we're doing here!"

"What are we doing here?"

"I have no idea!"

As Dawn held Michael, he began to regain consciousness for a few seconds. He got a brief look at the beautiful, gleaming, winged figure holding him in her lap and then promptly faded out again. She barely noticed. She was calling for me. "Ariel? Ariel?"

"Yes, Chief!"

She looked around, in vain. "Where are you? I can't see very well from this side!"

I came in as close as I dared. "This is the best I can do!"

"That's just fine! What's going on? Any threats?"

"None at all. We have them on the run, and the area is secure. We can break you out of there any time you're ready." I paused, then added, "It looks like you get your fifteen minutes, Chief!"

"He's hurt. I'll need more time!"

"I toooold you!"

"Ariel, please!"

"Right. In that case, I suggest you take him home."
"Home?"

"His home!"

"Oh. Right!"

"We'll set up around there and let you know when they start to make their move."

"Good. That'll work."

"Oh, and Chief?"

"Yes?"

"You might want to make yourself a bit less conspicuous. Just a thought."

She looked around and at herself and realized just where she was. "Good point!"

And with that, she picked Michael up and teleported out of the rail yard.

*   *   *

Last call at the Executive Center was 2 a.m. Some of the patrons had hung around a bit longer; management's policy was not to give them the bum's rush but at the same time the employees wanted to get dressed and go home. Now even the vacuum cleaners were put away and the only one there was the night watchman. Well, the only one that one of you would have been able to espy.

Dragora relished the thought of needling Dravang. "I hear you blew it."

"We had less than optimal success," he admitted.

"That Guardian, blowing that gun up right under your nose! How did you ever let her manage to get that close?"

"She was under restraint. She should not have been able to interfere. But she broke free...."

"Sounds like a feisty little thing!"

Dravang gave her The Eye. "The incompetents involved are already being disciplined."

"Why not discipline yourself? I could have found any number of humans more, shall we say, experienced in these matters. But no, you had to go with a bunch of rookies. You wanted to control them yourself!"

"You are wrong. Amateurs leave clues. Professionals do not. And clues can be traced. Remember our objective."

"Seems a little out of reach now."

"I have an alternate plan. I always have an alternate plan."

* * *

NATHAN HAD BUSIED HIMSELF SETTING up an unobtrusive but very strong defense in depth. They could have held off a full-on enemy attack for almost a full hour. With that kind of protection, Dawn had been able to let Michael rest.

Healing his injuries had not taken long, at all. Every Warrior is to at least some degree a combat medic and Dawn had taken her training further than most; she could have qualified as a journeyman Healer had she wished. The injury would have been serious had it been allowed to continue, but as it was the bleeding had lasted less than five minutes all told. She found clean sheets, telekinetically undressed him, and then, with a kiss, laid him down to sleep. Now he was snoring away.

This left her with some time on her hands. She looked around and decided to thoroughly clean the very messy house. She did use her special abilities to assist, but most of the work was accomplished with her own two hands—well, occasionally four. Now the former pig sty looked as neat as a pin. Mike was still sound asleep. What to do next?

You know, she thought, *he might like a really good breakfast.*

*   *   *

RAILROAD DISPATCHERS ARE NOT POLICE dispatchers. Now they are trained to keep track of the officers under their supervision, but their primary responsibility is the movement of trains over the railroad. Michael was supposed to make a roll call check once an hour, and he last did so at three a.m. Four o'clock came and went, and to be quite blunt the dispatcher working from the central office in Topeka was busy with a complicated meeting of trains farther down the line and just missed it. When five o'clock came he noted the blank line on his form and chastised himself, then placed a radio call for Mike.

It went unanswered. The dispatcher became nervous. A missed radio call is not necessarily a reason for immediate alarm—batteries do go dead out there in the field, after all—but it is a cause for concern. Then he remembered that this agent normally took his lunch break at five a.m. and sighed with relief. And at that moment a freight extra headed for an interchange track at Corsicana Junction requested a block which a manifest container movement was scheduled to occupy shortly and he reviewed the timetable and siding lengths to see where he could put one of them "in the hole" so as not to delay the premium cargoes any more than necessary....

But when six a.m. came and shift change with it, it was time to 'fess up. To be sure, he was sorely tempted to 'gun deck' the log and just write times in. To his credit, he didn't. "This one fell through the cracks," he admitted to his relief. "I think he's at lunch; he normally takes it now; but I don't remember hearing from him since three."

The incoming dispatcher frowned. It might be nothing major, but then again…. "We'd better find him right now," she said. "Does he carry a cell phone?"

Michael did indeed carry a cell phone. Dawn had powered it off so that he could rest undisturbed. After the third call to it went unanswered, the two dispatchers looked at each other uneasily. "Let's contact local law enforcement with his last reported position," the incoming dispatcher finally said.

The man she was relieving winced. If anything had happened…he'd never hear the end of it. And he had two girls in college…!

*　　*　　*

A REPORT OF A MISSING peace officer gets prompt attention. Two patrol cars were at the Old South Yard by 6:15 a.m. The dawn was just beginning to break on this brisk morning in early March. The first thing the responding officers saw was Mike's Jeep, quiet and undisturbed. That was either a very good sign…or a very bad one.

The yard was rather large, and filled with rail cars. These officers were trained, but they were not familiar with the safety requirements and practices of a railroad. They requested additional units and called K. P. & G. asking for some employees to assist them with their search.

*　　*　　*

Dawn is actually quite a good cook. Most of us are, for that matter. Please understand that, when you live in a realm where you can have virtually any material thing just by wishing for it, there is almost nothing which bespeaks love quite as much as a home-cooked meal, prepared entirely by hand from fresh natural ingredients. To you it may look and taste the same as something materialized or copied from an established pattern, but our eyes see the difference.

And the two of us were having fun. I knew of a family-owned pig farm and smoke house near East Anglia which had some excellent ham, bacon, and sausage, as well as an all-Jersey dairy in Bosbury. Dawn, for her part, had connections with a wonderful independent flour milling concern in San Antonio, a citrus orchard in the Rio Grande Valley, and a free-range egg ranch in Kilgore. Through some of Nathan's crew we had good leads on maple syrup, cheeses, and fresh fruit. The spread took shape, filling the dining table and then some. Yes, the talented chefs which keep the King's Table stocked could have done better—but not by much.

*　　*　　*

It was a quarter past seven and the sun was now up when Officer Jackson noticed the crowbar. He bent down to inspect it—and saw traces of hair and blood. Alarmed, he made an immediate radio call.

*　　*　　*

"You really shouldn't feed her at the table," I commented. "It's a bad habit!"

Yes, there was an obvious tone of jest in my voice. Sassy had made a friend. After a little initial hesitation—dogs really do have an innate gift of discernment—she was now showering Dawn's face with puppy kisses. Dawn, for her part, was reciprocating with bits and bites of choice delicacies. That little half of a link sausage wasn't going to do Mike any good now, anyhow, was it? Dawn gave the puppy another affectionate pat and set her back down, then washed her hands before returning to her project.

"So what's going on?" she asked presently. "How am I fixed for time?"

"Still nothing. You can let him sleep." I looked around at her handiwork. I retract my previous statement; even the King's chefs would have a tough time topping this. "Ah…isn't all this just a bit much?"

At the moment she was squeezing oranges into a pitcher, barehanded. "You only get one chance to do something the first time!"

Finished with the pitcher of juice, she took one of the bottles of milk, poured cream off the top into a small bowl, added a spoonful of sugar, and began to beat it with a wire whip. "My goodness," I commented. "Are we doing *everything* by hand today?"

She glanced around; the kitchen she just worked so hard to tidy up looked as if someone had set off a small bomb. But now it was spotlessly clean again. "Mmm… not quite everything!"

I chuckled. "Jolly good show!"

"I can't believe it's still so quiet. You'd think that they'd at least have started something by now!"

"Dawn, I'm beginning to think… I believe they might not realize what has happened."

Now I had her full attention. "What? You mean they don't know I'm here?" The excitement in her voice began to show. "Ariel, do you realize what this could mean?"

Yes, I realize it. A holy angel, free and undetected behind enemy lines—to us, it's rather like the Holy Grail. The speculative fiction about what one of us could accomplish in such a scenario makes your stories about first contact with aliens pale by comparison. It was time to bring her down to Earth—no, that's not right. But it was time to bring her down. "Don't get your hopes up, Chief. You know you don't belong there. Don't plan on staying very long."

She sighed. "I hear you."

She found a place for the last few miscellaneous items on the already overloaded dining table. I admired her creation. "I must say, it does look delicious. Do you mind if I make a copy and save it for later?"

"Help yourself." She looked around, considering. "Maybe I could make…."

"Chief, you're stalling."

"I guess so." She looked in the direction of Mike's bedroom and took a nervous breath.

"Go on!"

*　*　*

Detective Sergeant Estevez's tenure with the South Central Division began fifteen years ago. He and Rick were colleagues before Rick transferred to Narcotics, and Mike was once assigned to the division as a rookie cop with the department. The sergeant knew that the two men were friends, and gave Rick the unpleasant wake-up call that early Sunday morning. Now Rick was on site at the rail yard.

"Crowbar, found here," Sergeant Estevez said. "We took photos, then sent it into the lab for blood analysis. Found bloodstain here, not far away. Not sure how much blood yet; we haven't disturbed this rock base. It could have seeped down quite a ways."

"Now, look at this," he continued. "Streaks of blood over the gravel, about five feet worth. Somebody moved him. And that's it. No other evidence that we can find."

Another detective was about to belie that statement. "Look at this!"

They looked. Under a nearby boxcar, between the rails, there was a Colt M1911A1 pistol. Rick had seen it before, several times. Since Mike was a child and it belonged to his father, in fact. He sighed.

"That's Mike's sidearm."

"Looks like we'd better make some phone calls."

"I'll make the phone calls."

* * *

As Dawn stepped through the door of the bedroom Mike was just beginning to stir on the bed. "Ooooooh," he groaned.

"Good morning, Michael. Are you ready for some breakfast?"

The bedroom, which formerly looked like the set of *Hoarders*, was now spotlessly neat and clean. Dawn was in a normal human body and dressed in purest white.

Mike sat up, rubbing his head. "Ooooh. Oh, God. What happened?"

Dawn smiled and stepped closer. "Well, you suffered a blunt trauma to the head. Hairline fracture, moderate concussion. But I've got you all fixed up now. Feel OK?"

"Yeah, I think so."

"Good. Nice to know my seven centuries of training paid off!"

He did a take at that, then thought that he must have misheard her. He hadn't. And at that point, both Dawn and I got a signal.

*   *   *

IT'S REALLY THE HARDEST JOB that a police officer can face. At least with a fatal shooting there is closure. If there is injury but not fatality, there is hope of recovery. But when another officer is *missing*, under suspicious circumstances and with evidence of injury, it's the worst of all possible worlds.

Rick's first call was to the headquarters of Mike's department in Topeka. They would be responsible for making the official notification to the family, but they asked if he would be willing to assist. He was. They asked whether he knew of any other relatives besides Mike's mother, who was the only name on the emergency contact list. No, as far as he knew she was Mike's only living family.

Rick wasn't going to put off notifying her, not exactly, but he wanted to be able to provide her with solid information if at all possible. He called the trauma centers and major hospitals in the nearby medical center. None of them had any record of a patient matching

Mike's description that morning. Obviously. He called the fire department to see if an ambulance had been dispatched. Nothing. Of course Mike's cell phone still did not answer. He prepared to call K. P. & G. again, to arrange a meeting with one of their other local agents in order to make a check of Mike's home—just a formality, at this point—before notifying Martha in person, but then he hesitated.

There was one contact still untried. Mike, with his affinity for working antiques, was one of the few remaining persons who actually had a traditional landline telephone. Not only that, he was fanatic about protecting its privacy from telephone solicitors and nosy politicians. The number had never been listed and in fact it was not on any of his official contact information sheets. Mike kept the number private for family and close friends, only. And Rick had it.

He hadn't dialed it in quite a while; he couldn't remember it off the top of his head. Had it been transferred when he received his new cell phone? Yes, it was there in his personal directory. He placed the call.

*   *   *

THE WESTERN ELECTRIC ROTARY DIAL telephone at Mike's bedside rang. Dawn gestured at it. "That's the police. They're looking for you."

Mike picked up the phone. "Hello?"

*   *   *

AT FIRST RICK THOUGHT IT must be an answering machine. But when no recorded message followed, a surge of hope welled up in him. "Mike? Buddy? That you?"

"Yeah, it's me."

A wave of relief washed over Rick. Immediately he reverted to his normal happy-go-lucky self. "Hey, we found your truck without you in it and we got a little worried! You OK?"

"I'll be fine. Got jumped by a gang last night. Bit of a bump on the head. Woke up in the hospital, but I'm doing all right now."

Now Rick was back to being a professional police officer. "Which hospital were you treated at? Did they take a report?"

"Huh? What? I'm right here!"

He looked around the spotless room, then at the old rotary phone, and finally at Dawn. As he stared, little Sassy came in the bedroom wagging her tail and gave out a sharp yip. Mike began to realize that this *wasn't* the hospital. Dawn smiled and said, "I did a little cleaning up last night."

Rick was confused, then concerned. Head injuries can be tricky things. "Mike," he said, "You're at *home*, buddy. Are you sure you're OK?"

"Yeah...fine." Then Mike hung up the phone.

Rick still had concerns and questions about what was really going on, but he had to pass on this good news right away. He looked up the number of K. P. & G.'s police department again.

* * *

NATHAN AND I REALIZED IMMEDIATELY that we had loose ends to tie up. Much as we would like to take credit for a miracle, it would also send the enemy onto us in jig time. Fortunately, about ten miles to the south we found a suburban hospital outside the jurisdiction of the city and in fact over the line into the next county with an unseen management who was inclined to be coöperative. They didn't object at all as we quietly amended their records to insert an account of a railroad police officer being brought to the emergency room by a pair of good Samaritans—video footage would show that they looked a great deal like Nathan and Philip in human form—early in the morning with blunt trauma to the head, treated, and released to be taken home by a relative. The relative's name? Dawn Marie Mitchell. Sam Wilson's older sister Mary had once been married to a Mr. Thomas Mitchell of Kalispell, Montana; all were now deceased. Someone was really thinking ahead. But I digress.

When Rick and the two police departments received that report they bought it completely. So, apparently, did Dravang and the others on the side of the opposition. Shortly after the events immediately following the old phone would ring again; Dawn would speak directly with Mike's chief of police in Topeka and assure him that, yes, Mike was safe and recovering nicely; still a bit dazed and confused, perhaps, but she was there and taking good care of him. As the injury was sustained in the line of duty he gave Mike two weeks' leave with pay with the promise of more if necessary in order to recover; how nice. But back to matters at hand.

Mike had not objected to Dawn's presence in his bedroom one bit; it almost seemed as if she belonged there. But now he realized that she did not. "What's going on here? Who are you?" he asked after he hung up the receiver.

"I'm—hmm. Who do you think I am?"

I'm one of the good guys!

Mike blinked and leaned back, considering. "You know, that's a good one. I'm sure I've never met you before, but it almost seems like I've known you all my life…in the back of my mind somewhere." A hazy memory began to come back to him. "And then, last night…."

"Yes?"

He shook his head. "Nah. I was delirious."

"Oh. Delirious. I see." She moved in very close and sat down beside him on the bed, looking directly into his eyes. "Are you delirious now?"

"No, I'm fine."

"Are you sure?"

"Yeah, I'm sure."

"All right, then."

She stood up, then turned to face him. She spread her arms. Then….

The glory of Heaven exploded before him. It was as if she had caught on fire, and the thin human veneer on top had burned away to reveal the glorious, supernatural creature within. A jeweled circlet, like a diadem, appeared on her head and her casual shoes transformed into soft suede ankle boots decorated with gold and silver thread. Her raiment, although modest enough, was nonetheless somewhat daring at the same time; her tanned skin gleamed like burnished bronze. The ornate hilt of her dress sword hung at her side, shining with its own reflection of her glory. The wings transfixed him; large, powerful, and covered with silver feathers so bright that they might have been fashioned from the pure metal itself. Folded, the wrist joints were almost even with the top of her head; the tips of the primaries came within a few inches of brushing the floor. They made her look as though she was wearing a royal robe—nice touch, that. He was terrified, yet at the same time he couldn't get enough of her.

He pushed back and found himself falling off the back side of the bed. Still, he stared over the bed at her. She smiled, lifted off the ground, and floated over the bed, hovering beside him. She extended a hand.

"Don't be afraid. I'm one of the good guys!"

Chapter Nine

THE BIG DAY

WITH MORE THAN A LITTLE hesitation Mike took Dawn's outstretched hand. She helped him up and back to a sitting position on the bed. He managed to croak out a question. "Am I dead?"

"Good question. Let's just see," Dawn answered. She rested a hand on his neck as if to check his pulse. "Hmm. Pulse 135, respiration 32, blood pressure 190 over 90…!" She clucked at him. "Something must have really startled you. Any idea what?"

Then she pinched him on the cheek. Hard. "Ouch!" he cried out.

"Did that hurt? Y'know, in my best professional opinion I'd have to say you're still alive. Hope you're not too terribly disappointed or anything!"

His hand was still where she had pinched him. "Who are you?"

"Figure it out." When no response was forthcoming she added, "My friends call me Dawn."

"What are you here for?" Mike asked.

She made him wait for it.

"Breakfast!"

*   *   *

I SUPPOSE THAT IT'S NOT entirely fair to ask your charge and partner to join you for breakfast for the first time when you are glorified and impeccably attired and he is unshaven and in pajamas. But whoever said that life had to be fair? Heh, heh.

But Dawn had backed off a little. Don't noise it about too much, but although we do like to put on a bit of a show when we can, we also tend to tone it down somewhat when we are just relaxing with friends. And so Dawn's skin was now a normal flesh tone and her wings were purest white. Mike still stared; the back of her chair was in the way so she had simply phased her wings through it. Easy enough, of course, but I suppose it was entirely novel to him.

"Would you like some maple syrup?" Dawn asked him. *Dawn, no....*

"Uh huh," he managed to croak out. He seemed almost entirely to have lost the power of speech; I can't for the life of me imagine why.

A silver pitcher of syrup levitated off the table and over to Mike's plate, pouring out some of its contents on his French toast. "Say when!" she told him. Show-off. Now, if I were in her position...I would have done exactly the same thing, of course. Jealous much? "Is that OK?"

"Uh...."

Good enough. She directed the pitcher back to its resting place, looked him in the eye, and smiled. "Nervous?"

"Uh...uh huh."

Finally! Three almost-words from him. Now they were getting somewhere!

"Don't be," she told him. "Look, Mike, you can talk to me. I won't bite!"

This reassured him not in the least.

"Go ahead," she continued. "Question and answer, maybe? Anything you'd like to know?" I believe she was beginning to lose patience. "Say something!"

"Um...when did you die?"

She hid her face in her hands and laughed quietly for a few seconds before looking up again to answer. "You have a lot to learn!"

"I always thought, like, you die, you turn into an...."

"No. That only happens in the movies. I've always been what I am. Just like you'll always be what you are."

He looked rather disappointed. "That's not much to look forward to."

Oh, really? Redeemed soul? Heir of salvation, purchase of God? Dawn raised her eyebrow, then gave him that enigmatic smile. "Wait and see."

"Where did you come from?" he asked.

"Oh, I've been around," she answered. "Been keeping an eye on you every now and then." Then, with exaggerated casualness, she added, "It's a living."

I could tell that my best friend was quite literally over the moon this morning, but Mike wasn't picking up on it. Yes, she could have been more, shall we say, flirtatious had she chosen…but we girls do like to play hard to get. Yes, even in Heaven.

Mike chewed on her statement for a bit before responding, "You mean you're, like, my guardian angel?"

Dawn allowed herself an eye roll and a hint of the sarcastic. "And he figured it out!"

"So this is, like, your job?"

"Um, not exactly. I think I'd better clear something up here. Don't take this wrong; it's not that I don't want to help you out when you get in a tight spot, I do. But sometimes when I'm back on my own side of the Border it's kinda tough to reach through. I'm glad I could last night, believe me—but don't count on it every time. My real job is to guard your soul, not your tail."

"Oh. I guess I should say, 'Thank you.'"

Yes, Mike, you should. And that is something that we Guardians live for. Dawn simply gave him back the warmest of smiles and said, "You're welcome!"

Now, for the first time, Mike took the initiative. Things were looking up. "Uh, is there anything that I can do for you?"

"Well," she said, "it is Sunday morning."

No response other than the blankest of blank stares.

"You can't think of any place that an angel might like to go on a Sunday morning?"

More of the blank stare, but now the light began to dawn!

She looked up at the ceiling and with mostly mock frustration asked, "Is it too late to look into another line of work?"

*　　*　　*

MICHAEL HAD COME TO KNOW the Lord as a child in an older church off Park Place, not far from his home neighborhood. But now the old church was closed for good; the shell of the facility still stood vacant awaiting a buyer. Mike was now an occasional member at a much larger church farther down the freeway. It's not a bad church; I understand it was rated C-plus during our most recent evaluations. They think that their large size means that God is blessing them; I tend to think that it means that the enemy doesn't consider them worthy of concerted attack. But, anyhow….

An usher recognized Mike and called out to him, "Hey! Mike! Good to see you…it's been a while!"

Mike quickly and furtively turned to Dawn beside him. She does have a good sense of human fashion after all these years; she had morphed her outfit into a teal blouse and beige skirt which went well with her blonde hair. "Okay," he asked. "Nobody can see you or hear you but me, right?"

Sigh. Too many sappy movies; the look she gave him was one of utter disgust. "Get real," she said before calling out and introducing herself to the usher. First names only, of course.

They arrived while the early service was still in session; the crowds in the foyer and reception area were light. Mike headed towards the book store and coffee shop. I suppose I need to insert the requisite line about "houses of merchandise" and so forth. Truth be told, as long as they are run in a fair and honest manner, legitimate and plainly identified concessions do not cross our red line…but they do jiggle the yellow.

At any rate, they had a few minutes to while away. Dawn went into the book store and began to browse through the gift items. There were two shelves full of angel figurines and related bric-à-brac; Dawn was getting her first truly good look at them from your side. She sighed, then chuckled, and then finally called out to the clerk. "Excuse me, miss, I was just wondering. Do you have any that don't look quite so, um…ditzy?"

* * *

I'm accustomed to "A Mighty Fortress" and "The Church's One Foundation," not to mention some of the more recent works by Ms. Fanny Crosby and Charles Wesley—they continue to be most productive, you should know. So hearing the same seven words repeated eleven times and called "praise music" really doesn't do much for me. But the preaching was sound, albeit edited somewhat to fit within time constraints. Got to stick to the schedule for rebroadcast over the radio, don't you know. In general, though, it was a successful service; I rated it as a solid B.

"Now, that wasn't so bad, was it?" Dawn asked as they were exiting the sanctuary…excuse me, "Worship Center."

"I know, I know. It's just been a while. I've been so busy!"

"Excuses, excuses. When you join the team you need to make the practices." She looked around and recognized a familiar face. "Speaking of joining the team…."

It was Chuck, Mike's old Sunday School teacher who had given him such a good start twenty years back and now a member at this same church. Dawn made a beeline for him and gave him a hug which was warm enough and long enough to raise a few eyebrows. "Thank you!" she murmured.

"Well, you're welcome!" he answered with a touch of mild astonishment.

She released him and turned away, but squeezed his hand as she did so. "See you 'round," were her parting words.

As they walked towards the exit, the usher she had met before stopped her at the information desk. "Excuse me, miss," he said. "Would you sign our guest book?"

"Sure!" She picked up one of the giveaway ball point pens on the table and signed the book with the name we had arranged for her to use, then clicked the pen a few times. "Mind if I keep this?" she asked.

"Not at all; that's what they're for!" replied the usher.

"Thanks!" she answered as she tucked the pen away in her purse.

Mike looked a question at her.

"Souvenir!" she replied with a grin.

*   *   *

If you are in the Houston area in early March then you *must* visit the Rodeo; I give you no leeway in this matter. Dawn had been our commander in this region during the years when it was growing from a modest Fat Stock Show into the largest such undertaking in the known galaxy. The event was almost big enough to be seen from orbit, if you knew exactly where to look. And this would be Dawn's first chance ever to attend the event in person. Yes, I'm fairly sure that there are other things which she could have done in your world which would have excited her more. I'm also fairly sure that I could count them on the fingers of one hand.

Dawn had transformed her outfit yet again into Western wear: flannel blouse, jeans, and boots. And her hat, of course. She and Michael were negotiating their way through the crowds in the livestock hall. Aside from the rows of neatly groomed show animals being presented by the youthful members of the 4-H society there were also quite a number of concession and merchandise booths. One was a seller of handmade custom jewelry; to her delight Dawn found therein a silver pin of a winged angel which did not look ditzy at all. She paid for it—she had been allowed to draw some spending money; while we can't just 'make' cash at will we can act as our own ATM when properly authorized—and she showed her purchase to Mike. "Well? What do you think?" she asked.

Mike looked at the pin, and then took a much longer look at her. "I kinda prefer the real thing!"

Wonder of wonders, our boy was finally beginning to loosen up. Dawn chuckled and said, "That's sweet. I guess it'll do." She tucked it away in her purse. "Souvenir!"

They wandered out of the livestock hall and onto the grounds which held the enormous carnival midway. Perhaps it was a poor substitute for the Astroworld theme park which had once stood nearby, but it would do for the present. The two of them took a ride on a roller coaster and then a Ferris wheel. Then they passed a carnival barker's game stand.

"Don't waste your money," Mike advised. "These games are rigged."

Those games *are* rigged, you should know. Rigged to make them look easy, even when they may be impossible to win if you're not standing behind the line where the carny stands. But this wasn't quite one of those games. It was a milk can softball toss—and the milk cans all had rings welded into their necks to block anything other than a perfectly thrown ball. But, if you knew what you were doing, and if you had excellent aim, and if you knew exactly how much backspin to put on your toss to kill the ball's momentum and keep it from glancing off….

Dawn was highly qualified in all three regards.

She collected her prize from an incredulous carny. Mike reacted with exaggerated casualness. As they turned away he spoke in an undertone. "Showoff. You're cheating, right?"

She restrained her emotions—she was righteously indignant—but she let him know. "We don't cheat. Not about stuff like this. Not, at least, without very good reason. We *can't!*"

"Oh? Why not?"

"It's too important! If you'd been paying attention in church, you might realize that there's a war going on!"

"I thought that was already won. Resurrection and all that."

"The Resurrection is our clue that the war is *going* to be won, but it's not over until the last enemy surrenders! Which hasn't happened yet, as someone in your profession ought to realize."

"So? Fight them. Beat them. Happily ever after, then fade to black."

Dawn sighed. "If only it were that simple."

Behind them, an eight-year-old girl had seen Dawn win her prize and eagerly ran up to the game booth. Her parents were hesitant, but the carny was pointing to Dawn and doing an excellent sales job as to how easy the game really was. Her father was digging the requisite four dollars out of his pocket. Dawn turned to them and said, "Maybe you'd better let me try that for her."

Her father was willing, but the carny intervened. "Oh, no. See that sign? 'Limit One Prize Per Day!'"

Dawn nodded equably. "All right. Go ahead, young lady. Good luck!"

The ball arced up and landed squarely in the center of the can's ring. The disgusted carny reached for another large prize—this was the first time he had handed out two in the same day in the past five years. Dawn turned to Mike and whispered, "*Now* I'm cheating!"

He stifled a laugh.

*   *   *

THE TWO OF THEM HAD obtained good seats in the stadium for the Rodeo proper. Dawn applauded the skill of the ropers; praised the performance of the bronc riders; gasped at the daring of the steer wrestlers; admired the precision of the barrel racers; laughed uproariously at the calf scramble; cheered on the chuck wagon racers; and had to be almost physically restrained by me when an angry bull turned on a thrown rider. The very last thing we needed was for her to make the ten o'clock news, especially deep in enemy territory without a safety net! Fortunately, the rodeo clowns did their job well and the bull was distracted and the rider retrieved with only some painful bumps and bruises.

As the stage was being set up for the evening's entertainment, Mike made a run to the concession stand. He returned with a pair of Coca-Colas and a program. He handed the latter to her. "Here. Souvenir!"

"What? Oh, you didn't have to do that!" Dawn protested. But her shining eyes belied that statement.

"I wanted to give you something," Mike said.

"Well, thank you! Thank you very much!" she replied with delight. She took a sip of the soda, then hefted the program. It was almost three inches thick and the size of a big-city telephone directory. "Gotta be careful. This could put me over my baggage allowance!"

"*What?*"

"It's a joke, Mike! You know, ha ha?" She sighed. "Skip it."

"Oh."

The evening's entertainment began. Someone, somewhere, must have pulled some strings. It wasn't me! But if you ask Nathan about that evening—let's just say that his denials are less than convincing. But for whatever reason, the country singer that night opened with, "You Are My Special Angel."

The two of them repaired to The Hideout once the performance was over. Michael is not a very good dancer. But Dawn is, and she was a forgiving partner. The night couldn't go on forever. But, so help me, just before the venue closed at the stroke of midnight, the band concluded their set with the very same song.

*   *   *

PARKING, TRAFFIC, THE DRIVE BACK to Eastwood...well, at least neither of them had any pressing responsibilities the next morning. As the door closed behind them, Mike was still stunned by the events of that day. Dawn, for her part, was savoring the memory of every second.

"Ah, what a day!" she said. "Thanks for showing a lady a good time!" She squeezed his hand, then wriggled a bit uneasily. "Do you mind if I get comfortable?"

"Uh...no," he answered hesitantly.

She transitioned immediately back into her glorified form, letting the suppressed energy radiate out of her. "Ah," she sighed, "that feels so good!"

With no activities to distract him, and having got over most of his understandable inhibitions, he openly stared at her. He was beginning to admire her, not just as an angel, but as a girl. Yes, she was beautiful—no, scratch that. She was *beyond* beautiful. She was perfection in physical form, the very essence of beauty defined. It was as if someone had been looking over his shoulder all of his life, noting everything he had ever found appealing...the fall of *that* hair, the curve of *that* face, the line of *that* figure...and had distilled them all down into one incredible package. Or, perhaps it was the other way around? Maybe he had subconsciously known her all his life, and the reason he found those other women attractive was because they reminded him of her...who could say?

She had taken a seat on his sofa. The hefty program was still in her lap. The pen from the church was still in her purse. And some sheets of printer paper were on Mike's desk within her easy reach. She retrieved one and began to write. "*Dear Michael...*"

"Dawn?" he asked hesitantly as she wrote. "Can I ask you a personal question?"

"Yes," she replied. "I can read your mind."

That brought him up short. "Oh."

She smiled. "Don't be embarrassed. I'm actually kind of flattered!"

"Oh. I take it you can't…." His voice trailed off.

"I will admit I have always been curious," she replied enigmatically.

He didn't know exactly how to respond to that. Then he noticed her ongoing activity. "What are you doing?"

"Writing."

"Writing what?"

"A letter."

He leaned over to see better. Dawn hastily shielded it from his view. "Hey!" she said, "this is personal!"

He backed off. "Sorry. Who's it to?"

"Umm…a friend. Any *more* questions?"

"Yeah. How do you mail it, and can I have one of your stamps?"

She couldn't hold back all of the chuckle. But she collected herself, looked up at him, and said, "Actually, I wasn't planning to mail this one. After I'm all done here, with you…" (this was said somewhat dismissively) "…I think I'll go look my friend up and hand-deliver it. Maybe we can read it together."

"What good will that do?"

"Well, at least he'll know that, wherever I was tonight, I was thinking of him."

"So it's a he?"

Was that a hint of jealousy in his voice? Dawn replied with a slight, knowing smile. "Yes, it's a he."

"Lucky guy."

"I'd like to think so." She folded the letter and tucked it into her purse. "I can finish this later. It's past time for you to get to bed. *You* need to sleep!"

"You don't?"

"No, of course not."

"You're...what, just going to sit up all night?"

"Oh, I might stretch out on the couch for a while."

"So you do sleep."

She wrinkled her nose. "Well, it's like eating, kind of. I don't *have* to...but I *can*."

He paused for a few seconds to digest this. His next question was a bit more thoughtful; I think he was starting to look for the person behind the angel. "Do you dream?"

"Occasionally."

"What about?"

"Um, that's kind of personal."

"Oh. Sorry. Well, good night."

"Pleasant dreams!"

And as the door closed she blew him a kiss.

Chapter Ten

A WALK IN THE PARK

MICHAEL DID SLEEP WELL. VERY well; it was half past eight when he first opened his eyes. Bright sunlight was streaming in through the window. He yawned, stretched, looked at the alarm clock…and then he remembered.

Now he was wide awake! Had it all been a dream, or was it real? It must have been a dream—but the room was still clean and uncluttered. Light was streaming under the crack from the door to the living room. Was that sunlight, or was it…? He climbed out of bed and hesitantly put his hand on the doorknob.

It wasn't a dream. Dawn was there, hovering six inches off the floor, face to the morning sun, eyes closed in an attitude of prayer. Her wings were folded and she was attired in a flowing white robe. Outwardly she was silent with only a slight smile to betray her feelings, but inside she was overflowing with joy and praise and thanks and requests for wisdom as to what to do now. Much as I agreed with her, I sighed. Getting her out of there at this point would make extracting a 426 Hemi elephant motor from a compact Dodge Dart seem a simple task. (Mike's grandfather Glenn was a *serious* car nut. Still is, for that matter; it's just that deliveries of authentic original parts to his current Home are a mite convoluted.)

Very quietly, Michael came closer. But you're not going to succeed in sneaking up on a Warrior. Dawn's smile cracked just a bit wider, and her right hand clenched into a fist—middle knuckle extended. At closest point of approach she whirled around and "goosed" him soundly in the ribs with her knuckle.

He was caught completely off guard—again—and Dawn burst out laughing. "So I glow in the dark!" she said with eyes dancing. "Does that mean I can't have a sense of humor?"

"I didn't mean to disturb you," he apologized. "I guess you were...."

"Just checking in with Headquarters. C'mon, you can help me!"

"Help *you?* How?"

"Simple. You live here. You belong here. You have standing. I don't. When you ask for something, He takes you seriously. Me, I get the crumbs left after everyone's finished fighting over the good stuff. Come on, we've got a big day ahead of us!"

*　*　*

SHORTLY AFTER THEY SAID AMEN, the old rotary dial phone rang once more. It was Rick. "Hey," he said with a bit of frustration. "I know that you're still recovering, but are you ever going to turn your cell phone back on again?"

We angels have very good hearing. Dawn put her hand to her mouth. "Oops. Hadn't even thought about it." She reactivated the smartphone and sent it over to Mike. As it connected with the network it overflowed with chimes and messages and voicemails. Most of them were related to his unexpected absence the previous morning, of course, but the most recent....

"HPD requests your assistance with identification of criminal suspects. Please cooperate as soon as physically able. Thanks." It had come from headquarters in Topeka.

"I'm just now seeing this, Rick," said Mike as he read through the message. "What are you needing?"

"We've hit a dead end with identification of your drug suspects. The best match our computer came up with was in jail that night. Pretty tight alibi. Can you come in and go over mug shots? I don't want to rush you after you've been hurt, but I don't want the trail to get any colder."

Mike looked a question at Dawn. She nodded. "Okay, Rick, I'm actually feeling pretty good today. I can come in this morning. Say ten o'clock?"

"Oh, that's perfect! I'll have everything ready for you. We're not rushing you at all, are we?"

"No, no, I'm doing great. See you at ten." He looked back over at Dawn. "Will you...?"

"I'm coming with you. Here, let me put a bandage on your head. For form's sake, at least."

*   *   *

THE TWO OF THEM EMERGED from the elevator and entered the Narcotics offices. Rick was there waiting to meet him—and astounded to see him with the prettiest girl he'd ever laid eyes on. "Mike? Who is this?"

"This is Dawn." His voice dropped and became conspiratorial. "She's my gu…."

You must understand that, especially in a place like a police headquarters, there is an uneasy truce. We are present there, in force, as long as the officers in question truly are committed to observing the law and doing justice in accordance with it. But the enemy is there, as well. Most of them are the kind of spirits who recognize that a society governed with law and order will give them more and better opportunities than an anarchic free-for-all, and so the truce generally holds. But the kind of information Mike was about to divulge would be a game-changer.

Dawn's eyes flared wide. Mike's voice cut off; suddenly, he was unable to breathe. Dawn attempted to complete his sentence. "Cousin. Cousin, you might say. Distant family relation. Just happened to be in town."

"She's your *cousin?*" Rick asked with a new appreciation. Then he noticed that Mike was still unable to breathe. "Mike, buddy, you okay?"

"He'll be just fine!" Dawn answered. "I'm sure he just needs to step outside for some fresh air!" And with that, she hustled him outside the door into the hallway.

I'm sure that angels from both sides wondered why a team of Warriors suddenly barricaded them off from that corner of the hallway. But similar things happen behind the scenes in police stations all the time, so most thought nothing more of it. When a slight degree of privacy had been obtained Dawn released her telekinetic hold on his airway and demanded, *"What are you trying to do to me?"*

Mike recognized the real fear in her voice. "What? Nothing! Nothing!"

"Blowing my cover is *nothing?* You were about to spill everything!"

"What? I don't see…?"

"Don't you understand? *They don't know I'm here!* It's the only reason I've been able to stay! Usually, if we can get across at all, we have to fight our way in, take care of business, and get right back out! But this time I got past them and *they don't know about it!* By their rules, I shouldn't be here at all. But I am."

It was starting to become clearer to him. "So, you're, like, a secret agent?"

"Yes! Exactly! And if I get caught…."

"What? I mean, they can't kill you, can they?"

She gave an odd laugh. "No, they can't *kill* me."

"Then…what?"

"You don't want to know…and I don't want to think about it."

She let him chew on that happy thought for a moment and then continued. "Keep in mind: There *is* something out there! It is *not* all friendly! I've got to look human, act human, even *think* human! Don't blow it for me, okay?"

"I can't not think about you."

"I do have some cover. That's why I can talk to you now. But…." She considered. "We need a signal. King's

X." She held out crossed fingers. "When you see my fingers crossed, do your dead level best to treat me and talk to me just like any other human. Otherwise, we can talk. As long as we keep it discreet."

"Gotcha."

*   *   *

MIKE WAS AT A COMPUTER in the office, going through files of photos which the database had identified as a close match. Rick was talking with Dawn. When I had observed him slicking back his hair while those two were outside in the hallway talking, I knew we were in trouble.

"So, where are you from?" asked Rick.

"Oh, around."

"Around here?"

"Just passing through, actually."

"Well," Rick said with all the considerable charm he could muster, "As long as you're here, why don't you let me take you out and show you around the town sometime?"

"Thanks for the offer," Dawn answered as gently as she could, "but I think I'd better pass."

"Why? You strike me as a woman of the world!"

Dawn cocked her head and raised an eyebrow. "You might be very surprised."

Mike pushed back his chair from the computer screen. "Got 'em. Got 'em both. These are the two guys with the van."

"You're sure?" Rick asked.

"Positive."

"Thanks, buddy. Now we've got some work to do. Would you be okay with bringing that up in front of the DA and the judge?"

"Absolutely. We'll follow you there."

Rick turned back to Dawn. "Sure you won't change your mind?"

She smiled. "Don't take it personally. I'm afraid you're just not my type!"

* * *

YOU MIGHT THINK THAT SOMEONE like Amy who knows the two of us so well would instantly recognize her old friend in human form on the far side of the Border. You might be mistaken. Attractive young blondes who go by the name of Dawn are at least a thousand times more common in your world than are angels—any angels—in human form, and Dawn's physical appearance had only the most tenuous link to the spiritual identity Amy knew so well.

But what Amy did recognize from the obvious "fingerprints" on her soul was that here was a girl, whom Rick found attractive, who was intelligent, of pure character, a virgin, physically well endowed, and who gave every external indication of being a believer. Now she could not absolutely confirm that last without access to Dawn's private Records, which we of course were unwilling to give, but all the signs were there. In short, this was the kind of girl whom Amy had almost ceased to hope might come into her boy's life. She immediately set her considerable will upon making the two of them "an item." Sigh. Life just got quite a bit more complicated.

I was really hoping for some backstop from the Throne. Something rather like, "Wrong girl; not the one; back off and keep looking." I didn't get it. I sometimes wonder if He actually takes a kind of perverse delight in my occasional discomfiture. The thought briefly crossed my mind that perhaps I should let Amy in on the secret. No chance. Amy's background is as a Messenger, and asking her to keep news like this to herself—well, let's just say that we stood a better chance if we were to write it up as a press release and submit it to the Voice of America. I sighed again.

The deputy District Attorney signed off on the warrant almost as soon as Rick identified the case—the van bust was already legendary in their office—but the judge was not a pushover. While I'm all in favor of "law and order", sometimes judges who strongly identify with such run roughshod over the rights of the accused. Of course, I'm even less in favor of justifying the guilty. But he struck just about the right balance; after a few minutes' give and take with Mike and Rick he nodded and agreed to issue arrest warrants for Hector Ortega, aka Diego, and Demetrius Mack…better known on the streets as Leroy.

Now, to find them. Rick thanked Mike and Dawn, shook both of their hands…anything to justify physical contact with her…and then exited out one way as the two of them exited the other, taking the opportunity for one more appreciative look up and down at her form. I wondered whether it had been wise to manifest in that skirt which so emphasized her tanned legs.

"Want to have lunch in The Cloister?" Mike asked. "I can write this up as official business!"

"Sure!"

*   *   *

The Cloister is a cafeteria style lunch room operated jointly by a largish Episcopal Church downtown which provides the venue and a local restaurant who caters the food. It's quite good and service is quick; it appeals to those who work in the nearby courthouse complex and to those who have the dubious privilege of serving on jury duty. By the time Mike and Dawn arrived the lunch service for the day was winding down, but they both obtained a hearty dish of the signature red beans and rice with cheese and extra sausage. Dawn also asked for onions; Mike passed. They gave thanks and began to tuck in.

Mike had some more questions for Dawn—but, being inside a church, the unseen audience was rather more alert than elsewhere. Most of them were from our side, it's true—but not all, and we had already decided not to spread the news around to anyone without a real need to know. As Mike began to speak, Dawn tapped her crossed fingers on the table. Mike hesitated, and then spoke only pleasantries.

After lunch the two of them took a walk through downtown. They ended up in Sam Houston Park, easternmost tip of a stretch of green space which extends along the Bayou as far as the 610 Loop and then some. It is the oldest public park in the City of Houston; while Dawn was not yet the regional commander when it was created she was in fact a senior operative and threw her weight behind the initiative. Then, a half century later when she was fully in charge, she took a personal interest in the park and facilitated its further development. Now it housed a number of historic buildings from the 19th century which had been saved from various developers' wrecking balls and relocated to the site.

Dawn, of course, had a wealth of knowledge about the exhibits and was able to regale her appreciative audience with personal anecdotes about each of the various structures. I say "audience"; while at the start it was just her and Michael a number of visitors overheard her commentary and tagged along as she continued.

"When does the next tour start?" one asked as they ended up at the Kellum-Noble house. "We missed the beginning of this one!"

"Oh, this wasn't a tour," Dawn answered with a blush. "They don't give tours on Mondays. I just happen to know the park really well!"

"Showoff," I muttered to her as the crowd dispersed and the two of them began walking the path down towards the small pond.

"Well, there's no law against impersonating a museum docent," she replied *sotto voce* with a grin.

"Maybe there ought to be. You know you need to keep a low profile!"

"Who are you talking to?" Mike asked.

"One of my best friends, name of Ariel. She's keeping an eye on the both of us while I'm over here."

"Oh. Hello, Ariel," he said, ingratiating himself to me instantly. He was looking the wrong way, but I could readily forgive him for that. "What does she look like?"

"Well, Mike, for us looks are easier to change than clothes. But, generally speaking, she manifests a couple of inches smaller than I do; very nice figure; trim legs; green eyes; long dark hair. For most of the time I've known her it's been brown, but the past thirty years or so she's taken to wearing it red. You'll have to ask her why. When she wears wings, they normally match her hair."

"I'd like to meet her."

"Someday you will. Guarantee it!"

"So you've really been watching me my whole life?"

"Oh, yes. Ariel and I both have."

He became visibly nervous. Dawn laughed. "Yes, even then. Don't worry about it, though; the last thing I want to do is make you uncomfortable. I won't bring it up unless you do. Relax!"

He winced. "How did I end up with such special attention?"

"Oh, it's not just you! We've got at least one angel full-time on everyone out there."

"Everyone?"

"Everyone."

He seemed a bit embarrassed, but continued. "Ah… is it always a boy-girl thing?"

She chuckled. "Not at all. There's a whole lot of you who respond better to the big brother, big sister kind of touch."

"Who decides?"

"Who do you think?"

He was taken aback. "Is it really that important?"

"To Him? Yes, Mike, it really is."

He sighed. "I never even suspected. I mean, you read these stories about angels and such, but you never think of them as being really real!"

"Victims of our own success. We've done such a good job keeping the enemy at bay in this sector that you forget we're even here. But I could tell you stories from Africa and the former Soviet Union which would curl your hair!"

"Such as?"

"Later. Right now I'm enjoying the day. I'd rather not talk shop."

"But why is it that we don't hear from you hardly at all?"

"You hear from us when you *need* to. But, remember, we've already said a lot. It's written down; pick up your Bible any time and read it. Keep in mind there's a lot of tit-for-tat involved. If you heard from angels more often, you'd hear from demons a *lot* more often! On the whole, I'd rather things stay as they are." Then she looked him in the eye and squeezed his hand. "With limited exceptions, of course!"

"I guess I didn't think about there being another side."

"They're out there, for sure. And they're dangerous. But we have some ways to protect you."

"What?"

"If you become aware that the enemy is directly involved in a situation in your world...well, since you belong to us, you can tell them to leave."

"We can?"

"*You* can. This doesn't apply to the average Joe. But since you belong to us then, yes, you can. If you tell them to leave, they have to leave. You have that authority."

"Wow."

She raised an eyebrow. "I'm warning you, now, don't try to get fancy! They know exactly how far you can go, and if you go beyond that you'll never know what hit you! Just tell them to leave. They may bluster and bluff, but stand your ground. We'll back you up if we have to." She looked at the setting sun, then sighed. "Come on. We've got about ten minutes if we're going to beat traffic."

"I'm in no hurry."

"You should be. Sassy's about to leave another mess, and I can't risk teleporting!"

Guardian Angel

Chapter Eleven

A Rookie Officer's Nightmare

It was his fourth week of active patrol since graduating from the Academy. His Field Training Officer, a twelve-year veteran by the name of Darren King, assured him that he was coming along just fine. After four years as a Master At Arms, he had once thought that he already had a handle on police work. Still, after only a month in the meat grinder of an inner-city police division, he was beginning to realize just how far removed this life was from bringing drunks back to the ship on Shore Patrol.

There's no slow time for a police officer in the inner city. It was almost eleven p.m., a cold night in mid-February. As they cruised down Sampson Street, the radio crackled. "Unit 275, Dispatch."

He picked up the microphone. "Two seven five, go ahead."

"Two seven five, report of aggressive panhandler at Leeland Metrorail Station. Caucasian male, six-three, stringy blond hair, wearing a gray T-shirt. Verbal threats to passengers. Possible psychiatric case. Copy?"

"Two seven five copy. En route."

Darren slowed and looked carefully both ways before proceeding through the red light at Polk Street. But he did not activate his overheads; he didn't want to alarm the suspect. The cruiser pulled to a stop at the transit station in the median of the street.

"Gimme a dollar! Gimme a f**king dollar!" the man was hollering at the top of his lungs. It was in the thirties, just above freezing, but he was dressed only in a dirty T-shirt and light jeans. The half-dozen passengers waiting were cowering at the back corner of the platform, not wanting a confrontation but also not wanting to leave the relative security of the station. They showed visible relief as the two officers climbed from the patrol car.

No threatening moves. Establish a rapport, he thought, remembering the lessons from the Academy only a couple months back. He moved slowly; Officer King was doing likewise. Still, he had to protect these innocent civilians. "Hi there, buddy. What's your name?"

"I'm John." Then, again, before he could reply, "I'm John. I'm John! I'M JOHN I'M JOHN I'M JOHN I'M JOHN!!!!"

"Oh, Christ," Darren said under his breath. "We've got a duster!" In all his career on the streets, he was fortunate enough to have dealt with only one PCP addict close up. But that one had been enough. It had taken five officers to subdue him. One of them had ended up in the hospital.

The rookie had never had that experience, not yet. But his academy training had included exposure to dangerous hallucinogenics, and he recognized the distinct odor. *Angel dust!*

It was supremely important, now, to keep from escalating the confrontation. Darren was already calling, in a quiet voice, for five backup units. The dispatcher requested confirmation, but when he said it was a probable PCP intoxication they were dispatched without further question. Now, to keep this powder keg quiet until they could arrive. PCP is an anesthetic; it removes all feeling of pain. Normal compliance techniques are ineffective. And the subject can switch from passive to aggressive in a heartbeat, for any reason or no reason at all.

No threatening moves, sidearms holstered, hands out in the open. Relax. "A little chilly tonight, isn't it?" the rookie ventured to say.

"I'm f**kin' hot!" the man swore. He ripped his T-shirt off with one move; his skin was sweaty. "Gimme a dollar!"

"I'm at work, right now," Darren said in a gentle voice. "But if you just have a seat on that bench and wait a few minutes, I'll see what I can do!"

At that moment came a sound that neither of them wanted to hear, the horn of an approaching train. It was shift change time at the sprawling Oak Brook Dairy bottling plant just a block away; there must be at least a dozen innocent civilians who would be detraining into the danger zone. Officer King knew that he had to get this man away from the platform. "You know, I think I've got a couple of dollars in my car. Why don't you come with me?"

The man looked up at the veteran officer, took an unsteady step in his direction—and then something snapped. The rookie couldn't believe that a man could move that fast; it was like a striking snake. From somewhere in a hip pocket the man produced a switchblade knife. The two officers drew their weapons, but the duster was on top of Darren before he could aim. The knife was stopped by his body armor, but the maniacal addict was already taking another swipe...this time at his unprotected upper arm.

The rookie didn't have a clear shot without endangering his partner. Darren pulled the trigger on his Glock, but the shot went wild. Then he screamed as the knife slashed deep into his shoulder, separating muscles and ligaments as well as the axillary artery.

"Shots fired! Shots fired!" the rookie called over his radio. Officer King fell to the ground, writhing in pain and spurting bright red blood. Now a line of fire was open. The rookie pulled the trigger twice, aiming at the center of mass as he had been trained.

A .45 caliber slug can stop almost anything short of a tank—but it only made the duster mad. He turned and charged at the rookie, knife poised to slash again. He pulled the trigger four more times, scoring four direct hits on the torso; the duster kept coming. There was no time to reload, the addict was almost upon him. Then a thought from somewhere came to his mind, *Aim for the head!*

His marksmanship scores in training had been rated excellent to superior. Events seemed to unfold in slow motion. A neat entry wound appeared in the center of the duster's forehead. An instant later, the entire back half of his skull blew off and bloody brain matter exploded everywhere. But it made no difference. The dead eyes and face held a blank expression as the duster's hands reached for his neck. He could *feel* the maniacal death grip on his throat…

He sat up in bed, wide awake, breathing heavily. Dawn was there, hugging him. "It's all right," she said softly. "It didn't happen that way. Remember? Your last shot stopped him. You had fifteen witnesses testify that the attack was completely unprovoked. The surgeons were able to restore most of Darren's arm function; he took medical retirement on a full pension. Now he owns two Starbucks franchises and is looking to add a third. It's over."

"It could have," Mike said, still breathing hard. "It could have. I was so close…I just know it. It could have."

"Yes, it could have. But it didn't. And it's never going to. Try to relax. You're safe, now."

He sighed. "You never did tell me about your dreams. Better than that?"

She gave a wry smile. "Yes. For the most part."

Chapter Twelve

INVESTIGATIONS

THE MORNING MEETING IN THE Narcotics offices downtown was breaking up. Rick turned to Jake Higgins and Santos Martinez, the two detectives he had assigned to the van bust case. "Any new leads on Ortega and Mack?"

Jake answered first. "I haven't found anything on Ortega at all. Looks like he's gone to ground. Interviewed his family; they all pretended that they didn't speak a word of English." Jake smiled, so did Rick. Jake had the most Anglo face and voice that anyone could ask for…but he spoke better and more fluent Spanish than Julio Iglesias. "But, from what they chattered among themselves, looks like even they didn't have a clue. Got to keep looking."

"I did get a lead on Mack," said Santos. "I spoke with his grandmother last night. She said that he was working at the old coffee plant, but that she hadn't seen him for a week. She was upset at the thought that he might be getting back into trouble; sounds like she really wants to have him straightened out. I think she's being honest with me. I'm planning to head over there as soon as we let out, check with their personnel office once it opens. Who knows, maybe he asked to have his check mailed to him!" Stranger things had happened.

"You mean the old Maywell House place?" said Rick. "You know, I haven't been there in fifteen years. Wonder how much it's changed?" He paused, and then added, "Do you mind if I ride along with you?"

Now of course you're not going to tell the boss, "No" to a question like that. But Rick and Santos were on a friendly basis as colleagues; each of them looked forward to a morning of good conversation. Besides, you never know when another pair of eyes might see something you miss.

"So you've been in this plant before?" Santos asked as they drove south through the underpass from Texas Avenue to Harrisburg Boulevard.

"Oh, yeah! Lots of times. More than I really should have been, to tell you the truth. Had a neighbor, Rufus Johnson, used to work there forty years. My best friend and I would sneak in and look around. Used to be nobody minded that much, as long as you kept out of trouble and didn't do anything stupid."

"I hear they don't make coffee any more."

"No, haven't for a couple of years now. Not exactly sure what they're producing now. But they used to do all kinds of stuff. Uncle Benji's had a rice processing plant on the property. Also used to make Lemon Time and Coolerade. That's where old Rufus worked when I was a kid, the powdered soft drinks. He used to bring us up there; the boss would send us home with some free samples. It was a great place to visit." He sighed. "I'm sure it's all changed now. Liability and all. You can't get away with what you could twenty years ago."

"Where's the main entrance?"

"Hang a right here on Milby."

They drove up to the main gate and pushed the intercom button. "Houston Police. We'd like to speak with someone in Personnel."

You don't last as a cop for thirteen years and make lieutenant on your first try without developing some real instincts. As soon as they drove through the gate, something felt wrong. Almost as if a weight had descended upon him. Rick wasn't sure what it meant, but he was suddenly wary.

You also don't make it as a cop's Guardian for thirteen years without developing the same set of instincts and then some—as well as a real link with your partner. Amy immediately sensed that something was different. True, some of the old spiritual hierarchy was still in place here—she detected a couple of familiar presences—but they shunned contact. Almost as if they didn't want to acknowledge that they knew either her or Rick. That was a bad sign.

Amy tried to extend her senses. No dice; she was blocked in every direction. Rick actually had a better view of the surroundings than she did. If she tried to back off, as at the Executive Center, she would be separated, unable to help him. She elected to draw close, seeing only what he saw, but at a distance where no one could come between them. This was not good.

*　*　*

ANTONIO WAS AWARE OF A growing pressure in his bowels. *No hay problema;* it would be time for a break in only a couple more minutes.

But then, the blasted yellow light came on. Antonio sighed.

Quickly, the corridors outside were cleared and the doors to the room were locked. Inside were about a dozen workers…as well as Enrique and his two top henchmen, Luis and Carlos. They were making an inspection tour of the processing room. The room fell silent.

Enrique was not worried. His security precautions were tight. This was a nuisance, nothing more. Possibly an OSHA inspector, perhaps someone from the environmental commission. This room was isolated, far away from any legitimate activity. All they had to do was hunker down and wait for the light to turn green again in a few minutes. He felt safe here. "Go ahead; keep working," he called out. "*Quieto.*" Keep it quiet.

Slowly, the workers resumed pulling the kilos of cocaine from the totes and loading them into ice chests. Antonio was among them, taking the chests and stacking them in a small anteroom until the coast was clear and they could send them downstairs to the trucks. Now that he could not leave the room, the internal pressure he felt was even more insistent. He muttered a Spanish profanity which was the equivalent of the only appropriate English four-letter word, at the moment.

*   *   *

THE SECURITY GUARD REGARDED THEM with a neutral expression as they waited in the small lobby. They were in plain clothes, Rick in a suit and Santos business casual with a light jacket. They had no police radios or visible sidearms, but each man carried a mobile phone and a concealed pistol. Santos had a pair of handcuffs, but if they hit the jackpot and Demetrius was there on property he planned to call in backup units to make the arrest.

It took a few minutes for the plant manager to meet them at the front desk. They passed the time looking at the various photos and awards on the wall. There was a redevelopment award from the mayor's office, and a photo with the mayor, district councilman, and congressional representative shaking hands with the big shots from the plant management office. "Some serious voltage here," Santos commented. "They've made a lot of friends over the past two years."

"Yeah. You don't know the half of it. We… Well, let's just say I've sat in on some discussions with the Chief's office. The general tone is, 'back off.' Not that I mind; it's been good for the neighborhood. I used to live out here when I was a kid. Still…." Rick's voice tailed off as one of the men in the photo appeared in the doorway, all smiles. "Hi. I'm Lieutenant Smith; this is Detective Martinez." They showed badges and ID cards. "We're looking for information on a person of interest; we've received a tip that he was working here recently. May we speak with your personnel manager?"

"Certainly! I'm Alfred Nelson, plant manager for Advanced Chemical Specialties. I'll be happy to escort you upstairs to Personnel. Come with me?"

He led them down a long, narrow corridor and then down a half-flight of steps to the elevator. Stairs to the elevator? Santos shook his head. But Rick had been there before. Virtually every architectural oddity ever conceived could be found somewhere in these million square feet.

"So what are you producing here now?" Rick asked conversationally as the elevator slowly ascended to the fourth floor. "Used to be the biggest coffee plant in the world!"

"Oh, no more coffee, I'm afraid. Too bad; I heard they used to give out a lot of free samples!" He laughed. "These days we specialize in formulating paint bases, and we're also adding a new process for producing fertilizers." He was well versed on what to do in just this situation; be affable and friendly and just as helpful as possible. Let his underlings—most of whom truly did know nothing—be the buffer to protect the hidden activities. Such as the personnel office. *Sorry, but I can't make exceptions to policy…*

"I'm sorry, Lieutenant," said the personnel manager, "but our policy here is only to release personal information about employees through our legal department in San Antonio. I can give you their contact number…"

Rick was an astute observer of body language. Mike had learned, over the years, never to play cards with him. With Amy working alongside him as a team they were even better. He noticed the "helpful" and "affable" plant manager's reaction to this policy. While there was no suspicion to act on as of yet, it did light off his instincts. But the personnel manager continued.

"…Unless, of course, you already have a warrant. We cooperate fully with law enforcement if a warrant has been issued."

"Actually, ma'am, we do have a warrant," said Santos. "I have it with me, right here." He opened his portfolio.

138

Rick said nothing, but he watched the body language closely. When mention of the warrant was made, the plant manager grew tense. Then, as he read the name—Demetrius Mack—he relaxed again, noticeably.

The personnel manager looked through her files. "No, I'm sorry. I have absolutely no record of a Demetrius Mack being employed at this location ever since we took it over two years ago. Perhaps you should call the old coffee company and ask to look through their dead files?"

"Hmm," said Santos. "My source was pretty clear that this was very recent. Possibly you have him under another name? I understand that he's known on the street as Leroy."

Bingo. Rick had been watching Alf Nelson like a hawk. He'd been completely relaxed as long as "Demetrius" was the name on the table. But as soon as "Leroy" was mentioned, he tensed up again. In point of fact, the junior cocaine courier detested his legal given name and never used it outside of his immediate family. To everyone else, he was Leroy. Rick and Amy were blissfully unaware of this fact at the time, but now they both knew: Something was up.

"No, I'm sorry," the manager continued. "No record of a Leroy Mack either. In fact..." Truthfully, she knew nothing. She was genuinely being helpful. She searched the personnel database, then said, "No. No record of any employee here with a first name of either Demetrius or Leroy. Sorry, but I just can't help you."

The plant manager had relaxed, yet again. "Possibly I received some faulty information," Santos said slowly. He and Rick had worked together as detectives for five years; they had an unspoken code and turn of phrase. Rick knew that what he was really saying was, *...and* *possibly Walter Cronkite was lying about the moon landings, too!* Over the years, Santos and Maria had forged much the same working relationship as Rick and Amy. He was suspicious, as well, but knew better than to voice it openly.

But regardless of their suspicions, they were limited in what they could do now by the letter of the law. They couldn't very well go to the judge and say, "The plant manager seemed nervous." And without a search warrant, they couldn't legally go poking through the plant. Unless they had permission. And who better to ask for that permission than…Mr. Helpful and Affable?

"Sorry to waste your time, Mr. Nelson," Rick said with an affable smile of his own. "You've been very helpful." He turned to leave—and then, with an 'oh by the way' manner, turned back and said, "You know, I've always been curious about this place! Mind if we look around for a bit?" in his best 'aw, shucks!' voice.

"Mr. Affable" relaxed again. The plant was over a million square feet, built like a maze, and the only portion worth worrying about was in a few thousand square feet of an otherwise unused building. A year and a half back, a night watchman who had been here for three months took a wrong turn and ended up lost until morning. The chances that two outsiders could stumble on the real operation? Inconceivable. As I pen this account the thought comes to my mind, *You keep using that word…*

"Sure! No problem! Of course, I will have to escort you. Liability concerns, you know."

"Oh, of course. We wouldn't have it any other way!" By now, Rick could read Mr. Nelson like an open book. "Why don't you show us where we should start?"

Chapter Thirteen

Beaches and Buildings

Having awakened early, Michael had come up with the notion of watching the sun rise from Galveston beach. Dawn was more than receptive to the idea, although she insisted upon taking the ferry across to Bolivar Peninsula. By now the sun was well up; the weather was still mild but it had warmed into the low seventies (yes, I know, but after all the years I spent in Merrie Olde England prior to metrification I still prefer to think in Fahrenheit), enough to where Dawn had shifted into a bathing suit. It was a tolerably modest one-piece but, still, a bathing suit is a bathing suit; Mike and the half-dozen or so other men on the semi-deserted beach were enjoying the view. For his part, Mike had left the house in an athletic warm-up suit but by now had ditched the sweats and left his tennis shoes behind in the truck; now the two of them were walking through the surf, hand in hand.

"We might as well be heading back," she said. "Traffic has eased up, by now."

"How did you get me back to the house Sunday morning without a car?"

"Oh, I can teleport. But I don't want to do so any more than I just have to. The enemy can pick up on the activity. It's a little like setting off a firecracker in public; you might get away with it one time."

"I noticed you had your fingers crossed as we drove through Galveston."

"Yeah. I want to keep a low profile going through there. Some of the powers-that-be might recognize me. There's some hard feelings there."

"Why?"

"I wasn't always a Guardian. Before you were born, I had a leadership position over our forces in this whole region for almost fifty years. Fortunately I had a lot of good civic-minded humans I could use; we accomplished a lot. Freeways, Astrodome, space center, the big airport…a lot of good years. One of my initiatives—well, you've heard that Galveston used to be a 'wide open city.' I pushed to have it cleaned up. The other side still holds a grudge."

"You were here? But I was born in North Carolina!"

"Yep. And you think it was just a coincidence that your Dad was assigned here as a recruiter in '97? These things have a way of working out, if you're paying attention."

"My dad." He sighed. "Have you seen him?"

"Oh, yes. Lots. He asks about you all the time."

"I wish I could see him."

"I do, too. But that's a line that I just can't cross."

"Why not?"

"There's a strict prohibition on communicating between worlds with people who have passed on. I mean, really strict. It's just so easy to be taken in by counterfeits. Sorry. If I could, I would. But I can't."

Dawn glanced around, making sure that no one was watching her as she shifted the bathing suit back into casual street clothes. Other than Mike, of course. And, yes, he stared. "How do you do that?"

"E equals M C squared. It isn't just for breakfast anymore!"

"What?"

"Matter, energy…they're all linked. I can see and manipulate the patterns. Got to be a little bit careful when I do so; while they look the same to you one of us can tell the difference between something I zap and something made by hand the hard way if we look really close."

They took their seats in the truck; Dawn buckled in. Mike started the engine and shifted into gear. Dawn said, "Michael…seat belts?"

Mike looked over his shoulder and shot her a grin. "With my own guardian angel right here in the truck?"

Dawn sighed. "Please. Humor me. My job is tough enough as it is."

Chastised, Mike fastened his seat belt.

*   *   *

Affable Alf escorted them into the adjacent Building 12, where the old coffee roasting ovens had been completely replaced by equipment for mixing paint blends. He was droning on about vertical material flows from the storage tanks on the roof down through metering and mixing equipment on levels 4 and 3 to the packaging machinery on level 2. Rick barely heard him; as with the police radio most of the time it went in one ear and out the other. But a slight feeling of intuition came to his mind. And he had learned to trust those hunches.

Amy was busy. Messengers are *experts* at communications of all sorts—both verbal and otherwise. And one of the prerequisites for communication is knowing your audience. I've used combat imagery and the term "enemy" so freely that I'll forgive you for thinking that Fantar and Dravang, et al., are the rule rather than the exception. Frankly, the greater number of the fallen spirits merely want to be left alone. Oh, yes, there are some truly twisted types out there; more on that later. But while the deeper layers of Hell are a lot like the worst nightmare you've ever experienced, when one gets close to your world there is something at least approaching a sense of permanence and predictability. So a great number of those spirits, and especially those who haven't lapsed all the way into insanity, try to get as close to your world as they possibly can and attach themselves to a particular location, people group, or, in more recent years, sometimes a corporate entity. They can be quite protective of it.

Twenty-plus years previously, when Rick and Mike were first beginning to explore their neighborhood, Amy had succeeded in getting through to the spiritual presences here that these were good kids, that they meant no harm, and that we their Guardians would be able to keep them from doing anything terminally stupid—which promise we were able to fulfill, for the most part, although if you notice any gray hairs on the heads of the three of us let me assure you that we come by them honestly! And, as a result, Mike and Rick had gotten away with going places and doing things which, quite frankly, no youngsters should ever have been allowed to do in a dangerous industrial facility.

Some of this old guard of spirits were still here. They had been overwhelmed, these past few years, by Fantar's legion of hellions. Many, even most of them, resented the intrusion and remembered the days when they could feel that they were a real part of a vital and productive enterprise. Now Amy was reaching out to them again. They shunned direct contact; not wise to let their new masters see them in league with the heavenly Enemy. But what about indirect?

Amy noticed a pattern in the network of spirits which were blocking her senses. While the new presences were all around her, evenly distributed, the old guard was mostly clustered to one side...but with three distinct individuals positioned at about four o'clock from the main mass. She processed the information, taking into account the fact that the other side could not risk being seen extending any open measure of coöperation. The small group was on the third floor of Building 12; a passage to Building 10 was just now at their eight o'clock. *You need to go that way*, Amy transmitted to Rick.

He heard.

*   *   *

THE PICKUP TRUCK WITH THE two of them was northbound on the freeway nearing Dickinson when Michael saw the orange signs for the construction zone. One was an electronic billboard flashing the message, "LANE CLOSURES AHEAD — EXPECT DELAYS."

Sure enough, traffic was backed up. "I thought you said traffic had eased up!" Mike said with a bit of a tease in his voice.

"Actually, it has. This is about as good as it's going to get today!" she replied.

Mike gave a sigh. "Seems like this freeway has been under construction as long as I can remember."

"It has. I had been selected to take over our forces in this region in 1940, but what with World War II going on I waited until it had officially ended before I fully relieved Herman. This was one of the projects I pushed. Construction began in late 1946. It still isn't finished!"

"I don't suppose you could teleport us through this?"

"Not a good idea. Not here and now. It would be noticed."

"Well, then," he said in a tone of voice which clearly conveyed that he was joking, "perhaps you could pull a Superman, pick the truck up, and fly away with it!"

She laughed. "Oh, yes. Easily! But to star on a hundred thousand YouTube videos with my hair looking like this, why, it just wouldn't do!"

"Your hair looks fine to me!" He paused just a moment, and then continued in a more serious vein. "Just how strong are you, actually?"

"Strong enough."

"Can you be a little more specific?"

"Mmmm…not really; I haven't run up against my limits yet. Let's just say that if I wanted to rip this planet out of its orbit and throw it into the Sun, I might have to use both hands!"

He looked over at her. "What? Are you kidding?"

"Actually, no. Don't worry about it, though; I would never do something like that. God wouldn't want me to, for one thing."

"But what if… I mean, just suppose. Could you really?"

She nodded slowly.

He spoke in a very small voice, "Remind me not to make you mad."

She laughed, breaking the mood. "Works for me! Hey, go ahead and exit here. I think we can save a couple of minutes if we take Old Galveston as far as NASA One!"

*　　*　　*

As Alf Nelson droned on, Rick abruptly broke away from the group down a corridor to his left. "What's back here?"

Affable Alf was nonplussed. "Oh, that's just a passage over to Building 10. Used to be rice processing on this level; that's where we're in the process of building out our new fertilizer production facility. See?" He opened a door which led across a short span of roof; construction workers could be seen running conduit and pouring footings for equipment in the largish space beyond.

It truly was nothing of concern. Amy wasn't surprised; this was a test. And she managed to convey that fact to Rick. The three oddballs had by now rejoined their fellows; that was a signal too. Communication established.

The three humans descended a staircase to the second level of Building 10. A large open area, it hadn't been built out yet. "The packaging equipment for the fertilizer will be installed here," Alf said, "and the product will move by conveyor to the warehouse on the other side of that wall. Come with me, now, and we'll go back into the active part of the plant."

He led them around three sides of a square back into Building 12. There were several lines of packaging machinery taking in empty one-gallon cans, filling them with paint, applying labels, and sending them on their way down a conveyor to parts unknown. "Some of this equipment is actually left over from the coffee company," Alf said. "The manufacturers were able to convert it for our new application." He went up and over a pedestrian bridge across the packaging line; Rick and Santos followed suit.

Amy noticed a couple of the familiar presences edging their way from the main mass again. Another test? Perhaps—but she didn't think so. Maria picked up on the activity, as well. Not to the same extent as the experienced Messenger, to be sure, but she gave her partner a nudge of her own.

"Excuse me," said Santos as he pulled out his cell phone. "Just need to take care of some business hanging fire." He sent a quick text.

* * *

Sitting at his desk contemplating his next move, Jake got a chime from his cell phone. He pulled it out; there was a message from Santos. *Need you in area. Bring backup.*

He wondered about the cryptic message for a few seconds and was on the verge of calling back for more information—but there are many possible reasons why a narcotics detective in the field would choose to be less than verbose. Then he concluded that Santos and Rick must have developed a good lead to the suspect he was tracking down and began gathering his paperwork. He replied with a quick *OK*, then picked up the phone and called the South Central Division. They would know a suitable meeting place.

*   *   *

Rick broke away from the small group again and stuck his head through a plastic curtain. The large room on the other side was full of chutes and bins, many still wrapped with caution tape.

"Where are you going?" Alf Nelson called.

"Just curious, again," Rick called back. "Wanted to see what was in here."

Before, when Rick went off on his own, Alf Nelson had been nonplussed. Not this time. Affable Alf was quickly turning into Anxious Alf. Still, he was a good actor; he controlled his voice as he said, "There's nothing in here. This whole area is out of service."

"Oh?" Rick asked. "Why's that?"

"The equipment back here is just too specialized. We're not likely to be able to re-purpose it, not any time soon. We're talking agglomeration tanks three stories tall for making instant coffee granules, super-high-pressure CO_2 compressors for decaffeinating…."

"Wow, that sounds really neat!" Rick said with obvious interest. "I'd like to see that!"

"I've got somewhere I need to be right now."

"Please?" Rick asked in his most persuasive voice.

Alf Nelson was at a loss. He had been told what to do in just such a situation, but the consequences of actually carrying those orders out…? Then he remembered whom he was working for and the consequences of *not* carrying those orders out. "Well… All right. But give me a second." He pulled out a cell phone and pressed a hotkey. "Ms. Dinsdale? Cancel my ten-thirty with Mr. Fitzmorris. That's right, cancel Mr. Fitzmorris. We're running late."

*   *   *

IN THE FRONT OF THE large room, a light changed from yellow to red. Everyone watching went absolutely silent. Including Enrique, Carlos, and Luis.

Antonio was already silent. He was in an alcove in back, trying to stay out of sight of the big bosses.

Chapter Fourteen

The Vipers' Den

"Be careful; some of this area is still hazardous," said Alf Nelson. He started to lead the group to the south stairwell. Santos followed… Rick did not. He was proceeding into the southwest corner. Santos noticed and followed him; Anxious Alf belatedly realized and hurried to catch up as Rick opened a door. "There's nothing back there!"

Rick was examining the short corridor with a detective's eye. Abandoned? Then why were the lights on and air conditioning running? The floor was… not the sterile clean you might expect in a plant with an overzealous janitorial staff, but neither was there two years' worth of dust broken only by the occasional footfalls of a night watchman or maintenance worker. There was dust, yes, but it was obvious that there was regular foot traffic through here. And old memories were being stirred mightily. He entered the short corridor and climbed the six steps before it turned right into Building 20.

"Where are you going?" Alf asked. The anxiety in his voice was now palpable.

"Just hoping that there might be a men's room back here. Ah! Here it is!" he exclaimed, seeing the sign on a door immediately to his left.

Rick did relieve himself; he had a hunch that he might be here for quite a while longer. As he washed his hands, he also scoped the facilities out. There was fresh rubbish in the waste can; some of it was still damp. And this restroom looked to be cleaned and serviced regularly. The puzzle pieces were beginning to come together in his mind.

Let's be clear, here. At this point, neither Rick nor Amy knew what awaited them or the extent of the hidden activities here. Mr. Nelson had a Guardian, of course, but with no personal link he or she could not easily be raised. Even if he were he could not have been much help; one of the constraints upon Guardians is that we cannot divulge secrets which our partners wish kept. Not, at least, until the final Judgment Day. All Amy knew is that there were some spiritual presences, whom she had dealt with in the past and had a measure of trust for, who were encouraging her to revisit an old haunt. And Rick knew even less than that. But, upon emerging from the restroom, he saw and recognized Rufus Johnson's old stomping grounds.

Ahead of him, and still labeled as such, was the handling room for the powdered soft drinks. After being mixed on the floor above, they were processed through here destined for the packaging machinery on the first floor below. Off to his right was the old break room. "Hey, there's a water cooler!" he called to Alf. "Mind if I get a drink?" He entered without waiting for an answer.

Mindful that he was being watched, he didn't open the refrigerator. If he had, he would have noted several bagged lunches. But he did check the rubbish cans as he disposed of his drinking cup; fresh garbage in there, as well. He knew, now. Something was going on here. Something that Anxious Alf didn't want him to know about. But what?

Upstairs, Amy was transmitting to him. *Upstairs.* Forces from the other side were attempting to block her, but she was too close to him for them to wedge in. *You need to go upstairs!*

"I guess I've seen enough here for now," Rick said. "Let's see, where's the staircase?"

"Back over here by the freight elevator," Alf said with palpable relief. "Let me show you the way out; it's kind of confusing." He headed down, Santos following...Rick headed up. "No! That's the wrong way!"

It was a long staircase; there were twenty feet and more between floors in this building. Rick emerged at the third-floor level to find...things had changed.

Oh, some of it was still the same as he remembered. There was dehumidification equipment in the corner for the instant coffee process, now obviously unused. A corridor led to the emergency exit at the west end of the floor, past the switchgear. But where there had once been a lightweight roll-up door leading to the quite large mixing room for the powdered soft drinks, there was now a heavy-duty steel double door bearing a sign, "DANGER—HIGH VOLTAGE."

Santos emerged from the stairwell door behind him, followed by Mr. Nelson who was breathing hard. Rick felt an inner satisfaction. "What's in there?" he asked with a nonchalant tone.

The actor in Alf Nelson was coming to the fore again; you could tell he had rehearsed this. "Nothing. That's just the transformer room."

"Could I stick my head inside and take a look?"

"No. That area is off limits. I don't even have the key for it." Which was true, at least as far as the key was concerned.

*   *   *

ON THE OTHER SIDE OF the door there was no sound, no movement. Presently Enrique became aware that everyone was staring at him. This light had never been red before, not even once. He had given strict instructions: If the red light came on, dump everything incriminating down the floor drains and flush it away. And, had he not been there himself, those instructions would have been followed. But, as it was…everyone was looking to him to give the word.

He couldn't do it. There were *millions* of dollars' worth of cocaine in this room! Was the situation really, truly, that dire?

But another participant in the drama was making a decision of his own. Carlos had served nine months hard time out of a twenty-year prison sentence before a sharp lawyer had managed to have a key piece of evidence invalidated on appeal and, in so doing, overturn his conviction and set him free.

I'm not going back to the Big House, he resolved. *No freaking way!* (At least, I *believe* that's the term he used…) He patted the pistol under his leather jacket.

* * *

"You could call someone," Rick said. "I'm sure somebody in Maintenance or Electrical must have that key."

"No," said Mr. Nelson. Affable Alf was by now long gone. "Liability concerns, you know. I can't let you into that room without a search warrant. Furthermore, I need to ask you to leave, right now. My day has been disrupted enough."

Rick stepped to the corner of the passage. From there, he could keep an eye on both the main access door right in front of him and the corridor which led to the emergency exit at the far end of the building. "I'm sorry, Mr. Nelson, but my feet are hurting. I'm just going to have to rest right here. Santos, get Jake on the phone!"

* * *

Officers Jackson and Ross had been waiting for him in the parking lot of the small Mexican restaurant just across Harrisburg Boulevard from the plant when Jake Higgins pulled in. Being in plain clothes he flashed his badge; the two uniformed officers nodded. "What's up?" Jackson asked.

"Working a drug case; may have got a lead on a suspect. My partner and my boss are in the plant across the street; he asked me to wait here with backup. Could be anything."

"In there?" Officer Ross asked. He gave a low whistle. "Sure hope they know what they're doing. Those folks have a lot of friends at City Hall."

"Yeah, tell me about it," said Jackson. "We've been told to stand back and give them space. Very unofficially, of course."

"Did you hear about the anti-terrorism upgrades?" Ross asked Jake. "Reinforced fences. Riser bollard barricades that can stop a semi at all the gates. Seems a little overkill, but I guess it is a chemical plant now. Hey, do we have time to grab a cup of coffee?"

"Don't see why not," Jake answered.

It was the slow time of the morning, half past ten o'clock. Service was quick. But as soon as Jake finished stirring his sugar, his cell phone rang. "Figures." He took a quick sip, then answered the phone. "Higgins. What's up, Santos?" A pause, then, "Across the street with a couple of guys from South Central. Mind if I put it on speaker for them?"

Apparently the answer was affirmative, as Jake pressed a button and laid the smartphone down on the table. The three officers heard an excited Detective Martinez saying, "Jake, I'm going to need you to run back downtown and talk to the judge. We need a search warrant for this plant. Specifically the electrical area in the third floor of building 20, but make it broader than that if you can get it. There's definite suspicious activity going on here, possibly leading to our two suspects. Here's what we've seen…."

*　*　*

AMY KNEW FOR CERTAIN, NOW, that *something* untoward awaited on the far side of that door. It seemed as if all the forces of Hell were trying to block her out! A lesser spirit might have flown the white flag and called retreat…but she was bound and determined to crack through that barrier, even if it took dynamite.

As it turned out, dynamite wasn't required. The only necessity was one man who really, really wanted to go to the loo.

*   *   *

THE PRESSURE IN ANTONIO'S BOWELS was now becoming intolerable. He became aware that all activity in the area had ceased. Curious, he emerged from his hiding place in back to see everyone silently staring at the light.

It was no longer yellow!

*   *   *

ON THE LONG ARM OF the X-chromosome in human cells, in the position geneticists designate as 28, there is a gene which they have dubbed *OPN1MW*. This gene carries the molecular information which allows retina cells in the eye to manufacture a pigment which is sensitive to light in the yellow/green portion of the visible spectrum. Occasionally there is a mutation in this gene which disrupts this information and prevents the eye from manufacturing this pigment. Since women have two X-chromosomes in each cell, it is very rare for both to be disrupted at the same time. But if they are, or if they pass a defective X-chromosome along to male offspring who have only the one X-chromosome and thus no "backup copy" of this information, it results in a condition technically known as "deuteranopia." The eyes of the affected human are rendered unable to distinguish between otherwise distinct shades of color. They do still see colors, but whereas a normal human physical eye can distinguish from between two to ten *million* distinct colors, a physical eye with deuteranopia can distinguish between only two and three hundred thousand. Shades of red and shades of green, in particular, can look almost identical. For this reason traffic signals are designed and built to give indications not only by color, but also by position; "stop" indications are always top or left while "proceed" indications are always to the bottom or right. The layman's term for deuteranopia is, of course, "color blindness."

And nobody knew that Antonio was color blind.

*   *   *

THE EXIT DOOR WAS LOCKED—BUT the key had been left in the lock. Antonio turned it and flung the door open before anyone could stop him. Enrique yelled at him, but all that did was to draw even more attention from the officers waiting on the other side of the door. Not that this made a difference.

A surprised Antonio looked directly into the face of an equally surprised Lieutenant Smith. Behind Antonio, Rick could see tables and ice chests and bricks of cocaine and about twenty stunned faces.

The recently promoted lieutenant was first to respond. Immediately he yelled out, "Houston Police! Freeze! Everybody down, now!" while drawing his concealed sidearm.

But he couldn't cover everyone in the room at once.

*   *   *

The astonished workers were slow to respond. Many of them, including Antonio, didn't understand English at all and stared uncomprehending until Rick repeated his order in Spanish. Enrique and Luis, on the other hand, understood English very well and also understood exactly what that red light had portended. They were among the first to hit the floor. As they did, Enrique was struck with an ironic thought: the plant was actually making money! Oh, it wouldn't be as fantastically profitable without the smuggling activities, certainly, but the legitimate business was pulling in enough net revenue to cover the utilities and taxes, keep the local politicos paid off, and provide fat bonuses for his operation's senior management—including Alf Nelson. *I could have gone straight!* he mused as he lay there prone with his hands over his head.

Luis dropped almost as quickly as Enrique, but instead of thinking upon what could have been he kept a clearer head. Inconspicuously he reached into his jacket for his cell phone. What was normally the "mute" button between the volume buttons had been reconfigured on his phone into a panic button. He pressed it.

Carlos, on the other hand, was acting upon the decision he made earlier. From under his jacket he drew a 9mm Beretta and flipped the safety off. Rick saw the motion and turned to cover—but Carlos got his shot off first.

Most thugs seldom practice with their weapons, and their aim is lousy. Carlos's was not.

*   *   *

Lockwood Drive would normally be the quickest route to Mike's home, but there was major road work underway adjacent to his old alma mater, Austin High School. Instead, he detoured around to the north via Cullen. But there was a backup there, as well; he could see a train parked on the railway crossing with no indication as to when it would move. Not a problem, though; he knew a back way. He took a left on Coyle Street, then turned right on Milby. This would take him back to Polk, where there was an underpass which would let him cross under the railway back into his neighborhood.

When he arrived at Polk Street he saw that the underpass was not needed; the train was parked somewhat to the south, and the rail crossing of Milby on the far side of Polk Street was clear. It would be a slightly quicker trip home if he continued straight on Milby and then turned right a few blocks past Harrisburg. And so he did.

*　*　*

THE THREE OFFICERS ACROSS THE street were listening to Santos's account of the suspicious details he and Rick had observed while touring the facility. Jake set the phone to record the call, but he was also jotting down notes on paper as a backup. Then, in the background, he heard a surprised yell followed by his boss calling out for everyone to freeze and get down, first in English and then in Spanish.

Then there were sounds which could only be gunshots, accompanied with the sound of Santos's phone clattering to the concrete floor.

Immediately the three officers dashed out the door. Jake threw a business card down on the table, calling out to the waitress, in Spanish, that they would be back.

* * *

As soon as he turned the slight break to the right where Milby crossed the railroad tracks Mike saw that he had made the wrong choice. Up ahead, the railroad crossing where the Consolidated Pacific tracks crossed Milby was blocked by a northbound train. It was almost assuredly the reason why the other train had been parked; these tracks merged with the line of K. P. & G. just a few blocks to the north. Mike sighed, but at least this train was moving—and at full track speed, near as he could tell. The crossing would be clear in just a minute or two. He pulled up to the gate and waited.

Near on the other side of the tracks loomed the towers of the former coffee plant, now the site of more nefarious activity unbeknownst to anyone else on our side…although that was just about to change. "The old Maywell House plant," Mike said. "I know that place!"

"I remember. You used to go trespassing there."

Mike looked over at her. "Exploring."

"Whatever."

* * *

Amy was still blocked. But when Antonio's action flung the barriers wide open in front of her, she realized what was going on almost as soon as her partner did. Like him, her first concern was to get the word out as quickly as possible. She screamed out a message at the top of her telepathic lungs to every angel with whom she had even a tenuous contact.

Messengers are *experts* at communication.

* * *

THE FIRST TWO GUNSHOTS BELONGED to Carlos. The first impacted Rick's body just an inch and a half below the right clavicle. As he was in plain clothes and on a routine investigative visit Rick was not wearing body armor; neither were Santos nor Jake. The Parabellum slug penetrated a lung, creating a sucking chest wound. Very dangerous. The second was even more problematic. It impacted Rick's skull at his left temple, ricocheting off the inside of the parietal bone through his cerebral cortex.

The third gunshot belonged to Rick. But it was purely a reflex action, not aimed, and it hit nothing of interest. The lieutenant was rendered unconscious instantly by the bullet wound to his brain, and he collapsed to the ground bleeding.

The next seven shots fired all belonged to Detective Santos Martinez.

* * *

"OH, DEAR GOD!" DAWN CALLED out, putting her hand to her mouth.

"What?" Mike asked with concern in his voice.

"Rick has been shot!"

* * *

ANTONIO NEVER DID MAKE IT to the loo that morning. But his bowels were now empty. His pants were not.

Chapter Fifteen

BREAKTHROUGH, PART II

THE THREE OFFICERS RAN OUT the door of the restaurant at full tilt. Officers Jackson and Ross ran to their cruiser; Jake's vehicle was what the 1970s truckers would call a "plain brown wrapper" but it had a siren and police lights behind the grille. These he activated and followed the squad car through the red light onto Milby Street.

A train was crossing northbound just on the other side of the plant. The officers ignored it. The squad car pulled up to the main entrance gate, Jake's car right behind it. "Houston Police! Let us in! Let us in, NOW!" Officer Jackson called over the intercom.

There was no response. No verbal response, at least. But, to Jake's horror, a pair of stainless-steel bollards rose out of the ground just behind the gate. Even worse, other security barriers could be seen rising into position behind the internal gates into the production areas within. These barriers had been installed by the same company which serviced the security measures at the White House; they would laugh off an impact by a fully loaded tractor-trailer at sixty miles an hour.

Officer Jackson was still, in futility, calling out for someone to respond over the intercom as Officer Ross attempted to relay the gravity of the situation to their dispatcher. The SWAT team was being mobilized…but could even they break into this armored facility in time to make a difference?

He wondered.

* * *

"It's here! He's right here!" Dawn cried out to Michael.

"What? Here?" Mike replied.

"Yes!"

At that moment the south end of the northbound train cleared the crossing. Technically violating the law, Mike drove around the crossing arms without waiting for them to rise. There was a marked and an unmarked police car, lights flashing, at the plant gate just ahead. He could hear the siren cut in and then out as Officer Ross called, "Open up! Open up NOW!" over the squad car's bullhorn. It was no use.

A peace officer is never truly off duty. Mike skidded to a stop just this side of the plant gate and jumped out of his pickup, Dawn a step behind him. Although clad only in shorts, T-shirt, and sneakers, Mike was carrying a concealed firearm and his badge. He flashed the latter, calling out, "K. P. & G. railroad! Special Agent!" A precaution, but not strictly necessary; both Officers

Jackson and Ross recognized him from his days in their division not two years prior. "What's happening here?"

* * *

Fueled by adrenaline, Santos had emptied the six-round magazine from his Smith & Wesson M&P 40 Shield, plus the one in the chamber, in less than three seconds. Two of his shots had missed, but the other five had all scored hits on his target before it could react. Carlos, however, was young and in top physical condition; it took a few seconds before his body registered the damage. But those seconds passed, and Carlos collapsed to the ground. Panting, Santos reached for his backup magazine and scanned the large room for any more threats.

None were apparent, but…Detective Martinez was not watching his back.

* * *

Jake also recognized Mike as the agent who had ID'd the suspects they were tracking down. Quickly he brought both Mike and Dawn up to speed with a few brief sentences. Santos's phone call, by now, had cut off completely. "We've got to get in there, now!" Jake finished.

Mike looked across the street. "I can get in there!"

* * *

Santos was still scanning the room for threats when he heard…the sound of a pistol being cocked behind him. Then came Alf Nelson's soft voice. "Detective? Put down the gun. Put down the gun, now."

He turned. Behind him were four armed security guards, all with pistols pointed at his back, covering him from every direction. He hesitated.

"That's right. No sudden moves, now. Just put the gun down," came Mr. Nelson's soothing voice. Recognizing reality, Santos complied.

In the next room, Enrique and Luis were rising from the floor. Enrique saw that there was new life in the situation. "I'll take over from here," he told Alf Nelson.

"You're not getting away with this," Santos replied angrily.

"I'm not saying I need to get away with this," Enrique said calmly. "I just need to get away. You can have the plant. You can have the drugs. You can have the credit." Pointing at the bleeding form of Carlos, he said, "He got your man, but you got him. Let him take the blame. All I want is a two-hour head start for me and my top men. Just two hours. That's all."

Santos replied with a suggestion which would have been anatomically challenging even for a shapeshifter.

"The clock is ticking, Detective. You need to make your decision before the first police car arrives here."

"Uh, boss?" said one of the security guards. "They're already here!"

*　　*　　*

Diagonally opposite across the street and the Consolidated Pacific tracks from the old coffee plant is an even older industrial facility: The Milby Street Roundhouse. The actual "roundhouse" as such is now gone and has been for many years, although the locomotive turntable still remains. It was the central engine terminal for the former Houston Belt & Terminal railway for most of the twentieth century, eventually falling into the orbit of K. P. & G. when the old H. B. & T. was broken up amongst its owners following the mega-merger years which created the modern North American railway landscape. It still serves as their primary engine terminal and servicing facility in the Greater Houston area. A baker's dozen of locomotives were parked there in various stages of service, from covers off and vital parts removed all the way to Diesels idling and ready to head out on the road.

Mike's attention was focused on the latter.

*　　*　　*

MY UNDERSTANDING FROM INTERVIEWS WITH saints who have come Home is that, for them, leaving the physical body behind is much like waking up from a bad dream into a glorious eternal Morning. I have not had the dubious pleasure of speaking with those who have gone the other way, but I suspect that it resembles nothing so much as falling down a black hole into a bottomless pit of despair.

As previously recounted, Carlos was young and, up until now, healthy. It took nearly a full five minutes for his soul to completely relinquish its grasp on the physical. As the bonds broke away he became aware of a larger world which had heretofore escaped the notice of his senses. There were personalities here as well; deprived of physical means of detection, his soul struggled to make sense of his surroundings but eventually rendered them in an analogue fashion which he could comprehend.

There was an enormously fat…man?…with a look of desperation on his face, barking orders to all

167

and sundry. There was a masculine presence which appeared debonair and behaved obsequiously, but who seemed to be doing little to carry out the increasingly desperate and contradictory orders which he received. Beside him was a feminine spirit, just standing there with a subtle look of satisfaction on her face. Around them were underlings who looked around in confusion and who regarded Carlos as nothing more than so much furniture to trip over. But there was one presence who seemed sympathetic. More than sympathetic, he seemed almost like the older brother whom Carlos had never had. "Help me!" Carlos pleaded with him.

"It's too late. I can't," the other responded before turning away. There were tears in his eyes.

Around him, almost like demonic garbage collectors, several personalities converged. Carlos screamed.

Nobody heard him. His last rational thought was that he would rather go back to the Big House after all.

*   *   *

IN THE THREADBARE EMPLOYEE LOUNGE across the street at the roundhouse an engine crew, conductor and engineer, were preparing to take a locomotive set out on the road and down the line to the large container terminal in Pearland. Mike was explaining to them what he had in mind. Dawn was ignoring me. I have to admit that I was screaming, *"Are you out of your ever-loving mind?"*

"This will work," Dawn muttered under her breath. To me, mainly, but Mike heard it as well. He took it as encouragement. I didn't.

"It's not whether or not it works! It's what becomes of you! Do you have even a hint of what's waiting over there? If they recognize you there's no possible way that we can get to you before they do! You're not the bloody Lone Ranger!"

"I'll keep a low profile. Nothing 'special'," she replied in the lowest whisper she had.

As if I would believe that! "And what about Mike?" I responded. "Don't you both know he's putting his career on the line?"

Dawn sighed. Then she turned to Mike. "I'm not trying to talk you out of this, but—you do realize that, if you go through with this, you could be fired?"

Mike looked her straight in the eye. "And? If I do get fired, will you still stick with me?"

"You betcha!"

"Then let's roll."

*　*　*

THE SECURITY GUARDS HAD CARRIED handcuffs. Santos was now lying face down, arms and legs restrained behind him, teeth gnashing in fury. Enrique spoke. "No time to talk, Detective. It's a simple choice, really. *Plata o plomo.* If we get our two-hour head start, you get a pleasant surprise in a month or two. Delivered discreetly, of course. Otherwise, you get no time at all."

Nobody would have faulted Santos for pretending to go along with the deal. But he was a man of honor, and a man of his word. And the thought of crawling before this human snake was more abhorrent than the idea of taking a bullet. "See you in Hell!"

"As you wish." He stepped back. "Luis, do it."

Luis was loyal. He was also smart. He had no desire to be tagged as a cop-killer in a state which quite frequently makes use of the death penalty. "Boss, we gotta get moving! We gotta go now!"

Enrique hesitated. The bug-out plan for him and his men was work clothing and fake IDs concealed in an old locker room in the next building over. They would change, then mix in with the legitimate work crew and attempt to filter out in the confusion when law enforcement finally did break in. The plant's defenses had been designed to hold off anything which the local SWAT team could muster for at least thirty minutes, probably a full hour. But he had not expected to be surprised in his lair with the first police cars showing up less than a minute later.

When a railroad track abuts your property, locomotive horns are a frequent occurrence. But there was something different about this one....

*　*　*

THE TWO LOCOMOTIVES WERE SIX-AXLE SD40-2 units, each one older than Mike was. Substantially older, for that matter; they had been built in the mid-1980s. They were coupled tail-to-tail, push-pull style. The crew was in the trailing locomotive—which only makes sense, considering what they had in mind. The engineer slid the reversing lever into the control stand to unlock it. Oh, and before I forget, each SD40-2 had three thousand horsepower and weighed in at three hundred and sixty-eight thousand pounds. And, as previously recounted, there were two of them.

Even when your intent is to violate the rule book, there are still formalities to be observed. The track which he needed was actually owned and dispatched by Consolidated Pacific, but K. P. & G. held trackage rights. Mike picked up the locomotive radio. "ConPac dispatch, K. P. & G. agent Wilson. Need a light engine move from Milby engine terminal to Maywell House spur, requested by Houston Police. Engine 1821."

The K. P. & G. conductor—you've met him before; he works the spur into this plant frequently—spoke into the radio next. "K. P. & G. 1821, requesting light engine move to Maywell House spur. Standing by."

"Received," replied the dispatcher. He checked his board; it was clear. He set the switches appropriately, then keyed his microphone. "K. P. & G. 1821, light engine move from Milby Street terminal to Maywell House spur approved. Highball."

"K. P. & G. 1821, copy highball," the conductor replied.

"Highball," his engineer confirmed.

The two locomotives nosed their way out the north gate of the engine terminal and onto the Consolidated Pacific main line. When clear of the switch the engineer stopped the locomotive, allowing the conductor to step down and throw it behind them. Then, he climbed back aboard for a short backup move—not quite a quarter of a mile—to the crossover which led to the track that they needed. "North" of here...actually, west-northwest...the spur was used as a passing track and the first switch from the main line was operated by the dispatcher via remote control. To the south, though, it was all the old coffee plant. The conductor stepped to the ground as the locomotive passed the second switch and backed up onto the passing siding. Then he unlocked the switch and threw it so that the two locomotives could proceed forward onto the spur track. Once they were past the clearance point he threw the switch again, aligning it for normal use, and locked it.

He knew that it might be a while before they unlocked it again.

*　　*　　*

By now backup units and the core of a SWAT team were beginning to arrive in the area. Officers Jackson and Ross briefed them on what Mike and Dawn were planning, and warned them to keep clear of the railroad tracks on the south side of the facility.

Once they understood what was supposed to happen next, they complied without question.

*　　*　　*

"Ready?" Mike asked the conductor as he stepped back aboard.

"I've done my thirty. I'm ready to retire right now!" he replied.

"Always wanted to be a Hollywood stuntman," the engineer commented.

"Wonder if anyone's filming this?" Mike asked.

"Oh yes we are!" Dawn assured him.

"What's she doing here?" Jake Higgins asked.

"She can take care of herself," Mike replied. He picked up the microphone; this would be recorded by the home office. He transmitted, "This is Special Agent Michael Wilson. K. P. & G. 1821 on the Maywell House spur. On my authority…highball!"

"Highball," the conductor confirmed. The engineer released the brakes, put the reverser into REV, and advanced the throttle. The big Diesels spun up to power and the two locomotives began to accelerate down the tracks.

From their starting location to the switch which led to the spur into Building 10 was just over a quarter of a mile. A locomotive is no dragster, by any means—but six thousand horsepower with no trailing load does have its own measure of brute force. Emphasis "brute".

There was another track which continued straight back to the warehouse; it had once been used for shipping coffee out in boxcars. But that portion of the track had not been in service for more than thirty years, save to store the occasional rail car; all deliveries by rail went to Building 10 and the switch was already lined appropriately. The conductor confirmed this; the arrow on the switch stand ahead pointed to the left.

The engineer leaned on the horn. No long-long-short-long sequence as required by law; instead he sounded a continuous blast. By the time the locomotives crossed Milby they were already doing twenty-six miles an hour. It was too late to stop now; they were committed.

"How far do we take her?" the engineer asked.

"If she stays on the rails? All the way into the building!" Mike yelled.

*　*　*

THE GATE, AS PREVIOUSLY RECOUNTED, had been reinforced with heavy steel I-beams. But there were no riser bollards here; the possibility that they might be needed had never crossed Enrique's mind. Even if it had, whether a suitable barrier could actually be designed and built was a very good question.

There is a philosophical debate of long standing about what the results will be if an irresistible force encounters an immovable object. It is a silly question; the only truly immovable object and the only genuinely irresistible force is in fact God, and God is too sane to dispute with Himself. Still, based upon what I witnessed that day in microcosm, if the question is ever actually put to the test for real—my money is on the irresistible force.

I will say this much with confidence. Whatever the results may be, you certainly don't want to be standing between them!

*　*　*

THE STEEL I-BEAMS TRULY WERE strong. Stronger, in point of fact, than the tracks and rails upon which the large gate traveled. The lead locomotive crashed into the gate doing thirty-eight miles an hour, knocking the gate off of its tracks as a unit and causing major damage to the brick walls of Building 17 when it slammed into them. The shock actually registered on the instruments in the Seismology lab at the University of Houston a mile and a half distant; investigators putting together a time line later used that as a data point.

The two locomotives did in fact stay on the rails. I can't say whether or not Dawn "did" anything to facilitate that. I'm not saying that I don't *know*, I'm saying that I can't *say*. Hint, hint. The engineer made a full service locomotive brake application as soon as the gate was penetrated; he knew that by comparison the roll-up door into Building 10 itself would be like slicing through a sheet of paper.

174

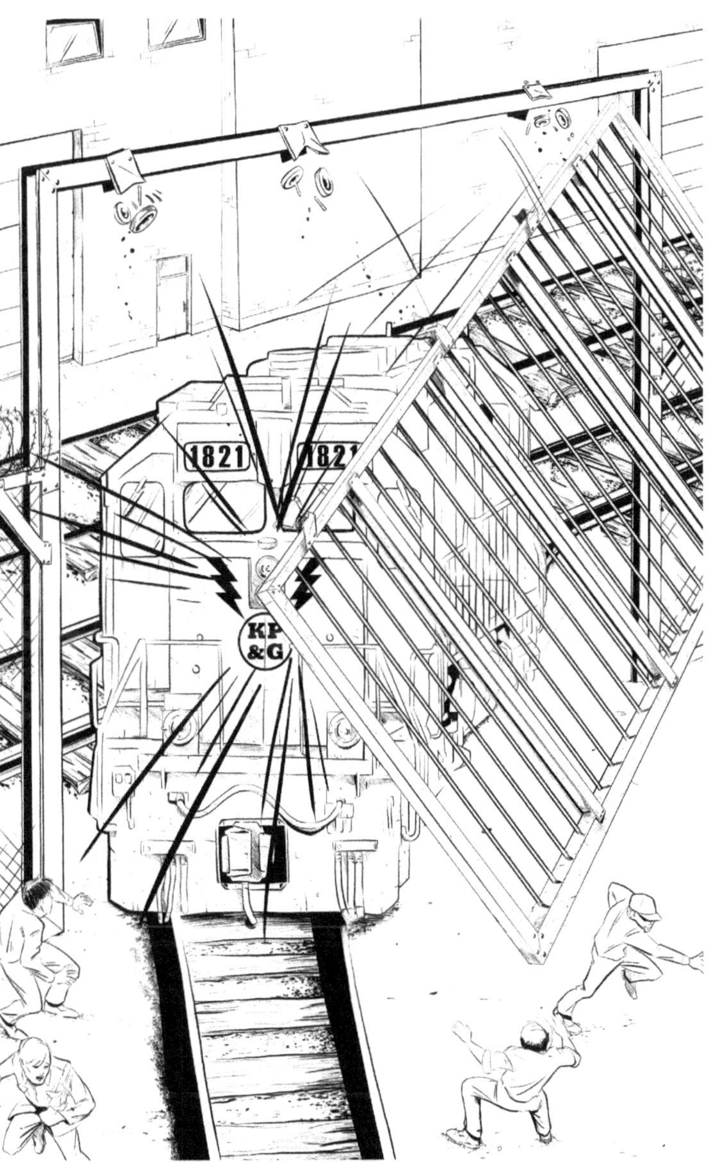

Irresistable Force, Immovable (?) Object...!

It was.

* * *

THE EXTENDED HORN BLAST WAS followed by a tremendous crash. Enrique and his men *felt* it. "What the hell was that?" one asked.

Enrique was rattled. Had SWAT used explosives to penetrate the perimeter? He had considered that eventuality likely, but always thought that it would take at least the better part of an hour to assemble a team of demolition experts and obtain the necessary permission to proceed. It had been less than seven minutes since the gunfire was exchanged. "I…."

Luis took charge. "Boss, get moving! We gotta get out of here now! I'll take care of this!"

Enrique, Alf Nelson, and the guards hustled out of the door. Behind them, they heard two gunshots.

* * *

SANTOS WAS STILL LYING FACE down on the floor, seething. He heard Luis telling the others, "I'll take care of this!" and steeled himself. Then Luis knelt on the floor beside him, and he heard, "Count to two hundred," in a very low voice. But, before he could get started or understand, he heard the two gunshots at very close range.

They were close enough that his skin was peppered with cement shards from the concrete floor. But he was alive. It wasn't until he heard the door slammed and locked behind him as Luis left that he finally understood.

Luis might still go down for narcotics offenses. But he would not go down as a cop-killer.

Chapter Sixteen

Sic Transit Gloria

The locomotives had slowed, but not enough. They crashed into the end of the loading dock, breaking up the concrete and exposing rails which had not been used since Henry Ford was loading Model Ts from this same spur track. There was no fire; Diesel is nowhere near as combustible as gasoline and even cars do not burst into flames nearly as often as Hollywood would have you believe.

"Call it in to the office and prepare to face the music," Mike told his conductor. Then he turned to Jake. "Where is he?"

"From what Santos said before the call cut off, he was on the third floor of building 20. Wherever that is."

"Third floor of building 20?" An old memory came to the fore of his mind. "I think...."

"We know exactly where that is!" finished Dawn. "Let's move!"

K. P. & G. equips all of its locomotives with a very comprehensive industrial first-aid kit. Before clambering down out of the cab, Dawn grabbed it.

*　　*　　*

Back on my own side of the Border, our forces by now had been fully alerted as well. We truly had had no idea of all that went on in that little corner of Hell... but now that events in your world had breached the enemy defenses, that was changing. As police cars and ambulances flooded in through the opening Mike and Dawn had created in the plant perimeter, so too angels were pouring in through the corresponding gaps in our realm.

It's not as though we stumbled upon Fantar's innermost sanctum, however. That was too well protected and hidden by layer upon layer of decoys. Instead, we had the net effect of wedging in between Fantar's empire and your world, rendering him... irrelevant. And that was the most crushing blow of all. Straightforward defeat in battle he could have endured, biding his time and plotting eventual revenge for the insult. But irrelevancy was more than he could bear.

More than his superiors could bear, too, as it turned out.

*　　*　　*

Mike and Dawn raced each other to the stairwell in the south corner of Building 12, with Jake Higgins a step behind them. The two police officers had their weapons out, while Dawn was still carrying the large first-aid kit.

Dawn allowed Mike to take the lead after they reached the second floor; he remembered where to go. For the most part; he was briefly confused by a second, closer door leading to the old quality control lab which looked much like the door he remembered.

"Other door," Dawn prompted. He broke to his left, in the far back corner about thirty feet away was the proper door. They went through it and climbed the same six steps Rick had taken not twenty minutes past and the turn to the right past the men's room. "Left," Dawn prompted again. Mike remembered and found the stairwell, taking the steps two at a time.

The heavy steel door was now locked; the fleeing felons had secured it after the expendable pawns had fled their erstwhile workplace. "Locked," Mike said with frustration.

Hollywood would have you believe that, in such a situation, two or three rounds fired into the lockset from a pistol acts as a universal key. The two experienced peace officers knew better; such is more likely to jam the lock and render it inoperable save by the use of dynamite. "Is there another way in?" Jake asked.

"Here, let me try," Dawn said from behind him. She set down her first aid kit, wiggled the knob back and forth for a couple of seconds...and it opened. I was beyond sighing. "Maybe it was stu-uck?" she said with a Texas twang while giving her most oh-so-innocent dewy-eyed little girl facial expression.

Jake yanked the door open; he could see bodies on the floor beyond. He raced through the doorway, pulling out his cell phone to call this in to dispatch. Mike paused long enough to look Dawn in the eye and give her a muted, "Showoff!"

She grinned. But the grin did not last. From her position on the far side of the Border, she began to become aware of the full extent of the forces arrayed against them. It was enough to give even the experienced Warrior pause. But she paused for only a moment; there were injured men in the room beyond and she was trained and equipped.

"Triage" is derived from the French for "sorting things out." In a medical context it is used to refer to the sorting of patients by urgency. There are some patients whose affliction is minor; they are in no immediate danger and can be dealt with at leisure. Santos fell into this category; aside from a few minor bumps and scrapes he had no real injuries at all. There are some patients who are so far gone that expending resources upon them is just a waste of time and effort; this described Carlos's situation perfectly. But then there are some patients whose life is in grave danger, but who can be saved by quick and drastic action. For Rick, quick and drastic action was called for. Dawn broke open the first aid kit, grabbing blood packs to sop up the mess and scissors to cut his suit off him. The head wound...it was a mess, but that sucking chest wound took priority.

Mike and Jake both carried handcuff keys on their key rings; fortunately Smith & Wesson Model 100 cuffs are fairly generic. Santos was freed and sat up; after assuring Jake that he was all right he told them that the bad guys went that-a-way...indicating the door leading outside into the third floor extraction area. But before they could follow Dawn called out, "Mike?"

He turned towards her. As it turns out, Philip had gotten close enough to feed her some inside information. In a soft voice intended for Michael alone she said, "Locker room. Building 19, second floor. Hurry!"

Jake and Santos were struggling with the locked door. No good. But Mike remembered another way. He stood up and said, "Follow me. Let's go!" leading the two detectives down the ramp and through the curtain into building 15.

* * *

FANTAR WAS IN FULL-BLOWN PANIC mode, looking around for someone to blame. Dravang was convenient. But the latter had a hole card of his own, and now was the time to play it. Alert for the entry of the presence, Dravang was first to drop to his knees. Dragora was just a heartbeat behind him, and the other spirits in the room quickly followed suit. Fantar was the last to realize what was going on. Belatedly he prostrated himself and said, "Your Majesty!"

I want to say that it was Mister Big himself. I know better than that. I can't begin to tell you how many times we have thought that we had the Evil One over a barrel at long last, only to find that we had actually latched on to an underling and that the real power behind the throne had escaped to wreak havoc on yet another day. Such was the case now. But there was a link to Old Scratch here, that I'm sure of, and it was a close link. Closer than anyone in the room had ever experienced before. They did not find it comforting. Even less so when aides loyal to the potentate followed, quickly outnumbering and outgunning the forces of the one-time demonic prince.

"What is going on here, Fantar?" the newcomer asked. The omission of any of his titles did not bode well for the demon prince. Not at all.

"A temporary setback, my lord. Just a tem…."

"Temporary?" the other interrupted. "The humans have smashed a promising operation. Our Colombian and Mexican activities may be threatened. And you try to brush this under the rug as a 'temporary setback?'"

"We can rebuild, my lord. We can rebuild. I know these people; I know this territory. They will be back in my power as soon as…."

"Silence!" the overlord thundered. Then, in a more measured tone, he continued. "We have been contemplating a change of strategy in this area for quite some time now. It would appear that this is the opportune time to implement it. Your services are no longer required."

Not what any demonic prince wants to hear. Fantar was whimpering. "No, my lord! I can still be of service! Let me prove…."

"Remove him," his master commanded.

His powerful aides promptly obeyed. "NO! NO! NOOOoooo…!" screamed Fantar as he tried to claw and scrape away, to no avail. Then came a sound, and a scene, like the very final slamming of a door. Fantar's former minions grew deathly silent.

"Dravang," spoke the overlord.

Dravang does have other talents…more on that later… but one of them is groveling. He prostrated himself yet again. "Yes, my lord?"

"Arise. You are now our prince in this sector. We have seen your proposals. We encourage you to implement them."

Dravang rose, and then bowed. "By your command, my lord!"

"We also thank you for your reports of your former commander's performance. They were most helpful. Take care that no one under your command has cause to send us similar reports about you."

"But of course, my lord."

And just like that, the overlord and his entourage were gone. Dravang surveyed the scene with some satisfaction. "At last! Command! Now I am the power in this principality! Arise, my subjects. Let us give our masters a triumphant first impression. I want to be able to report some kind of a victory by midnight. Spread out and survey the area. Find some way for us to strike back. Go!"

There's always someone ready to toady up to a new boss. In this case, it was Helspeth. He had managed to reach out and re-establish a link with the former stronghold after Nathan's forces had successfully neutralized it. "My prince?" Helspeth asked.

"Yes?" Dravang replied. Helspeth directed his attention through the viewing warp back to the third floor of building 20, where Rick lay on the floor bleeding as Dawn fought to keep him from slipping away. "Yes. That will do nicely," Dravang said. "Get him!"

*   *   *

Mike led Jake and Santos through building 15 into building 16, and then through a doorway into building

17. This one was supposed to have been locked as well, but most of the illicit "employees" had their belongings in an old locker room on the second floor of that building and, well, underlings can be less than diligent, especially when they are fleeing for their lives. All of these buildings were connected on this, the third floor, and a passage led to the right through building 18 into building 19.

Essentially, Mike had led the detectives around three sides of a square which the fugitives had cut straight across. The stairwell door here was locked as well— major fire code violation; have to write them a ticket— but Mike kept going into building 22. This "building" was actually more of an open tower extending upwards some fifteen stories; the coffee beans had been hoisted to the top of it for storage and then weighed and processed on the way down. Here there was an open stairwell leading down; the three officers descended it.

Only to be met by a trio of SWAT officers in full ballistic gear, one clutching a shotgun. "Police! Freeze!" SWAT officer Nelson ordered.

Mike froze; it doesn't look good to be in shorts and sneakers carrying a weapon at a known crime scene. Fortunately the SWAT officers were not trigger-happy; their dispatcher had alerted them to the presence of plainclothes officers on site. "Houston Police! Purple!" shouted Jake, 'purple' being the code word for the day which had been received at morning roll call. "Jake Higgins, narcotics."

"Santos Martinez, narcotics. This is Mike Wilson, K. P. & G. special agent. We're following him; he knows his way around here."

"I got a tip," Mike said without giving details. "This way!"

*   *   *

Dawn was torn. The link Helspeth had reconnected ran both ways; he had a clearer view than she had but she was aware of the forces arrayed against her. Still, although she had sealed the chest wound, Mike's best friend was on the verge of slipping into tension pneumothorax—collapsed lungs; life-threatening—and not something that her first aid kit was equipped to deal with. Yes, if she used her full 'toolkit' she could handle the problem…and also the head wound, which was even nastier than she had thought upon first glance…but it would put her into imminent danger of recognition and capture.

I had my hands full extending my being to keep an eye on both Mike and Dawn at the same time. I do believe that she was on the verge of throwing caution to the winds and doing it anyway—but she was saved, for the moment, by the bell. Jake Higgins had been able to give the dispatcher enough information to allow the paramedics to find the scene; well, after a few false starts and a little 'help' from our side. Two of them, accompanied by two officers with weapons drawn, burst from the southeast stairwell behind Dawn.

She let them take over and gave them a quick briefing. "He needs a needle decompression, and he needs it now!" she told them.

"We'll take good care of him, ma'am," one assured her. "Does this freight elevator work, and where does it go?" he asked.

"Yes, it works. Have your ambulance come around to the front loading dock."

* * *

ON THE SECOND FLOOR OF building 19 was the old locker room. On its door was a sign, "DANGER—KEEP OUT—ASBESTOS." "Look in there," Mike ordered.

The door was locked, of course. But the shotgun which Officer Weiss was carrying was actually a 'breaching gun.' Developed by the military, it uses special hardened ammunition intended to wreck and open locks, hinges, and door frames. Of course, it's Just Too Bad for anyone who may be on the far side of the door, which limits its use in normal law enforcement scenarios. But very little about this day was 'normal.'

Weiss fired. The SWAT officers burst in to the door, with the three plainclothes men backing them up.

Enrique was, quite literally, caught with his pants down.

Chapter Seventeen

On the Edge of Forever

THE CROWN JEWEL OF THE publicly supported Harris County Hospital District, and really one of the finest trauma centers of its kind which you may find anywhere, is Ben Taub General Hospital in the midst of the Texas Medical Center. Rick was in the care of the surgeons there for five hours. In the meantime we had been busy. Nathan and I called in every outstanding favor we had. Before Rick had been wheeled out of the operating room there were emailed letters on the desk of Mike's police chief in Topeka, as well as the corporate CEO, from the commander of the Narcotics division, the Houston Chief of Police, and the Mayor's Chief of Staff praising Mike for "quick thinking and decisive action which may well have saved the lives of two of our officers." With voltage like that supporting him Mike would retain his position and even earn a muted commendation. Not a bad day's work, if I do say so myself. The downside—

there is always a downside—would be that from this day forward Mike would be known amongst his fellow officers in the company by the sobriquet of, "Trainwreck." Oh, well. At least he has a sense of humor about it. On balance, we'll take it.

Speaking of overworked...the fire department's ambulance technicians in this city never rest, either. While Mike and Dawn were outside the Emergency department waiting for the official word on Rick's condition—barriers again; Dawn and I knew no more than Mike did at that moment—the same two paramedics who had treated Rick earlier emerged after having brought in a heart attack victim...who would, by the by, live for several more years after receiving a successful emergency coronary bypass. Although Mike had detoured to his home mere blocks from the old coffee plant to change into his uniform and Dawn had shifted her attire as well, the two paramedics recognized her. "Hey, aren't you the girl who was working on that narcotics officer at the old coffee plant?"

"Yeah, that was me. How is he?"

"They aren't saying. He's still in OR. But that's some damn good work you did on him at the scene. Where'd you get your training?"

"Oh. I was in the Army."

"Were you? So was I! What's your MOS?"

"Does it matter? I was a Warrior; that's all that counts."

"Guess so. Well, if you're looking for a job, we could really use someone like you!"

"I've already got a full-time gig. Sorry. Thanks anyway!"

"No problem!" And they left.

"So what do you think about that?" Mike asked as the paramedics turned the corner.

"About what?" Dawn asked.

"Getting a job. Maybe an apartment. I mean, you're welcome to my couch, but people will talk. Be a secret agent for real!"

I didn't have to be telepathic to know exactly what was going on behind that blonde hair. *Is there any possible way I can present that to the Throne as a prayer?!?!* Then she saw the expression on my face. If looks could kill…well, let's just say that I would be defending myself against charges of assault with intent to maim. Dawn sighed. "Mike, there are factors which you don't understand yet. It's just not that simple. We haven't been able to keep any angels in this world long-term, not for thousands of years at least." She paused a moment and then added, "Or, if we have, it's classified well above my pay grade. But if I could, I would." *In a heartbeat,* she added silently.

Just then there was activity in the corridor. The news hounds had not been allowed to bring cameras inside the hospital proper, but an impromptu press briefing area had been set up on the grassy lawn outside. A hospital spokesman and a doctor had entered the corridor and were pushing their way in that direction. Mike and Dawn followed.

I suppose that I could spend the next five pages giving you an exact transcript of the media briefing which followed, including detailed explanations of the medical jargon involved and an irreverent examination of the repetitious and mostly inane questions posed by the ladies and gentlemen of the press. But the abridged version is: the surgeons had accomplished all that their skill would allow. However, Rick remained in extremely critical condition. The bullet wound had caused severe damage to his cerebral cortex; cerebrum activity as measured by electroencephalogram was almost nil. Even so, his cerebellum and brain stem had largely escaped injury so his autonomic functions—breathing, heartbeat, and so on—continued on in almost a normal fashion. He showed no signs of regaining consciousness and, when asked, the doctors admitted that the chances that he would ever regain consciousness were less than fifty-fifty. At that, they were being conservative. Further, Rick had an advance medical directive in effect which limited the life-support measures which the doctors could employ. He had no need of a ventilator, but if there was no anticipated medical improvement after a period of one week the directive was to remove all feeding tubes and IVs and allow nature to take its course.

If even that is too much information, the "Too Long; Don't Read" version is: Mike's best friend now had no detectable higher brain function, and the chances that he would ever recover were almost nil—barring a miracle. It took Mike a measured total of seventeen seconds to realize that a miracle was standing right next to him.

"Dawn!" he exclaimed. "Do something! You've got to do something!"

She glanced around with some trepidation and gave a nervous laugh. "Well…keep your fingers crossed!"

"Don't give me that! You healed me; you can heal Rick! You have the power!"

Dawn looked around in a near-panic and grabbed Michael by the arm. "Not here!"

*   *   *

HELSPETH TOOK HIS RESPONSIBILITY TO "collect" Lieutenant Smith seriously. That's where most of his attention was, but a peripheral portion of his awareness extended to cover the crowd of reporters and police officers who were filling every available public space. He wasn't focused on Mike and Dawn, by any means, but was dimly aware that there had been an emotional outburst between them. *What was that?* he wondered with curiosity.

*   *   *

THE HOSPITAL CHAPEL WAS SMALL, and in accordance with the dictates of political correctness had been stripped of any overt trappings of religious belief. However, a Catholic chaplain had just concluded a Mass for a worried Hispanic family and the altar and crucifix he had used had not yet been taken down by the hospital staff. I can't say I'm a fan of the symbolism; our Boss is most certainly no longer on that Cross; but it was useful as a reminder of Who is ultimately In Charge. At least the space was private and defensible. Dawn hustled Mike inside and shut the door. "Okay. We can talk."

"Dawn. He's dying! Even if he lives, he's likely to be a vegetable! I know you can do something to help him! You've *got* to!"

There were tears in Dawn's eyes. "It's not that simple."

"Why not?"

"They're watching him. I can't get to him without being noticed. Remember, I'm really not supposed to be here!"

"So you're just going to let him die? Why am I not surprised!"

"Michael!"

"Why should you care? What does it matter to you? Death is your business!"

Dawn was righteously indignant. "How can you say that? My 'business'? My business is *life!* What, you think I like concentration camps? Cancer wards? Do you think I enjoy tearing apart husbands and wives, friends and relatives?" She gestured at him. "Do you think I get some kind of kick out of knowing that a little boy is going to have to grow up without his father? What kind of *monster* do you think I am?"

That last line almost looked to register with Mike. Dawn took a deep breath and tried to calm down. "I hate death! If I had my way, there wouldn't be any death. Or sickness, or pain, or…"

She realized that she was getting on another roll and broke off. "Well. There is one good thing about death. If you belong to us. If you belong to us, it means that it's the last time you ever have to feel pain, or fear, or heartbreak, or loneliness. It means you'll never see sickness or poverty or crime or injustice, ever again. It means that you can come Home with me. And I won't ever have to hide, ever again."

Mike was internalizing that—or at least beginning to. "So. All right. At least, if he goes, he'll be a lot better off."

Dawn was struggling to keep control and not entirely succeeding. "No. No."

"*No?* What do you mean, no?"

"Rick…he doesn't belong to us. He…"

Mike grabbed her by the shoulders. "*What are you saying?*"

"He never surrendered to us like you did. They've been able to claim him since he was twelve years old. If he goes, he's…gone! He belongs to them. He ends up wherever they end up!"

"But Rick is a good guy!"

By now Dawn was losing it again. "Don't you understand? It's not how 'good' or 'bad' you are, it's who you belong to! I'm not here to keep *score!*"

Now Mike was losing it, too. "Then why didn't you do something? My God! You talked to him! You sat down and talked with him! If it's so important, why the hell didn't you say something?"

"Mike, I was with him for twenty minutes. You've known him for twenty years! Why couldn't you just…."

"That's right, blame me! How should I know what to do?"

Dawn gestured at the crucifix on display. "You know who He was! You know what He did! That's all you need! Believe He was who He said He was, believe He did what He said He would do, pledge allegiance to Him, then get out of the way and let us do the rest!"

"That's all?" Mike asked. "Then why didn't you just tell him? Why didn't *you?*"

"I CAN'T TELL HIM!!! I want to! Oh, God! How I want to! I sometimes feel like I'm just about to explode! But I can't say a thing!"

"Why not? You talk to me!"

"Of course I talk to you! You already belong to us! I can tell you anything I want! But if I tell someone who's not already part of our Family—if I even *hint* at it too strongly—it would break all the rules!"

"Rules? *What* rules? Is this some kind of a game?"

"It's no game," she replied in deadly earnest. "It's war!"

"There are no 'rules' in war!"

"Oh yes there are! There have to be! There are some things you just can't do! I mean, maybe you can...but you *can't*, not without destroying everything you're fighting for! Mike, don't you see? It all ties in together! Everything He did, He did for *you!* You're the ones who have to pass it on, one on one, brother to brother, friend to friend! If it's not important enough for you to do it yourself, what you're saying is, 'It's not important!' We can help you—we *do* help you—but we can't do it for you, not without breaking our own rules!"

"So? Break them!"

"Mike, you're missing the whole point! Do you think we're fighting this war to see who's stronger? *No!* We already know that! But it's not enough. We're out for something even bigger! We're out to stop all this pain, all this death, all this evil from ever happening again! Mike, some day when this war is finally over there's going to be a trial like this universe has never seen. We've got to be able to show that we won, every step

194

of the way, because we were *right!* We're out to prove for all time that there really is such a thing as right and wrong! That's what we're fighting for! Right and wrong! It's bigger than you; it's bigger than me…and it's bigger than Rick. I want to help him, really I do, but I can't break the rules to do it!"

Mike was burning white hot, and Dawn's impassioned speech made no more impact on him than a single ice cube would make on a blast furnace. "Look. I don't care about your rules! I don't care about your war! All I know is that I've known Rick since second grade. He's lying in there right now, dying; you say he's going to Hell, and you're not going to lift a finger to stop it! You don't give a damn, do you? You really couldn't care less about him or me!"

Ooof. That hurt. That really hurt. Dawn looked as if she had just been sucker-punched in the gut as she responded, "Mike, I'm the second best friend you've got!" It should go without saying that she and Mike had differing ideas about who the first best Friend was.

"Oh, right! Give me a break! What am I to you, really? A pet? A toy? Some kind of plaything?"

Dawn's eyes were wide as saucers. "No! No, not at…."

"Waitaminit. I know. I know! *I'm another souvenir!* You want to keep me under glass for the rest of forever? Who else do you have in your personal zoo? Do I get the spot on your mantel? Or do you plan to just toss me in the garage?"

"No, Mike, no!" She reached out for him as if wanting someone, anyone to cling to.

"Just get away from me! Leave me alone! I said, get the hell away from me!"

Dawn was on the verge of completely breaking down, eyes moist, jaw trembling. But he had told her to leave. In accordance with his command…she disappeared.

Chapter Eighteen

ᴛᴡᴏ Sʜᴀᴛᴛᴇʀᴇᴅ Hᴇᴀʀᴛꜱ

Tᴏ ʙᴇ ǫᴜɪᴛᴇ ꜰʀᴀɴᴋ, I had been stunned by the suddenness with which events had gone south. When Dawn teleported out of the room, I was slow to react and her trail had grown cold enough in that second and a half or so that my own skill was unable to follow. And Nathan's contingent outside had been fully involved with guarding their privacy; they knew no more than did I.

I put out a call on our private telepathic channel but received no response. Had she returned Home? No, there were no indications of a Border penetration. Then she must be somewhere on Earth—or, at least, somewhere within Earth's physical universe. But where?

It didn't take me that long. The old sanctuary had not been tended to in years, but the polished wood paneling and high vaulted ceiling still lent an air of spectacular elegance to the space. The setting sun streamed in through the windows, with a ray of dying light illuminating the pulpit area where Dawn knelt, in tears. I moved in closer, watching, not intruding. My best friend needed comfort right now, not advice, and I very gradually let her become aware that I was there for her. "I thought I might find you here," I said gently.

She snapped to attention, momentarily forgetting her own problems in her concern about her partner. "Ariel? Who's watching Mike?"

"I left half a squad with him. Right now you need me more than he does, Chief."

"Maybe so." She sighed. "I just feel so…."

"Strange? Silly? Incompetent? Sick?" I spoke with droll humor to soften the import of my words.

"Torn, more than anything else. I just never thought that things would go so bad so fast."

"Do you think you're the first one it's ever happened to?"

"No. But it is the first time it's ever happened to me."

Now I tried to be as reassuring as possible. "He didn't mean it, you know. Not really. He needed a target, and you were convenient."

"I know, I know. I just…." Her voice trailed off and she sighed.

"You really ought to be flattered. He thinks you're supposed to be the answer to all his problems!"

"Hah. I wish."

"So do I, but unfortunately it's not time for that yet. And I know you don't want him using you as a crutch. Maybe it's time for you to come on back."

Her face took on a set. "No. Not until I can find a way to take care of Rick."

"Dawn, it's much too dangerous. They have a death watch on him!"

"I've at least got to try!"

"No! It's not your job!"

"I am in position! If not me, then who?"

"It's not that simple! Now just calm down for a minute and let's talk this out."

She took a deep breath and let it out slowly. Then she turned towards the large, polished wooden cross which hung from the wall behind the high glass baptistry. "What do You say?" There was a brief pause, and then she turned back to me. "You heard? He's not going to stop me."

"No, but He's certainly not encouraging you either. Now, listen. There are other ways that we might be able to...."

"Don't tell me what I can't do. Tell me how I *can* do what I'm going to do anyway!" Then she added, "And not get caught!"

"I just think you ought to...."

"Ariel. Please. Look me in the eye, and tell me that you don't want Rick to have another chance."

I flushed and looked away for a second. When I did look back in Dawn's direction there was a thin smile on my face and I was nodding slowly.

Guardian Angel

*   *   *

Ben Taub Hospital is really not far from Eastwood as the crow flies, but it was now rush hour in the city. To make matters worse there was a major accident on the freeway; traffic was horrendous and the backup spilled out onto the side streets. And Mike was a tangled up mess of swirling emotions.

Nathan's crew is largely Warriors, but he does have some highly competent Counselors on his staff as well. I know most of them; we became friends during Dawn's fifty years as regional commander. Mike was not consciously aware of their gentle ministry; all he knew was that memories of the past three days kept coming unbidden to the forefront of his thoughts. At first he struggled, trying to justify his anger. But before long his self-righteousness cracked, and he realized how much he had come to love his Guardian in just the short time he had been privileged to know her. And he began to get a hint—just a hint; he could not have borne the whole load—of how deeply he had hurt her. It was more than he could take. He needed a diversion. He reached for the switch of the satellite radio.

Nathan truly is a frustrated disc jockey at heart, and a senior Commander has all kinds of connections: Somehow, he was able to arrange for The Four Seasons to sing "Dawn" at exactly that moment. *Do you really want her to go away back where she belongs?*

Michael almost slapped the "off" button at that, but then he clenched the steering wheel and his eyes grew moist. *So, what do I do now?* It's not as though he could call her up on the phone and apologize. But Nathan was just getting started. Next up was dear Petula and her classic standard of "Downtown".

Mike was torn. Was this a sign? Nathan had yet one more ace up his sleeve. After Miss Clark finished, The Drifters began to croon of going "Up On The Roof"...

Mike swerved to his left, cutting off a driver who answered with a petulant horn, and headed for the exit to Chenevert Street.

Chapter Nineteen

A Battle Plan

Dawn was back at Michael's house, sitting at his desk, writing a letter. While that was the prime focus of her attention, she also spared a glance for me, Nathan, and his elite Warriors. "So. What's the plan?"

"Standard rescue insertion," Nathan responded. "Only difference is, you'll be our ace in the hole. When you're in position, we move in as though we're trying to open a hole for Philip here. They fight back. In the confusion, you get started taking care of Rick. If Phil makes it through…"

"…I back off and act as surprised as anyone else while he finishes the job. Right."

"Whatever happens, as soon as it's over you pack your little tail feathers out of there at once!" I remanded her. "Understand?"

"I understand." She finished with the letter, folded it in thirds, wrote the date on the outside…then hesitated. She pulled three more letters, written over the previous two days, from her purse and hesitated again. Finally she pulled open the bottom desk drawer and hid the letters there under some miscellaneous paperwork. "Ariel," she said. "If anything happens…make sure he finds these."

"I'll do my best," I promised her.

"And…take good care of my kid."

"Right."

*   *   *

"I'M VERY SORRY, BUT INTENSIVE Care visiting is for immediate family only," the nurse at the window said gently.

"Please!" she wailed. "There's just so much I never got a chance to tell him!"

"He's not conscious, you know, honey. He's not expected to regain consciousness."

"I've heard. Still, if I can only see him, touch him, talk to him…I just know, wherever he is, he'll hear me!"

My goodness. Maybe Dawn truly is a ditz at heart. She was certainly putting on a convincing impression of it. Did I really know her that well after all these centuries?

The nurse was not without compassion. She began visibly wavering. "Still, I can't…."

"Please! You've just got to let me see him!"

"All right," the nurse decided. "Five minutes. Come with me."

Click. Dawn's demeanor changed from ditzy blonde to commando-dangerous as she followed the nurse into the ICU. I faded in for a quick aside. "Did you want your Oscar now, or can you wait until next March?"

*   *   *

AMY WAS, TO PUT IT charitably, in shellshock. She had vowed to herself, some time before, that if circumstances ever became this hopeless she would withdraw, go Home, and not wait around to watch the end. She couldn't do it. There was nothing she could do to help—Rick's soul was well out of her reach—but she was simply unable to leave. It was as fascinating as watching yet another train wreck unfold…in slow motion, this time.

Come into the light, my son. Do not be afraid. Death is but a door…

Dragora was a good actress. She had plenty of experience appearing as an 'angel of light.' *Let go, my child. A new world awaits…*

"Curse this 'modern medicine'," Dravang growled as he looked on. "Twenty years ago we'd have had him by now!"

"I miss the old days," Helspeth commented. "Remember how it was? Sometimes we'd actually drag them down to the Pit while their bodies were still breathing!"

"Yes, and if they got away from us at the last second they generally woke up screaming for the nearest preacher! This new policy may not be as viscerally satisfying, but it has cut our losses rather substantially… What?"

Dawn had entered the room and immediately knelt by Rick's bed in an attitude of prayer. She began to sob.

"Oh, this is not good! Who is she?" Dravang demanded.

"Some girlfriend, I sup… *INCOMING!*" Helspeth screamed.

*　*　*

Nathan's forces had surprised the enemy, but Dravang had a defense in depth of his own ready. Ownership does make a difference in such matters; here in a public space it could not be as effective as Nathan's similar shield around Mike's own home but as Rick belonged to the enemy it kept their barrier from being penetrated by the first wave.

"Rescue mission! Let us through!" Nathan demanded.

"Not a chance!" came the reply.

As Amy became aware of the new developments she quickly aroused from her torpor. She reached out towards her partner's soul with renewed desperation. She scored a partial success almost immediately; between her efforts on the one hand and the assault of Nathan's forces on the other, Dragora's mask shattered and, for a fleeting instant, Rick saw her as she was. He recoiled spiritually from the vision.

Dawn observed the developing conflict with the experienced eye of a general officer. It was rapidly turning into a pitched battle—but Nathan had no more reserves which could be spared. Dravang, on the other hand, was calling in support from every possible quarter. Against the forces which the newly crowned demonic prince personally controlled Nathan's team would have prevailed, but Dravang was essentially mortgaging his soul to buy reinforcements from any power or principality which might be enticed to assist. His ranks swelled. *Now or never*, Dawn thought to herself.

We angels cannot actually travel through time, not without Divine assistance at any rate, but we can locally change its slope; slow events down. Dawn now did so as much as she dared. There was much work to do here. We also have a real ability to look backwards into time and see things as they once were; while this can be thrown off by enemy interference Dawn also knew Rick and his soul better than anyone else save Amy…and the Lord, of course. She locked in on a clear pattern as she began her rebuilding.

Her first priority was to restore the structure of the blood vessels. The surgeons had actually begun the work; it was essential to saving Rick's life. But their tools were quite limited compared to those which Dawn had the capability to draw upon. Where they had cauterized and sutured and trusted to the body's amazing ability to then repair itself, Dawn re-opened passages and rebuilt connections between arteries, veins, and capillaries. With circulation back to normal she then began to restore the glial cells, the essential scaffolding for the higher brain functions.

Lastly, and trickiest, was repairing the network of neurons. This involved risks from two sides; errors in making connections would disrupt pathways and force skills to have to be re-learned. More critical, though, from our perspective was the fact that, as I mentioned earlier, many of the enemy spirits are trying constantly to get closer to your world. A damaged brain is in many regards like a computer without a password; it's easy to hack in. Your physicians have noted the frequent occurrence of personality changes following brain injury; while it's rare for a core personality to be completely supplanted it happens quite often that you can end up with a mélange of ninety percent of the genuine article and ten percent unwanted interloper. Dawn was determined to leave not even a razor-thin opening for the enemy to wedge into the soul of Mike's best friend.

During all this time she was outwardly and physically maintaining a posture and attitude of intense prayer. And, make no mistake, she actually was praying; even for one as skilled in healing as Dawn a job like this takes all the help one can get. While Amy did not key into the altered time slope and the other interventions Dawn was surreptitiously making—Warriors are quite good at covering their tracks—she did see that there was new life in the situation and threw herself into the fray with the vigor of desperation. Amy's efforts succeeded in distracting the enemy forces and only aided Dawn in her efforts.

Connections restored, Dawn reached in and applied a touch of energy—a "jump start", if you will. As Rick's soul reconnected with his body and began to move towards consciousness, Dawn began to relax her shielding. Rick opened his eyes and looked into her face. She said, "Hello, Rick."

"What? Who?" Rick said in confusion.

"One more chance. Use it wisely!" she said just before dropping the shield completely.

Back in the spiritual realm, Nathan's forces were withdrawing. The enemy began to celebrate. Dravang cried out in victory, "That's right! Run! This one is *ours*, do you hear? Ours!"

But he suddenly broke off as the ICU nurse ran into the room, alerted by renewed activity on the monitors. "What's going on here? I saw…" Then she saw Rick lying there, eyes opened, looking around.

"Oh, Nurse, it's a miracle! A regular miracle!" said Dawn the Ditz, now back in rare form. "Oh, I'm so happy!"

"You need to get out of here," said the nurse. "We've got to run some tests!"

"Yes! Run all the tests you want! Oh, isn't this wonderful? And I thought I might never get to speak to you again…." Really now, old chum, you truly were laying it on thick.

At this point Amy was over the moon and it was Dravang and his forces who were in shellshock. Actually, it was the forces who were stunned into inaction; Dravang himself was apoplectic. With good reason, I might add; he had obligated himself with debt up to his eye teeth and now had absolutely nothing to show for it. "Who slipped up? One of them got through! Who slipped up? Admit it now or it'll be worse for you later!"

At this time I should turn aside from the action to remind you that, after multiple thousands of years of life, many of us have well-developed skill sets in several areas. For me, it is the divining of Truth and the use of that truth to counsel souls, both angelic and human. For Dawn, it is combat skills and healing. In addition to his quite genuine talents in these same areas, Nathan has a better-than-average aptitude for music (although I would daresay that each and every one of us Holy

Ones is musical). Dragora is a rather good actress…and a seductress, if I haven't spelled that out sufficiently by this point. And Dravang, in addition to having an inordinate ability to work his way through the nefarious politics and hierarchies of the kingdom of darkness, also has a great measure of skillcraft in a related area: Deception. Disguises. Dissimulation. Not only practicing those skills on his own, but recognizing them when they are employed by others. He looked after the retreating figure of Dawn who was now in the process of exiting, stage right. "No," he said. He shook his head, unbelieving. "No."

Chapter Twenty

RECONCILIATION

DAWN WALKED QUICKLY AWAY FROM the hospital and headed towards Hermann Park Drive. The sun had well set; the Zoo and the golf course were both closed and there was no activity whatsoever at this southern end of the park. No observable activity, of course. Dawn looked around and then directed a question my way. "Am I clear?"

I scanned the area as well. "I believe so. All right. Time to get you out of there."

"I can't leave without saying goodbye."

I surrendered to the inevitable. "I suppose not. Very well, then. One last quick visit, then Home!"

* * *

MIKE WAS ON THE ROOF of his office's skyscraper building, leaning against the parapet wall, looking to the southeast. The former coffee plant was visible in the distance, not quite two miles away. Its parking lot was filled with the flashing red and blue lights of the squad cars of officers still scouring the facility for evidence, and his own neighborhood was just beyond. The night was crystal clear and cool, and the city lights shone through it like millions of jewels in every direction.

"I hope you're not planning something precipitous," came a voice from behind him.

He wheeled to look. "Dawn? I thought you were already gone!"

"Just about. But I wanted to say goodbye, first."

"So you're going?"

"I guess I'd better."

There was no response for a second and Dawn turned away, expressionless. But then Mike spoke up. "Look. About what I said. I didn't really mean it the way it sounded. You know that, right?"

Dawn sighed. There was a brief pause, then she said, "Mike, you know, I may not be human. But I am a person! I have feelings!" She looked away, then spoke more quietly. "They can hurt."

"I…I'm sorry. I just… I didn't think… It's like, all those times you see something. Something wrong. And you say, 'God, why are you doing this? Why do you just let it happen? Please, can't you stop it?' And it's like, nobody's listening!"

Dawn gave a sad laugh.

"What?"

"I was just thinking of all those times I've seen somebody about to do something. Something wrong. And I'm trying to say, 'No! Don't do it! You'll hurt someone! You'll hurt yourself! Please, can't you just stop?' And it's like…nobody's listening!"

Her eyes began to tear up. Mike stared at her, then moved in closer. "I guess I never really thought it might cut both ways."

"Uh huh."

"I hope you're not…mad."

She took a deep breath and began to collect herself. "You know, there's one thing even I'm not strong enough to carry."

"What's that?"

"A grudge." She turned to look him in the eye, a hint of a smile on her face. "I couldn't stay mad at you if I tried." Then, very dry, "But you don't have to keep giving me chances to prove it!"

"So…friends?"

"Hey, we're a team…partner!"

She extended a hand. Mike took it, and she placed her free hand over his hand. A beat later, he did likewise. As the handshake broke up they came out of it holding both hands. Mike stood there for a second, uncertain of what to do….

It wasn't much of a kiss. But it was, most decidedly, a kiss. Mike was surprised, and didn't know how to respond for a second. She released one of his hands, then turned aside to look over the rail at the city below. Mike looked at her, then down and away. "How did someone as wonderful as you ever get stuck with someone like me?"

"You want to know?"

"The truth?"

"What else? I volunteered."

"You…what?"

"I volunteered. I could be out there hopping galaxies. I'd rather be here."

"Why?"

She just shrugged and smiled. But Mike was not about to be put off. "There's got to be something. Do you get paid, or anything?"

"I get to see your face the first time you see His face." Then she hesitated. "And…well. Haven't you ever wanted to bring someone up here to see something like this for the first time? I've seen your home town. I'd like to show you mine."

"It is beautiful up here."

"Uh huh."

"You see it like this all the time, don't you?"

"Hmm. Not lately. You've kept me kinda busy, kid. Not much time for sightseeing!"

"I wonder what it's like?"

She looked a silent question out into the night, asking for permission. That is, she must have asked for permission. Mustn't she? Right?

She opened up a portal into the next adjoining layer and stepped backwards into it, rendering herself invisible to human eyes and cameras. But she left enough of an opening and filtered it selectively so that Mike could continue to see her. She rose off the rooftop about a foot and transitioned into her glorified form. "You want to find out?" she asked softly, extending a hand.

With more than a little hesitation, Mike took it. They rocketed up into the sky.

*   *   *

I LITERALLY COULD NOT BELIEVE this latest turn of events. What in Heaven's name was she thinking? Didn't she realize the danger, how exposed she was while she was here? Now the two of them were off gallivanting through the skies! Wasn't she ever going to return Home? Why, she had been there for almost… three…

!!!!!!!!!

Oh, my goodness!

I am so STUPID!

I smiled, and looked out at the two of them. Yes, it would be hard on his friends and his mother, but as a Counselor and otherwise unattached I could stay behind to ease the transition. That is my job, after all. I detailed a small facet of my awareness to keep an eye on the lovebirds, then turned most of my attention to making the necessary preparations.

There was much to accomplish to-night!

*   *   *

THE ROOF OF THE SKYSCRAPER was now vacant. Or was it?

From the walls of the elevator penthouse there came an unseen disturbance, as of a mist opening up to allow someone to emerge from deep concealment. The invisible figure of Dravang stepped from it over towards the railing and looked out into the night pensively. "So," he said with quiet malice. "I'll get you, my pretty." He paused a moment and then added, "And your little dog, too."

Chapter Twenty-One

DATE WITH AN ANGEL

WITH MIKE IN TOW, DAWN rose about a thousand feet above the rooftop. Then she plunged downward, down into the concrete canyons of Downtown, pulling out of it at the last second and skimming along the streets so close that she could have reached out and slapped a traffic signal. She skyrocketed back up into the air, looping an enormous loop before coming down over the light rail tracks on Main Street. She broke right on Lamar Street, following it as far as the Sam Houston Park before pirouetting and streaking back between the Library and City Hall. A hard left past the Esperson Buildings, then right above Texas Avenue following the path of the old cattle drives past the former Union Station and present-day ballpark. She arced up and then back down over the green lawn in front of the Convention Center, then past the big hotel and around it to cross up and over the Houston Center complex. She swooped back down, aiming for the ten-foot gap between the towers of Pennzoil Place and hitting it dead center at such a speed that she would have generated a sonic boom…had she been but one layer closer.

Did I ever mention that Mike truly enjoys roller coasters?

Now, though, it was time to relax and do some flightseeing. She ascended to an altitude of about fifteen hundred feet, and slowly circled the towers of the center city. Off to their left were other towers; the hospitals of the Medical Center were but a couple miles away and Greenway Plaza and the Galleria area lay farther in the distance. Mike turned to look Dawn in the face; she was smiling. So was he. It resembled nothing so much as a scene from a certain superhero movie. Perhaps Michael was reminded of that. "Um," he asked, "what happens if I let go?"

Dawn came to an immediate stop, hanging there in midair. She regarded him gravely. "Oh, that would be very serious," she replied in a most sober voice. "You would become…*it.*" Her voice dropped an octave on that last word.

Mike didn't understand. "Become…*it?*"

"I'm afraid so."

"Um…what exactly does that mean?"

Suddenly she ripped her hand away from him, leaving him hanging there in midair. He looked from side to side frantically. She reached out and touched him on the shoulder. "Tag," she said in a sepulchral voice.

Mike looked back at her, unsure as to whether he was in deep you-know-what or if he was well into the process of being royally had.

"You're 'it'!" Dawn exclaimed as the twinkle came back into her eyes.

Laughing, she streaked away. Mike suddenly realized that he was able to follow. And so he did. "Yoo-hoo!" she called out. "Over here, slowpoke! Come on, you can do better than that!"

She teased him, of course, but interspersed with the teasing were shouts of encouragement and instruction. Such as the time when he was closing in on her—and she suddenly teleported about a quarter mile away. "Hey! No fair!" he called out.

"Oh? Come on, now! You try it!"

And he did…to find that she had popped to a new position, giggling. "Too slow!"

If it's not blatantly obvious by now, this was not simply a romp; it was a training session. But both teacher and student were having a blast. Eventually Dawn let Mike catch her. "Gotcha!"

"You got me. Not bad for a first try, youngster!"

"This is incredible. How?"

"Pixie dust," Dawn replied…deadpan, of course.

"What?"

"Just think of the commercial applications."

"You're pulling my leg again, aren't you?"

"Oh, however did you guess? Actually, though, it's not that tough. You already have all the wiring. It just never got plugged in. Right now I'm giving you a 'jump', so to speak."

"Whoa."

"Um, don't get too used to it," Dawn cautioned him.

"Sure," Mike acknowledged.

"Come on," Dawn said. "I want to show you something!"

And she led the way, higher and faster, faster, faster… until they were in space. In an orbital plane, actually, but at an accelerated velocity which a spacecraft could not have maintained without expending ruinous amounts of energy. The terminator at that point was over the eastern Mediterranean; she streaked towards it so that Mike could be treated to the view of a sunrise from orbit. Over the Holy Land, no less.

Mike was still a bit self-conscious. "You know, I'm not supposed to be able to breathe up here," he said.

"Let me handle the technicalities, okay? What do you think?"

"Uh…it's spectacular!"

"Mmm. Want to see something really spectacular?"

*　*　*

"So, how does it feel to screw up your very first day on the job?" Dragora asked with an edge of pleasure in her voice.

Dravang gave her that patented narrow look. "We have a situation."

"What kind of 'a situation'?"

"That Guardian—the one from three nights ago—is loose on our side of the border."

"What? Impossible!"

"I saw her."

"How could she have ever made it across without us noticing?"

"I was just thinking about that. I was 'reaching through' that night, when that firearm exploded. And I can't help but think that it didn't feel like any explosion I've ever felt before."

"What? You think it was her? Breaking through?"

"I am forced to consider the possibility."

"Let me get this straight. You opened the hole. You let her slip through it right under your nose. You gave her the chance to run around loose for three days and rescue a pawn which we were just about ready to harvest? Just wait until the high command hears about this!"

"They don't have to know. Not yet."

"Oh?"

"If I go down you're going down with me."

"You think so? You've got *nothing* on me, next to this! They'll have you shoveling coal! I ought to turn you in myself…."

"Before you do, listen. There are ways that we can take advantage of this. And all of us can come out ahead."

"I'm listening."

*   *   *

"Don't rush things," I told them. "Make sure that he has time to acclimate. It takes a while to shed habits and ideas learned after thirty-plus years on Earth. Give them plenty of space, but be just as helpful as you possibly can, whenever you get the chance."

The servants regarded me with eager anticipation. Some of them had been training for this since Mike had first come into our possession, twenty-plus years previous. Servants? Oh, yes. They were all volunteers; one of the fastest and most certain paths of promotion to an eventual position of great responsibility is to prove yourself in loyal and joyful service to another. By the by, this applies to you too; there are many one-time corporate presidents and CEOs who will wish that they could exchange places with their former housemaids, gardeners and janitors in the Kingdom to come. I addressed the chef and his helpers. "Keep in mind that he likes onions, but only if they're well caramelized. Don't give him any raw onion. And we can take our time introducing him to our foods. But I do believe that he's curious about manna, so have some handy to snack on."

*   *   *

Dawn had given Mike the Grand Tour. First the inner planets, coming so close to the Sun that he could feel the corona. Then outwards again, past Mars and the asteroids, to Jupiter and the rings of Saturn. They had another merry little game of tag there before continuing onward; Uranus, Neptune, and he was curious about Pluto even though the little iceball and its tiny moonlet really aren't all that compelling. "I don't believe this!" Mike exclaimed as they looked backwards towards the Sun, now no more prominent than any other first-magnitude star; he would have been utterly lost without Dawn's help. "Thank you!"

"Oh, don't mention it. You ought to know your way around your own backyard!" She took his hand. "Now, hang on!"

Space and layers and dimensions folded and unfolded around them in ways which he never would have believed. The two of them emerged in a realm of spectacular nebulae and a brilliant canopy of stars. "Where are we now?" he asked.

"My universe!"

She led him towards a point of unspeakable brilliance. "What's that star?" he asked, shielding his eyes.

"That's no star! Look!" she exclaimed.

At her command, he looked. His eyes adjusted; the unspeakable glory was now cool light. There was an enormous planet; many times larger than Earth. And, on the side facing them, a City of majestic brilliance some fifteen hundred miles square. From the center of the city four rivers led out; north, south, east and west; they each fed an immense fan-shaped lake. The overall effect was that of a giant Bolnisi cross. There were the calm freshwater lakes, but no oceans; gentle green rolling hills, but no mountains. After all, this was a park...but make no mistake; there are other worlds just a short flight away upon which you can find mountains to climb and ski and oceans to dive in and sail which make the best of what you know upon Earth to pale by comparison.

They flew closer. Now he could make out the City walls, upon their rainbow foundation of colored jewels, and the immense gates each hand-carved from a single pearl. In the center of the city the towers rose to impossible heights, the tallest as high as the city was square…but here near the walls the buildings were almost of believable scale; some might have seemed at home in Kuala Lumpur or New York City. Speaking of which….

As they came closer he could make out an area near the walls which had been set aside as a park. There were…buildings he recognized! That had to be the Empire State Building and the Chrysler Building, and in a small lake off of the North River a twin to the Statue of Liberty. There…that had to be the Eiffel Tower, and was that large building the Houses of Parliament and Big Ben?

"Look. A little farther!" she commanded. In an area past the Eads Bridge and Gateway Arch he saw…no! It couldn't be!

It was an amusement park. Tiny, by the scale of this place, but he could make out an even dozen of roller coasters…and a river ride, and a steam train, and a skyway, and the layout looked somewhat familiar….

It was Astroworld!

But not the Astroworld he remembered, cramped by space limitations and bowdlerized by years of cost-cutting corporate accountants. This was Astroworld as it could have been, should have been, with the best ideas of all the years together in one place. He could make out people, couples, families strolling the pathways and longed to join them….

He turned to look at Dawn. It took his eyes a moment to adjust; he had been viewing the scene with the telescopic vision of an angel. The two of them were still well outside the City walls. "How…?"

"I made a copy. Souvenir!"

"Can…we?"

She shook her head, sadly. "Sorry. Not yet. Got to draw the line somewhere, kid. Once you pass those gates you don't belong to Earth any more. And you've got quite a bit left to do there, I expect. But don't worry, we'll be back. I'll buy your ticket!" She looked behind them and sighed. "Come on. We need to be heading back."

*　*　*

"Ambitious. Very ambitious!"

Rankar was a demonic prince, of sorts; a peer of Dravang's. His domain included Mike's neighborhood and its environs, which meant that in recent years his influence had been overshadowed by that of Fantar and his forces. He was only dimly aware of events which had transpired, but he knew that Fantar had recently been replaced by the spirit who was now addressing him as—almost—an equal. He was flattered by that, and was inclined to be coöperative even before he heard Dravang's proposal.

But while the two demons had similar portfolios, they moved in very different echelons. Dravang dealt with businessmen, politicians, civic leaders, those of influence. Rankar, on the other hand, was intimately acquainted with every prostitute, drunkard, and petty thief who plied the streets and bars of the East End. Which is why Dravang had sought him out. "We need a pawn from you, Rankar. One which can be depended upon."

Rankar considered. "I have a few who are suitable."

"We may have to use him up."

"No great loss."

*　　*　　*

MIKE AND DAWN HAD RETURNED to Earth—well, the general vicinity, at least. At this moment they were walking, hand in hand, across the surface of the Moon. Dawn was still keeping the both of them a layer back; they were leaving no footprints which human explorers might later find. Not that this was all that much of a risk; the solar wind is much more erosive than science fiction writers of the 1950s ever considered. Even now, a mere fifty years after the Apollo missions, about the only way to recognize the landing sites is by the hardware and detritus left behind; that trope about the human footprints of the astronauts outlasting humankind itself turned out to be, uh, not quite so.

It was dark; the sun had not yet risen here in the Taurus-Littrow valley and would not do so for another two Earth days. And cold, although Dawn's talents were more than capable of coping with that technicality. Still, the low sun meant that the Earth which hung above them was bright and full; the view was, again, spectacular and the Earthshine provided more than adequate light…even without Dawn 'supplementing' it with a touch of her own glory. She was happy. More than happy, in fact; she felt fulfilled in a way which she never could have imagined. "Ah," she said. "This is the way it was supposed to be."

"What?"

"You. Us. Together. Just friends. This is the way it was supposed to be. This is the way it's going to be. Someday."

"It's like a dream come true."

Dawn absently murmured assent, then turned towards him, surprised. "For you, too?" She paused a beat and then continued. "The other night, you asked me what I dream about."

"Oh. Sorry."

"No, I'll tell you. I dream about what it's going to be like when we finally do take your world back. When Earth and Heaven are so much alike that it's hard to tell the difference—and I'll never have to hide who I am or what I am, ever again. About moments like this. And—I dream about you."

"Me?"

"About the things I see you doing, and becoming. About the fine young prince I see you growing into before my very eyes."

"Me? A prince? Ha."

"You are an adopted son of the King of all Kings. That makes you a prince in my book." The wry smile again. "Now, if I could just get you to act like one!"

"O-kay. Well, I guess I can run around, have a sordid affair or two, get into a messy divorce...."

She laughed. "*Touché!* But I think you know what your father would want."

"You mean my dad, or...?"

"Both of them, actually."

He sighed. "I miss him so much."

"I know, and I'm sorry. Someday that barrier will fall, too. But not today. Unfortunately."

"So." He paused a second, and then asked, "So what's it like to die?"

"Well, I can't say that it'll be easy, because sometimes it isn't. And I can't say that it won't hurt, because it usually does. But I can say this." She looked him square in the eye. "When the time does come, don't be afraid. I'll catch you."

He looked into her eyes. Yes, both of them were thinking about that swimming party all those years back. Then he sighed. "And what about Rick?"

"Well, I guess we'll just have to see." The hint of a smile came across the corner of her lip. "But, at least he still has a chance!"

"What?"

"He's in the process of being released from the hospital even as we speak. The doctors are still scratching their heads over it. Some are even calling it a miracle!"

"You…you did it? Thank you!"

"Why, you're welcome. Just keep in mind, Mike, that what I did for him is only temporary. To do something permanent, we need to get him into the Family. And I need your help with that!"

"All right." The two of them looked back up at the beautiful blue Earth. But then Mike looked back at her, a strange expression on his face. "Wait a second."

"What?"

"I remember something. I thought I had seen you before."

Telepathy can be somewhat unreliable; there are many threads of thought and it takes skill and experience to pick up on those which are immediately relevant. So we do speak, between ourselves, to clarify our communications. But the thoughts which he had now were very plain to anyone who had been a long time observer. "Thinking of this?" she asked.

When Mike was a young child his mother had an ornament of a crystal angel which she displayed each Christmas season. Not cheesy or ditzy as most such items are, but one which actually looked intelligent, strong, and lovely. We liked it. Michael also liked it, very much. It was when we saw him opening the Christmas decorations one July in order to find and admire the figurine that Dawn made the connection. As he looked now, he saw in her hand the same figurine he remembered from so long ago. "I kept a copy," she said. "Souvenir!"

He looked back up at her, astonished. "It's...it's you!"

"Sure, why not? You liked that little angel so much that I thought I'd use her as a model."

"A model?"

"Well, if I'm going to wear a human—well, mostly human" (as she rustled her wings) "body, I might as well put on something appealing!"

"You mean this isn't the real you?"

"What?" There was genuine puzzlement in her voice. This line of questioning was so alien that it had never seriously crossed her mind before.

"This isn't what you really look like?"

"Mike, I'm a spirit! I can 'look like' anything I want! I really don't have to wear a body at all, any kind of body!" As she spoke, she dematerialized into nothingness—although she left a wisp of glowing energy that his eyes might be able to follow. Hardly necessary, but a simple courtesy. She danced around in that form for a second or two as she continued, "In fact, up until just a few thousand years ago I didn't. It always seemed like such a strange idea." Then she rematerialized, very close to him, and ran her fingers through his hair. "Having tried it, though, I must say that it does have its advantages!"

He sighed and turned away.

"Okay. What'd I do now?" she asked with a hint of frustration.

"Nothing."

"Is there something wrong with this look? Care to make some suggestions?"

"No."

"Oh, go ahead. Be creative! I could use a good workout."

"No. No."

"Mike, what's wrong?"

"Nothing. You're beautiful. You're *perfect*. But if it isn't the real you, then…I want to know the *real* you, but…what if it's not this good? But, then—oh, I know I'm not making much sense here!"

"I think I understand." She stepped close, but did not look at him. Instead she looked out into the distance, and took a deep breath. She was about to take off the last piece of the mask, and she still wasn't sure she was ready. "Michael, just suppose. What if what I really am, at rock bottom, is someone who loves you so much that I *want* to be everything you've ever dreamed of?"

He looked at her, his face a question. She half met his gaze and nodded slowly. Mike reached out to take her hand. She gave it a gentle squeeze and cracked a smile in reply.

Kiss her, you twit! I muttered to myself.

For a moment I thought he was going to try. But he misread the signal, or else just grew self-conscious, and turned away. Dawn appeared mildly disappointed. "I don't think that's possible," Mike finally said.

"Well, maybe we'll just have to wait and see."

"But…you're an angel. You can't…I mean, you just *can't.*"

"Um, actually—I can. Some of my, ahem, former colleagues proved that a few thousand years back, quite conclusively." She paused a second and then continued. "It was one of the reasons we had to have the Flood. A lot of the human race wasn't entirely human, anymore."

"But…."

"Yes, of course, right now it's out of the question. It'd be breaking the rules, that's for sure! But I wonder, sometimes. After the war is over, could the rules change? Will we even need rules, anymore?"

"What, exactly, does that mean?"

"Well, when I find out…I'll let you know." A bit coy, there. Then she looked back up at Earth. The terminator was now over Merrie Olde England; it was sunrise in my old stomping ground. "Come on," she sighed. "It's time for me to take you home."

Chapter Twenty-Two

BREAKTHROUGH, PART III

DAWN AND MIKE LANDED ON the roof of his office building. It was not quite one o'clock in the morning. She reverted to fully human form, then stepped out of her portal and closed it behind them. I was surprised; I thought she would find it blocked and that her obvious remaining option was for the both of them to return to Heaven right there and then. Someone, somewhere, must want them to use up the full seventy-two hours. But upon a moment's reflection I realized this was all for the better; if I could only persuade the little perpetual motion machine to shut down for maintenance and close her eyes for a few hours the two of them would awaken together in Glory. I mused on how best to arrange the wake-up call. I have some friends in the Choir (who doesn't?); possibly a small ensemble—say sixty-four thousand voices or so? An intriguing question....

"All right, Mike," Dawn said sadly. "It's time."

She broke off her 'connection.' Mike went shaky at the knees for a bit. "Whoa. Withdrawal. You know, that could get addictive!"

She nodded agreement. "I know. One reason it's so dangerous in the wrong hands. If you're okay, I guess I need to be going."

What? No! Not now! My plans were suddenly in danger…

"Are you sure?" Mike asked.

"It's not that I don't enjoy your company. But I've already been here longer than I ever really thought I could. No need to be greedy."

"Maybe not," he said, "but it feels like I'm just now getting to know you!"

"I bet you say that to all the girls!"

"Uh…" That put Mike at a loss for words.

She patted his hand, and that coy look came back into her eyes. "You know, maybe I don't have to leave just yet!"

Very good, old friend. Very good.

*   *   *

"Last call! Closing time!"

"Louie, I'll take one more for the road!"

"Tequila on the rocks? Coming up!" Then the bartender leaned over and spoke conspiratorially. "Hey, Pete…better take a back way home. They've been setting up roadblocks around here come closing time."

"Thanks, Louie! Cheers!"

Rankar broke off his connection, this portion of his mission accomplished. Louie was so very, very receptive. Pete was not far behind. Now for the next stop….

*   *   *

I WAS NERVOUS. IT WAS now fifteen minutes past two; I was looking at a hard deadline of not quite an hour from now. But I didn't dare rush her, lest it expose and spoil my plans. I wanted this to be a complete surprise to the both of them.

Mike was in bed now, and fast asleep. Now to get Dawn to follow suit. But there was one thing which had to be taken care of first, of course. She sat down at his desk and pulled out a blank sheet of paper and her pen. That was fine; this shouldn't take long. She held the pen to her lips, musing upon how to begin.

Suddenly a horn blared from somewhere outside down the street, and there was the sound of a collision. Dawn jumped up and sprang for the door. I attempted to follow, of course. Funny, I couldn't seem to see anything past Nathan's outer shield….

*   *   *

A PAIR OF TAILLIGHTS WAS disappearing into the distance as Dawn ran into the street. Three houses down, and just outside the perimeter of Nathan's defenses, a fifteen-year-old pickup truck was wrapped around a large tree. From the looks of the impact he must have been traveling at least twenty miles an hour over the speed limit. She ran closer. The air bag had deployed—no! It had exploded! This must have been one of the vehicles equipped with defective safety equipment; it had been recalled but never properly repaired. The driver was still alive, but just barely. She looked back again at the fleeing hit-and-run driver, now turning a corner, then shook her head and tried to open the driver's door. It was jammed shut. She then made an understandable but very rash decision. She reached for the door handle and ripped the entire door free from the truck.

"You see?" said Dravang as he looked on. "Phase one. Execute!"

Dawn was engrossed with the problem of extricating the driver without causing further injury. She never noticed Dravang's forces reaching through…until she felt their grasp, and then heard maniacal laughter….

* * *

"WHAT'S GOING ON OUT THERE?" I demanded.

"There's a Barrier. It's tight. We're trying to penetrate, but so far no luck," Philip responded.

* * *

"PHASE TWO," DRAVANG COMMANDED.

Through the weak spot which had been left by Dawn's abduction, the spirit of Dragora flowed. She re-formed into a human physical body—and then shifted into the form of Dawn. Humming nonchalantly, she walked up to Michael's front door.

* * *

"DAWN?" I ASKED AS A familiar-looking figure entered the front door. "What happened out there?"

There was no response. I thought of speaking "louder", in a way more likely to attract attention, but thought better of it. Instead I reached out on our

236

private telepathic channel again—but received no response. Worse than that, it appeared to disappear into the darkness without trace. Translating it into the terminology of the telephone, it was the difference between a ringing with no answer and, "This line has been disconnected or is no longer in service."

I was still unsure; Dragora's imitation of my best friend was *perfect*. Even I could not tell the two of them apart. By physical appearance or even by physical mannerisms, at least. But then she walked past the desk where the pen and the blank sheet of paper lay. She gave them a cursory glance and then moved on. I have been watching Dawn write letters to Michael for literally all of his life and then some. Now I knew.

"Dawn? *No! Oh, **no!!***"

Guardian Angel

Chapter Twenty-Three
THE PIT OF DESPAIR

Dravang was taking no chances.

He remembered how Dawn had escaped his forces before. So he reinforced the bonds which held her to such an extent that even the strongest of Warriors could not have breached them without outside aid. At that, he was just on the mark.

As she realized that she was being abducted, Dawn had desperately attempted to reach out and establish a connection with Heaven, or even indirectly to any of us. But Dravang had anticipated that and planned accordingly, and her efforts had been in vain. She had attempted to keep track of the various dimensions and portals which she had been shuffled through, but that effort had been successfully blocked as well. Now she became aware of her surroundings; although what is fearful to an angel might not quite resonate with you, if you picture a dimly lit, rat-infested dungeon from the worst of Hollywood horror movies you will not be far from the mark. Around her was a ring of guards, the fiercest fighters which the enemy could muster, who had no task other than to hold her back. And, standing over her, the suave and evil figure of Dravang, with a look of triumph on his face.

"Well, hello," the gloating demon said. "Such a pleasure to meet you again. I understand that you go by the name of Dawn?"

"Let me go!" Dawn demanded.

"No, I don't think so," Dravang replied. "Unless, of course, we can secure your cooperation?"

"No, I don't think so," was her answer.

"Think again."

Imagine Dravang's hand morphing into a large claw and plunging into Dawn's body near her shoulder, and then ripping through her chest diagonally from upper left to lower right. The pain was excruciating—in the most literal sense. Her training had been, in such a situation, to conserve her energy in hopes that a window of opportunity to escape might appear. But even she was unable to hold back the reflex of her body to heal itself, which manifested as an explosion of visible light. She damped it down as much as possible, but the wound closed leaving behind a jagged, glowing scar. She didn't bother to waste any energy repairing her torn clothing, though.

Dravang raised an eyebrow. "I'm impressed. Whenever I try that out on our newly procured humans I get the most delightful screams. But not you. You are very brave." He paused. "Stupid, but brave."

He reached out again with the claw and completed the X-pattern. Again she held back the scream, but it cost her more this time.

"There," Dravang said. "You've put up an admirable resistance. I'm sure that even your self-appointed King couldn't expect any more of you. Now, talk to me."

"I have not yet begun to fight!"

She began to twist and try to tear away, using every trick she had ever learned in seven hundred years as a Warrior. It was to no avail. The guards were anticipating these moves, and they succeeded in siphoning off even more of her energy until she was visibly weakened. This had been her last, best chance to break free—and everyone in the chamber knew it.

"Poor choice of words," said Dravang softly. "What do you have to fight with? You see now, you cannot get away. We have you, and we have time. All eternity, if need be. Think about it."

While no longer sassy, Dawn was far from being cowed. Her voice now was low but steady and her attitude grimly determined. *I will outlast you.* "You cannot keep me. I am not yours."

With that infuriating meditative attitude, Dravang materialized a walnut between his fingertips and regarded it. "We can keep you for as long as we can hold you," he said. "You know that. And every spirit has its breaking point. We need only apply pressure until you crack—," demonstrating with the walnut, "—then pick out whatever we want from the pieces. We will know what we wish to know. The only question is, how much of your personality will survive the experience intact?"

He turned towards the guards. "While she's thinking about it, why don't you soften her up just a bit?"

*　*　*

TORTURE. DESPAIR. SCREAMS. FIGURES WRESTLING. Was that Dawn? Why was she wrestling with a redheaded angel who exactly matched her description of her best friend? Flames. Rats. A tidal wave of floodwaters bearing down upon him….

He sat up, wide awake. "Only a dream. Remember that. Only a dream."

Chapter Twenty-Four

An Epistle

Dearest Michael,

I feel out of sorts writing this to you; almost like an interloper. But a tradition has been established, and I do not wish to be the one who breaks it.

Someday, sooner or later, you will find out what happened tonight. Frankly, I'm torn as to whether I wish it to be sooner or later. If later, there will be more damage left behind to deal with, but if sooner then it almost certainly means that you will be leaving your world behind…and whilst I would welcome you Home, it would break my heart to do so without Dawn here to welcome you first.

Knowing you as I do, I'm sure that in some way you will want to blame yourself. You mustn't do so. Dawn was in your world of her own free choice; indeed, it was the fulfilment of a heart's desire which burned so strongly that it was felt at the very Throne itself. She loved you, truly, and all of those lives around you. You didn't have to ask her to help your friend; she wanted to do so from the instant she knew he had been wounded. She was fully aware of the risks involved; indeed, given her background she was even more cognisant of them than was I. She accepted those risks willingly, and whilst perhaps she might have taken some steps differently had she known at the time what we all know now, I firmly believe that even so she does not regret the choices which she made.

You see, you are unaware at this point as to just how special, as a redeemed human, that you are. Dawn never told you, but there are a very, very great number of we angels. Oh, we all know the big human names, the Peters and the Lukes and the Daniels and the Pauls, but the odds that any given one of us has spent one-on-one quality time with one of you humans is about the same odds as you as a human have of spending quality time one-on-one with an astronaut.

That's actually a very apt analogy. For the greater number of us, perhaps ninety-nine percent or so, Earth holds about the same attraction as the space program does for you. You may say, "Oh, that's great" following successful completion of a mission or mourn at the tragic loss of a spacecraft, but your real day-to-day interests lie elsewhere. Then there are a few of you who have a genuine interest in and working knowledge of your space program; you know the names of all of the various spacecraft and missions and those of the astronauts; you may even have briefly met one of them at some public function. And then there are the fanatics; those who so reorder their lives as to specialise in science or engineering or aeronautical proficiency so that they might possibly wangle their way into a situation at Cape Canaveral, Langley, or Houston...and, perchance, dare to dream of one day having that rarest of opportunities to leave the world behind and personally join in the great adventure.

It is from this latter group that Guardians are chosen.

You have heard that God loves you. You do not comprehend the half of it. He loves you so much that he arranged for someone like Dawn to be an active and integral part of your life before any human even knew that it had begun. You do not realise this, but Dawn was a powerful personage even by our own standards. Yet she willingly, nay, even eagerly set that aside to take on what is, in truth, the role of a servant. She did not regret it, not even for an instant. In all of this universe and beyond there is no one who can ever know you better and no one who will ever love you more than does Dawn...save only God himself. You might say that her love for you specifically is, in microcosm, the love which our God has for all of fallen humanity.

It is now time for me to bring this to a close for the night. Our attempts to track Dawn and to discern her whereabouts before the trail grew cold have failed, utterly. She is my best friend among my peers, and it breaks my heart to know that I now can do nothing more tangible than to pray for her. That, and to carry out what she stated as her final request to me. The ironic thing is that my own dream has now come true; I am now, at long last, officially a Guardian. It is what I have wanted more than anything else I could have imagined for a thousand years and more. But not like this. Oh, dear God, not like this.

Love,

Ariel

Chapter Twenty-Five

War is Hell

Michael had just awakened from his nightmare in a cold sweat. The first light of morning was visible through his bedroom window—but light was pouring through the crack under his doorway again. He smiled.

*   *   *

Dragora, manifesting as an angel of light, hovered a foot off the ground looking out the window. That is, her body was aimed in that direction; her eyes were tight shut. It wasn't easy maintaining her connection; our team was doing everything we possibly could to disrupt it. Still, it was a private channel and even Nathan's best Messenger was unable to listen in and divine the conversation.

"How are you doing?" Dravang asked.

"One big problem," Dragora answered. "The…"—well, the noun she used would have been technically correct for little Sassy, but I do believe she was referring to Dawn—"…has friends. They're blocking me. I can't read him."

"At all?" Dravang responded.

"I can tell something happened. Something big. But not what. How are things on your end?"

"She is a strong one. It will take some work to break her. Of course, that makes it all the more satisfying."

"Absolu…AAAAH!"

Michael had succeeded in sneaking up on the faux Dawn and 'goosing' her soundly. "Gotcha!" he exclaimed.

With an enraged cry, she flung him across the room and into the sofa. The sofa fell over backwards and knocked over a bookcase, which dumped its contents onto him. Sassy yelped and disappeared into Mike's bedroom. Mike sat there staring stupidly at 'Dawn' for a second. "Huh?"

"How *dare* you disturb me when I am in communion!" she exploded.

"What, you can dish it out but you can't take it?" Mike asked.

Dragora froze. She abruptly realized that she had made a misstep and shifted gears. "This is not a time for levity. I was in contact with the infinite principle of the cosmos. Your disruption was ill-timed."

"Oh. I'm…sorry," Mike said. "Um, could you help me clean this up?"

"Do you think that I have nothing better to do with my time than to keep *house*?" she asked as she walked out the front door.

Mike watched her leave, eyebrow raised with curiosity, and then began to straighten up the mess.

* * *

DRAGORA WALKED AWAY FROM THE home quickly, onto the pedestrian trail. A fence which Diego had crashed into just last week had still not been repaired. She headed southeast, towards a nearby park. As soon as Dravang's forces could give her some cover she spoke. "This is not working!"

"It will work. It has to work!" he demanded.

"Suppose I just forget him completely and head out on my own…"

"If you do that *they* can capture *you*," he reminded her. "You are taking her place. That's how we have to do this."

"I don't like it. I still can't read him, and now he's suspicious. She was with him for, what, three full days? How can I be convincing if I don't know what's been going on?"

"What do you need from me?" Dravang asked.

"Details. I need to know what she said, what she did, how she talks, how she behaves. Everything!"

"She's not talking yet."

"Make her talk. Fast. Or I'm out of here. Got that?"

"It shall be done."

* * *

By now, after a few hours of the tender ministrations of Dravang's guards, Dawn looked rather the worse for wear.

I must say, though, that there is one indignity which they did not subject her to. Not out of any sense of chivalry, but rather out of cold self-preservation. I know that such has frequently been used amongst humans as a weapon of war and even government policy on occasion, but the kingdom of darkness has come to learn that the Kingdom of Heaven recognizes a distinction between fallen humans being ravished by other fallen humans and an assault upon and defilement of its own sinless Holy Ones. The former is disgusting and stomach-turning and cries out for Heaven's justice, and although circumstances may not at present permit I assure you that justice is coming with penalties and interest due in full. The latter, however, is likely to trigger a massive retaliation from our side upon the instant—as the men of Sodom learned to their dismay. So there is that one line which Dravang demanded that his torturers not cross. Whilst thoroughly evil, he is not stupid.

At present he was stepping up to Dawn's side. He changed his fingertips into small claws, then idly tore gashes here and there in her body. At first there were small flashes of light accompanied by partial healing, but then the new wounds began to ooze blood. *Good*, he thought.

"I see your strength is going fast," he commented. "Pity. You can't even heal yourself, let alone anyone else. An interesting position, don't you think? Do you want out? It's not that hard. Talk to me."

"I am a servant of the Most High God," Dawn answered in a dull monotone.

"Yes, yes, I know that already," Dravang responded with a testy air. "You've made it perfectly plain. But you do know what happens if this goes on long enough, don't you? You can get so weak that even your own senses shut down. Just imagine. You can't hear, or see, or even feel a thing—except the pain. You still feel every bit of the pain." He gave that evil smile again. "It's like being trapped inside your own worst nightmare, and you haven't even the strength to wake up. It can drive even spirits like you and me quite insane."

"So that's what happened to you."

"Oh, come now. Let's not take this personally." Then he paused, acting as if something had only just now occurred to him. He was lying, of course; he had spent the past several hours frantically combing through dossiers and intelligence in order to glean every possible bit of information about his quarry. "You know, I do believe that I know you! You were an Enemy commander in this area for quite a number of years, weren't you? That would make you, what—a colonel, the humans would say?"

Name and rank are two subjects we are always permitted to divulge. "You're about two stars short," she answered with an obvious hint of satisfaction.

"Really!" He acted surprised. Possibly he was; the details of Dawn's final promotion were not widely known. "And you gave that up to wet-nurse that sorry, sweaty, smelly, slobbering sack of slime? Why?"

"Oh, yes. I never turn down a promotion."

He shook his head, uncomprehending. He was simply incapable of understanding. But then he continued. "Come, come now. I'm not asking for any details of grand strategy or tactical deployments. I just want to know what you were doing in our territory. If you have nothing to hide, why hide it?"

"I have nothing to hide. I have everything to protect."

"Oh? Look, it's not as though we keep you out completely. We let you through to do your stupid little rescue missions now and then. But you were behind our lines, in disguise—a very good disguise, I might add!— without our knowledge. Or our consent. Do you know what that makes you?" He paused for emphasis. "A *spy*. Spying is *wrong*."

"No. Not wrong. Just dangerous."

"It doesn't have to be. All you have to do is cooperate with us, just a bit. Why be so stubborn?"

"I am a servant of the Most High God."

"My, my, my. This is going nowhere. Well. Perhaps it's me. After all, I'm only an amateur at the business of interrogation. But I have a special surprise for you! Orville! Wilbur! Come here!

Dravang had gone into hock yet again in order to obtain—specialists. Two hideously deformed creatures from the worst of nightmares stepped forward from the shadows. They regarded Dawn with eager anticipation. One licked his lips.

"No relation to the two humans, of course," Dravang said with a smile. "We just call them that because they're so, um, *inventive*. They practice on the humans we, ahem, harvest, but you—you are opening night at Carnegie Hall!" He turned to the two monstrosities. "Give her a sample. A short sample."

* * *

When Dravang returned Dawn's body was a hideous, barely recognizable mess. He motioned the guards back from the immediate area, without loosening their grip on her bonds, of course, and leaned on the table, looking thoughtful.

"Are we feeling better now?" he asked.

Dawn opened her one functional eye and looked at him. Her voice, although weak and slow, was at the same time measured and deliberate. "May God judge you as you deserve."

"Oh, I am so scared," he replied with more than a note of sarcasm. "If you insist upon using these primitive human languages at least learn to put some feeling into them! Express yourself! There are all kinds of colorful phrases you could use. You might start by telling me to, 'Go to Hell!'"

"It's not the time for that. *Yet.*"

"My. So nasty. Hardly in character for one of Heaven's purest and holiest. So called." He leaned over her. "You're all hypocrites, you know. All that righteousness and purity is just a façade. We know it. Someday we'll prove it!"

Dawn closed her eye for a moment and sighed. Then she addressed him again. "Go right ahead. If you can—you're free. Or as free as you can be in a universe with no law, no justice, no final authority to cry out to for help. Where the strong enslave the weak, a universe ruled by brute force forever and ever. Do you really want that? Do you?"

Now he lowered his voice and acted a bit conspiratorial. "You might be surprised. I'm not completely at odds with your position. I can even see where you might have a point here and there. You know, if you were just wanting to isolate the truly twisted types like Wilbur and Orville there, why, I might even be willing to get behind you, a bit."

But what he was selling, Dawn wasn't buying. "I would rather be in their shoes than in yours. At least they aren't fooling themselves into thinking they're normal."

Dravang eyes flared with rage at this, for a moment—but it passed. He became thoughtful again, possibly genuinely so. At the very least, he asked the next question as if he seriously wanted her advice. "What would you do if you were in my shoes?"

Dawn saw the barest glimmer of light in this dark situation. With a wild, almost desperate sound of hope she answered, "Surrender. Stop fighting us. Stop fighting Him. Spare the universe that much more pain. Surrender!"

"Surrender? And what would I get in return?"

The moment had passed, and Dawn knew it. Still, with a sob she gave him an honest answer. "Justice!"

"Justice? Whose kind of justice?" Dravang asked. "His? Yours? That's not good enough. Now, if you were to offer some kind of quid pro quo…?"

"We don't make deals."

"Now that's your weakness." Dravang gave a thin smile. "You're so dogmatic. 'No Deals – No Compromise – Unconditional Surrender.' You've got to learn to be flexible, to give a little here and there! We aren't as one-sided as you are. We have our dark side…"—here he demonstrated with his best Count

Dracula impersonation—"… and our light side." Now he appeared as an angel of light, momentarily, before reverting to his accustomed form…much closer to the former than the latter. "We are complete!"

"I call it contaminated."

"I'm sorry you feel that way. Perhaps you need a little more persuasion." He motioned to the Wrong Brothers, who began to move back towards her. As they closed in, Dravang gave that evil smile. "War is Hell!"

Dawn didn't even try to hold back the screams.

Chapter Twenty-Six

Intruder Alert!

At Dravang's insistent prodding, Dragora had returned to Mike's home. He welcomed her in, but there was a strained silence between them.

He attempted to break the ice. "So. Um, are you hungry?"

"My sources of energy are not physical," she replied.

Now his frustration boiled to the surface. "Dawn, what's happened to you? You've changed!"

"Is it that I have changed, or is it that your perception of me has changed?" I think we may add double-talk to Dragora's skill set, hmm?

"Oh. Maybe. I guess. But you just seem so different. And I can't quite figure out why!"

"Ah, but now your situation is different. Perhaps we need to talk."

No, Mike! No! Yes, I was being blocked, but I have a better pipeline to our boy than anyone else save Dawn.

"No. Not tonight. Tomorrow, maybe." He turned to leave for the bedroom, and then spoke under his breath. "I thought I knew you."

That's good, Mike. Leave. You know something isn't right. That's not the person you know. Tomorrow you can tell her to leave.

But then I caught the spiritual equivalent of a foul odor. Dravang had succeeded in making connections with those of us so anxiously engaged behind the scenes. He entered, but not to do battle. To parley.

"Do you really feel it necessary to have so many of you here?" he began. "After all, there are just the two of us. And I don't plan on staying. Really, we're quite outnumbered. I think it's most—unfair."

At the magic word, Nathan turned and gave Dravang a dirty look. But he motioned to his troops to back down. He and I remained.

"Now, that's more like it," Dravang said with self-satisfaction.

"We are not going to stand for this!" Nathan said with more than a little heat. "She is not supposed to be there. We have an agreement. We don't preach to humans. And you stay out of their world!"

"I didn't make that agreement," Dravang replied languidly. "As I recall, it was imposed upon us rather unilaterally."

"We could take her right now," Nathan warned him.

"On what grounds?" Dravang countered. "As far as we're concerned, your spy is the one who shouldn't have been there to begin with. We're only taking her place." While Nathan attempted to formulate a response, he continued. "You know, I've always known that all your talk of right and wrong and all that rot was just pure window dressing. Sure, you believe in law and justice when it suits you. But when it doesn't, like now—well. Go ahead. Show your true colors. Throw her out of there. Brute force, that's all it will take. Go on. I dare you."

Nathan and I exchanged an uncomfortable look.

Dravang gave a smile of triumph. "Too weak to follow through. I knew it."

At this point I had taken just about all that I had a mind to. "We are not going to let you take and twist him around…"

"That ought to be up to him, not you, don't you think?" Dravang interrupted. "Excuse me. I wish to speak to my colleague. Privately."

Nathan and I silently followed Mike into his bedroom. Behind us, an impenetrable Barrier sealed off the living room.

*　*　*

"Well?" Dravang asked.

Holding the form of an angel of light didn't suit Dragora all that well either. She reverted back to her accustomed appearance with an air of relief. "I can't keep it up any longer if I don't get anything solid to work with. They've got him too well protected!"

"Well, in that case," said Dravang, "we've just got to move him out from under their umbrella. If he does something which he knows he shouldn't, then they won't be able to protect him anymore."

"What do you have in mind?"

"Quite simple, actually. I think I'll go down to the archives and look up everything I can find on…Samuel Wilson."

Chapter Twenty-Seven

Masquerade

The room was light, airy, and pleasant. Flowers and artwork were present, in abundance. There was still pain, but it was the ache of pains past. Her bed was surrounded by the somber faces of friends. And, in the midst of the scene, the familiar figure of Sam Wilson bent over her with a concerned look.

"Sam!" Dawn cried out as she recognized him. She flung her arms out to embrace him.

"It's okay. You're safe, now!" came the reassuring reply.

Dawn attempted to climb out of the bed. "I've got to get back. Michael…he needs me!"

But she was held back. "Hush!" she was reproved. "He's in good hands. Just rest, now, and then you can tell us all about it!"

"Oh, I will. I will!" she assured him. "But first, let me hear you pledge allegiance to the one true God. So I know this isn't a dream!"

But, to Dawn's horror, "Sam" and the "angels" exchanged uncomfortable glances. The beauty of the room melted away to reveal the ugliness of her dungeon. And, in the midst of it all, Dravang stood shaking his head. Dawn choked back a sob. She didn't want to give him the satisfaction—but she couldn't help herself.

"I just can't put one over on you, can I?" the suave figure commented with bemusement. Then, maliciously, he gloated. "Too bad your young friend isn't as wise to our ways!"

"*What*?" she exclaimed.

"Oh, you haven't figured it out yet? Here, let me show you some 'home movies'!"

An image shimmered and took shape....

*   *   *

"MICHAEL!" 'DAWN' EXCLAIMED. "I HAVE wonderful news!" The excitement she affected and enthusiasm she pretended to show put Mike in mind of the Dawn he thought he remembered. "You're going to get to speak with your father!"

This brought him up short. "But I thought you said…"

An even broader smile. Mike had just confirmed that he knew that what she planned to entice him to do was forbidden. "Perhaps I spoke too soon," Dragora/Dawn said softly. "Exceptions can be made, now and then. You will see!"

Michael, motivated by longing and loss, bought it. I was screaming, "No! No!"…but that did no good at all. "When can this happen?"

"Why, right now," Dragora purred. "If you just call out to him!"

Some of my protests were getting through. "Uh, wait. That just doesn't seem right."

"Oh, it's the way these things are done," the false 'Dawn' said reassuringly. "Call to him. He will answer!"

"Dad?" Michael said tentatively.

"Oh, no. You must use his name!"

*   *   *

IN THE OFFICE, AS CLOSE as possible to spiritual 'neutral ground', where such things are adjudicated, Dravang had filed an official claim to be 'also known as' Samuel Lane Wilson. A patent lie and falsehood on its face, but in that court a good lawyer could drag the dispute out longer than Michael's remaining Earthly life expectancy before it was finally resolved…and, you may rest assured, The Devil Is A Lawyer. Should you raise an eyebrow at that, allow me to remind you that at present the Earthly realm is legally disputed—and, while I'm confident that our claim will ultimately prevail, at present it is still under the jurisdiction of those whom we regard as the enemy.

Claim filed but still awaiting final resolution, Dravang had legal standing to respond to a call to that name. The real Sam Wilson, forbidden by our agreements to ever return to the Earthly realm while it remained in dispute, could not.

* * *

"OUT OF MY WAY!" DRAVANG thundered at Nathan and me. "He calls. I answer!"

"He's not calling *you!*" I retorted.

"But he does call. So you cannot protect him any longer. Stand aside!"

* * *

IF THERE'S ONE THING HE'S good at, it's disguises, I thought to myself. *Doesn't something about this hug just feel… wrong?* I attempted to transmit to Michael.

"I cannot remain," Sam/Dravang told Michael as he detached from the embrace. *Of course you can't; if you stay there's any number of ways that the impersonation might fall apart. Get them hooked, then turn them over to the big fish and bail…Standard Operating Procedure.* "But she can! Stay with her! Learn from her! Think of her as your spiritual guide!" Dravang told him.

With the steps Michael had taken away from obedience we couldn't shield his thoughts and memories any more; not effectively at the least. Dravang, Dragora, and the rest of their team were digging into the treasure trove greedily. *She did…WHAT?*

* * *

FROM HER TORTURE CHAMBER DAWN watched her doppelgänger take up the siren song. "There is infinite power in the cosmos," the counterfeit said. "You were given a taste of it already. I can teach you its hidden secrets. It will be yours to command, to control!"

The real Dawn was really losing it. "What? No! No!"

But the mendacious voices continued on. "What she teaches you, you shall someday teach others," 'Sam' said. Followed by 'Dawn' who continued, "Together we can lead your people to their destiny. The destiny we have always had in mind!"

"No! God, no!" Dawn sobbed. The torture, the abuse she had endured had been as *nothing* compared to this!

"You see?" Dravang gloated. "Humans don't want leadership, or righteousness, or justice. They want power! The kind of power we can give!"

"He belongs to us!" Dawn cried. "You can't have him! He's ours! You can't use him!"

"Oh yes we can," Dravang assured her. "Do I have to go back to the Inquisition and quote you the precedents? Oh, you can have him back someday—after we're finished with him. I'm sure he'll have brought in enough followers to keep us amused for quite some time!"

"No! This isn't true! You're making it up!" she wailed, clinging to a fragile thread of hope. "It's all just another lie!"

Dravang smiled. He had timed this just right. The "home movies" he had just shown her could have been faked; we do have those capabilities. But not this. He opened up a direct corridor—one-way, of course—to where she could observe Michael 'practicing' as an evil spirit in her very own body coached and made helpful suggestions. As realization and horror flooded into her, Dravang began to laugh triumphantly. Dawn—the *real* Dawn—broke down in tears.

"Well, it looks like we have things wrapped up here, now," the demonic prince gloated. "We have your boy well in hand, and I don't think there's anything more that I need from you. So go ahead, boys," he said to his assembled demons. "Have fun!"

The sobs of anguish which ensued were much deeper than physical.

Chapter Twenty-Eight

Unmasqued!

Nathan's defenses by now were in ruins, but some remnants remained. The small home was still unfriendly territory. So on Friday, after dinner—which he materialized under her direction—"Dawn" announced that she needed to take a short walk to commune with her master. Mike watched her go with mixed feelings. He wanted to be with her, yes, but at the same time…it was almost as if his head suddenly felt clearer as soon as she stepped out the door.

As she turned the corner onto the pedestrian trail along the old railway right-of-way he suddenly realized that she had not asked him to pray with her for almost three full days.

*　　*　　*

"So how are things going?" Dravang asked after she had arrived in the small park and opened a channel.

"Better than we expected," Dragora responded. "He's quite a student. Want to see?"

And she replayed a memory from earlier that same day. Michael was attentively watching as Dragora, in disguise, said, "Empty your mind. Become one with the universe! Feel the power flow through you. The very essence of reality is yours to shape, to control! Open your eyes. That chair is now part of you. Move it!" And the chair moved.

"And he really thinks he's doing it himself," she chuckled. "There's one born every minute!" They both laughed at that. "Too bad we can't keep him," she continued. "Same plan?"

"Basically. We need you to stay with him, in her place, until events have firmed up. After that, we want to make him a complete embarrassment to their side," Dravang said. "Experience shows that they're likely to remove him for us; you won't have to do a thing. And then, with him gone, we'll be free to put you to work in more strategic areas in that world. Without interference."

"Don't be in too big a hurry," she purred. "I want to have some *fun* with him first!"

Dravang frowned. "That would be extraordinarily unwise."

"Maybe." Dragora changed the subject. "So how are you doing with her?"

"I'm finished with her."

"You didn't let her go, did you?"

"No, of course not!"

"Excellent!" And then they both laughed again.

Unmasqued!

*   *   *

THE DISHES FROM DINNER WERE still on the table. Oh, it had been edible enough, but, still, when he compared it to the meals Dawn had prepared those first couple of days, something was lacking. What?

It occurred to him that he ought to be able to use his new-found powers to help in cleaning up. He attempted to empty his mind, extend his consciousness as she had said—nothing. He sighed and picked up a handful of dirty dishes.

It's not going to work, Mike. She's lying to you. It's not your power, it's hers! Can't you tell something is wrong? Am I getting through to you at all?

Nathan looked a question at me. I shrugged helplessly. "I can't get through to him. He's not listening to me," I said in a weary voice.

"I hate to say this," he said, "but I'm looking at contingencies."

"Stop," I said. "I don't want to think about it."

"You won't…?"

"I didn't say that." If one has to shoot one's own dog, best that he do it himself. "If it has to be done, I'll be the one to do it. But I'd rather not think about it up until that point."

"I understand," Nathan answered.

One thing we decided, thousands of years back, was that there was a limit as to how much of a loose cannon we would allow one of our own to become. It's every Guardian's nightmare. If push came to shove and I was ordered to do so, I would kill Michael myself. And it would just about kill me to have to do it. Yes, he'd still belong to us—but no triumphal entry, no "well done" from the Lord, an eternity of using the back stairs—it would ruin everything that I and the others had ever planned for him. And, someday, having to look Dawn in the eye and explain it to her…I couldn't bear the thought. I needed a break.

Mike needed a break, too. The dirty dishes were now in the dishwasher, and he came back in the living room intending to plop down into his recliner. On the way, though, he passed his desk. The pen and paper were still where Dawn had left them at quarter past two of that early Wednesday morning which now seemed an eternity ago. He stared at them curiously, then sat down. Little Sassy emerged—she had been reluctant to leave his bedroom for the past two days—and cuddled up against his leg. He patted her head absently.

He was going to put the pen and paper away, and pulled open the top desk drawer. Or tried to, at any rate; it was stuck. *Got to fix that,* he thought to himself. Maybe if he opened the bottom drawer…

What's that? Oh, it was his homeowner's insurance policy. Wait a minute, wasn't it just about up for renewal? Had he missed the notice? They were very bad about not sending reminders until the very last week before it was due to lapse. He pulled it out to check the dates on the declarations page. Good; he had time to get in another two paychecks before the payment had to be made. Satisfied, he started to set the packet back in the drawer.

What are those?

Unmasqued!

He was looking at four sheets of paper, each neatly folded in thirds. On the outside of each sheet a date was written in an unfamiliar but very beautiful, even calligraphic, hand. Curious, he picked the first up to take a closer look. With a start, he realized that the date was that of Sunday earlier this week! He unfolded the page to see what was written within...and his jaw dropped.

Dear Michael,

> *I still can't believe that I'm actually here, with you right there in the next room! I've been looking forward to this all your life— all my life, actually! I've been studying you every moment of the time, and I know you better than you know yourself...but you don't even know I exist! What do I do? What do I say? I only get one chance to make a first impression...Lord, help me to make it a good one!*

The letter continued on in a friendly style for the remainder of the page; as it was a bit personal I will leave it up to Mike to share with you if he should ever be so inclined. He read the next one, recognizing it as the one he had seen her writing literally under his own nose.

Dear Michael,

> *I met you today for the first time, and you should have seen the look on your face! Oh, it was rich! Oh, Mike! There's so much that I want to tell you, so much I want to say—but I'm still not sure that I should, not just yet at least. So I think I'll stick with my letter writing for at least a while longer. Still...*

WHAT a day!

He read it to the end, flipped on through the third, then hungrily read the last one. Although it didn't cross his mind to dwell on it, he was feeling spiritually clean for the first time in the past three days. But there, towards the bottom of the last letter, he read:

> *...I'm about to do something that's a little dangerous, and if something goes wrong—well, I may have to leave without saying good-bye. I don't want you to think I'm leaving because of what you said in the hospital. Maybe it's hard for you to understand, but I really do want the very best for you and yours. We all do. Remember that.*
>
> *Always and forever,*
>
> *I love you,*
>
> *Dawn*

He read through the letters again. And again. He almost began to sob, for a moment—but, then, like any normal red-blooded American male, stifled his emotions and sought a way to channel them into action. The pen and the sheet of paper were still right there. He picked them up, and then began to write himself. While his penmanship was somewhere between laughable and atrocious, the thoughts were eloquent:

> *Dear Dawn,*
>
> *I found your letters, and I read them. I'm not really sure I was supposed to, but I did. They just reminded me so much of what I saw in you those first few days! I do appreciate all that you're trying to teach me now; I really*

do—but I'd give it all up this minute if I could just have you back the way you were when I first got to know you...

"What are you doing?" 'Dawn' asked from behind him. With a whimper, Sassy retreated to her hiding place under his sofa.

Mike scarcely noticed. "Writing," he answered. A slight hint of a smile, there.

"Writing what?"

"A letter."

"Oh? Who is it to?" she asked with puzzlement.

"Guess!"

Her face clouded up. "I have no time for guessing games. There is much work to do. Put that aside, and come here!"

Mike tore the letter he was writing in half. He then stood up, a strange look on his face, and regarded her. "Who are you?" he asked. And then, a beat later: "And what have you done with my friend?"

YES!!!

With a start, Dragora realized that she was in trouble. The gaps which had opened up in our shields were closing again, and quickly. She slipped back into her warm, friendly, used-car salesman mode. "Michael, you know me. I am your friend!"

"It's almost like you're two different people! Like somebody switched the...waitaminiit. Maybe that's what this letter is about!"

"What letter?"

"You don't know? You don't know! You really ARE someone else, aren't you! But who…? Wait. It's got to be. You're one of them!"

"Michael, Michael, trust me!" Dragora said soothingly. "I really am an angel…"

"Yeah," he interrupted. "But what kind? How did you ever…of course! That *is* what this letter is about, isn't it? Dawn was doing something; it went wrong; and you took her place!"

"I can explain everything…"

"You get out of here!" Mike commanded.

With that, Dragora dropped the pretense. She still maintained Dawn's physical form, but the voice was her own. "Let's not be too hasty, now. I want to stay here. You want power, the kind of power I have, and to spare. Just think of what you could do with access to it! We can work out a deal…"

"Oh, right!" Mike interrupted again. "You expect me to trust you? No, thanks! Now get out of here! I say as a believer in Jesus Christ, get out of here!"

And with that, Dragora lost it. "Now wait just a minute, little man!" she hissed. "*You* listen to *me!*" She reached out and grabbed him by his collar, then lifted him off his feet and held him by one hand at arm's length with ease. "Do you know who you're talking to, little man? I could crush you like an insect…"

The look on Mike's face was pure shock. Dragora was pleased…for a moment. Then she noticed that the room had grown intensely bright…and realized that she wasn't doing it. She looked over her shoulder.

"Oh, do go on," I said to her.

Chapter Twenty-Nine
A MEETING

DRAGORA DROPPED MIKE TO THE floor and wheeled around to face…thirty fearsome Warriors and one admittedly rather smug Counselor. *"What?"* Then she growled, "This is *our* world! You are not supposed to be here!"

"Oh?" I replied. "You're quite right, of course, except for one thing." I possessively cupped a hand around Mike's shoulder and helped him to his feet. "This is our man. You were aware of that, were you not? And he told you to leave. But you didn't leave. So…"

"We're here to *make* you leave!" Nathan finished for me.

"Now, if you were here as a spirit," I said continuing on, "like *you're* supposed to be, why, then, we could have handled everything from behind the scenes." I reached out and touched a lock of her hair. "But you appear to be wearing a human body." Time enough to flash a wry smile, then say, "One must do what one must do!"

Mike was finding his voice again. "Who…who are you?" he asked.

"Oh, introductions. But of course. You may call me Ariel, and this gentleman is Nathan. And one of the squads he commands. Pleasure to make your acquaintance at long last, although I had hoped that it could be under happier circumstances." Then I regarded the false "Dawn" with a steely look. "And we are all servants of the One True God—unlike this counterfeit."

What happened next was much like arm-wrestling, although it took place mostly on the spiritual level. I grasped "Dawn's" upper arm firmly and set my jaw. She resisted, and she was considerably stronger than I'd realized at first. I wasn't worried, though; I had Nathan's entire team backing me up. It didn't take long before Dragora lost and her "mask" fell away completely. Back in her accustomed form, she looked around frantically. No help was to be seen.

"Are you looking for somebody?" I asked with more than a hint of satisfaction in my voice. "They're not coming. You broke the rules, my sometime colleague. You gave Him an excellent excuse to let us just walk right in. And your friends don't know a thing about it. They're not coming. So now you get to come back with us and cool your heels in a nice, quiet cell until Judgment Day." A very cold and thin smile. "And, no, I think we shouldn't like to talk about bail!" This time, taking a prisoner was worth the risk.

Mike had found his voice. "Who…who are you? What happened to Dawn?"

"You want to know?" said Dragora. "Maybe we can work up a deal...."

"Michael, NO!" I interrupted. "Nathan?"

Nathan grasped Mike by the shoulder and drew him away. As he did, two of his choice Warriors took Dragora firmly in hand...very mindful of how she had blindsided Gregory just a couple weeks back...and disappeared with her. Nathan, for his part, read Mike the riot act. "Michael...never, ever try to get information from these characters. For one thing, they lie. For another, they can claim that you owe them one. And they always collect at the worst possible time!"

"But I just want to know what happened to Dawn!" Mike pleaded.

"I'm afraid Dawn has been captured. A prisoner. Probably being tortured even as we speak."

"Can't you do something?"

"We can try sending someone in after her." Nathan was forcing himself to sound optimistic.

Philip, on the other hand, thought Mike should know the real score. "Yes, and every time we get close they'll bounce her off to some new hiding place."

"I'm afraid Philip is right," Nathan admitted with a heavy sigh. "We'll get her back eventually, that I'm sure of, but it may take some time."

"How long?" Mike asked.

"Maybe forty, fifty years," Nathan answered.

"More likely two or three hundred," Philip muttered.

Even at that, he was being optimistic. Dawn, wherever she was, had no connection back to the heavenlies which we could trace. Our best hope was some kind of exchange—but whom could we possibly trade for an experienced general officer? A low-level thug like Dragora? Don't make me laugh. Even Dravang himself would draw no more than a yawn from his high command. Fantar, had he not been disgraced? Maybe. Unfortunately, though, once away from the choking spiritual miasma of Hell the enemy spirits, even though held prisoner in our territories, soon lose any desire to return. The man who said, "Better to reign in Hell than serve in Heaven" obviously never spent significant time in either. It's quite a remarkable compliment to know that even your own enemies would choose imprisonment under your rule instead of release and return to their own accustomed sphere. But it makes it deucedly difficult to arrange a prisoner swap under those circumstances.

By way of amplification, we have learned from bitter experience that the connection 'cords' run both ways and that in many cases the principals involved aren't even aware of their existence—their own superiors were the ones who set the hook. And they're much harder to detect between spiritual realms than they are crossing the Border into the physical; without the Divine shielding we currently enjoyed Nathan's entire team would be in big trouble right about now. It's true that not much information and/or energy can be exchanged through such a slender thread, but 'not much' does not mean zero. Many of the enemy spirits who have willingly surrendered to us and demonstrated good behavior for a century or more have wondered why we are so reluctant to grant parole; well, that's why.

There was silence for a moment. Then Nathan turned to me. "Well. With your permission, Counselor, I need to see about putting together a penetration team. Your pardon, ma'am?"

"Just a moment," I replied. I turned back to Mike and gestured towards his desk. The torn pieces of the letter which he had begun to write reassembled themselves and returned to their place. "You may finish that at your convenience, if you like," I told him. "If we get her back...*when* we get her back," I corrected myself, "I'll see to it that she gets a copy. It will help."

"Are there any more of these?" Mike asked, indicating Dawn's letters.

"I should say! Almost...yes, almost fifteen thousand, at last count, I do believe."

"Fifteen...*thousand?*"

"Some nights she writes more than one."

Mike began to cloud up, but then like a Proper Red-Blooded American Male, channeled his emotions into action. "Isn't there anything we can do?" he asked. "Anything at all?"

Nathan sighed. "Look. You're a police officer. I want you to imagine that you've tailed the Bad Guys to a certain building. You know for sure that they're in there. The building has a million floors, and there are a million rooms on each floor. There are ten thousand elevators and staircases, and four thousand exits spaced evenly all around the first floor." He was simplifying matters unbelievably, of course, but Mike's human brain couldn't have grasped the true number of interconnections and dimensions in multispace. "To conduct your search, you have as many officers as I have angels with me here in your living room. How long before you apprehend the Bad Guys?"

It was beginning to sink in. "So there's nothing we can do?" Mike asked.

Nathan shook his head sadly.

But, at that moment, the germ of an idea occurred to me. It was—well, let's just say that I had ample reason to question my own sanity. But my vocal cords lived a life of their own. "Maybe… maybe there is," I interrupted.

All eyes were on me. I looked Mike up and down and asked, "How would you feel about being used as bait?"

Mike looked distinctly uncomfortable.

Chapter Thirty

A BRIEFING

"*Bait?*" Nathan asked incredulously. "What can you possibly be thinking!"

That last was not intended as a question. I held up a hand. "One moment." I turned to Michael. "Dawn only alluded to this briefly, but you ought to know that she was quite a prominent personality, even among we angels."

"She did say…"

"A leadership position, yes. Roughly equivalent to a major general, in your terms. But let me be even more blunt. Dawn had advanced *as far as it is possible for one of us to go* without extensive training in…shall we say, strategic considerations."

"Okay, but…"

"I am acting in her stead now, as her former assistant. But you should know that I have been involved with the human world not quite three hundred years longer than she has. My 'career track', as it were, was entirely different. But, towards the end, I was involved with the affairs of nations and had some significant education in those matters myself."

Nathan started, and regarded me with new respect. For a moment. Then he remembered. "You are not supposed to be here!" he warned me.

"Oh? You're absolutely right; I'm not supposed to place myself in any situation where I am in danger of capture. Are you ordering me out?"

He thought about it for a few seconds and finally said, "Keep talking."

"Very good. Michael…and Nathan, you need to know that history is not linear! Oh, it *looks* that way, certainly, from a distance, but from down inside of it there is a very great deal of backing and filling. Those flashes of insight which you get, those 'lucky breaks,' those nightmare situations which turn out to only be bad dreams—in many if not most of those incidents you are dealing with echoes of events which could have been, but weren't."

I looked around at the faces which surrounded me, human and angelic. This was news to Michael, of course. It was even news to Nathan and Philip. But it was not news to Nathan's chief of intelligence, that I could tell—that angel was shaking his head slightly, taken aback that I was venturing to discuss such sensitive matters so freely in this time and place. Such is life. "In the final analysis," I continued, "events are shaped by choices.

282

But not just your own isolated wishes, fairy godmother style. I am not a genie." And glad of it, too! "No, it is the summation of both your choices and the choices of those around you, limited by what you are willing and able to endure. When you reach the limits of that endurance there is a split—and then your future from that point is shaped by the choices you have already made."

"I don't understand," Mike said. I could tell he was speaking for Nathan, too.

"Then let me simplify it for you," I responded. "Michael…*you're dead!*"

"*What?*"

"You're six feet under. You're pushing up daisies right now. You bled out there in the rail yard, and weren't found until it was much too late. Your funeral was day before yesterday; it made the bottom of page 8A in the local news. You and Dawn are picking out curtains in Heaven even as we speak. Your mother is still in mourning, of course. And Rick—since you were never able to positively ID the druggies he never went to that plant."

"But…"

"Oh, wait, it doesn't look like that right now, does it? I almost forgot. You remember that incident five years back, when as a rookie you got that well-aimed shot off just in time to keep that duster from choking the life out of you? Well—you didn't!"

"Hey! Dawn said…"

"Oh, I'm just getting started! Remember that night in Thailand, when you were late coming back to the ship and took that wrong turn down the blind alley?

You thought you just barely escaped being mugged. So sorry! And all of those times you've changed lanes without signaling? In quite a few of them you hit the jackpot. Not wearing your seat belt certainly didn't help. I could keep going, all the way back to the time when you were two years old and decided to see what would happen if you stuck that paper clip into that electrical socket. Now, that's the earliest you personally remember—but think about the odds of that particular one of 375,297,168 sperm being the first to find its way to your mum's egg!"

He was silent. I continued. "You truly are crucified with Christ—yet you live! There are so many branches, so many possibilities. We have to put someone on you 24/7 just to keep track of all the twists and turns!"

"So, how does this…?"

"Choices, Michael. This most recent chain of events began with someone wanting you dead. They got their wish. But the dispatcher who was fired for not keeping track of you desperately wished that things had turned out different. Tension. But what you finally experienced made him happy, and you happy, and Dawn happy… but."

"What do you mean, 'but'?"

"But if it were that simple then angels would be openly intervening in the human world every single day. And we would call that 'Heaven.' Doesn't happen that way, as you've noticed. Because there is another set of choices, those made by the enemy. For some reason, someone among them—probably the same someone who wanted you dead—was more pleased by this turn of events than by either you bleeding out in the rail yard or you being found in time to be taken to a hospital and saved. I can only guess that what this someone was so pleased by was the opportunity to capture a holy angel. And, so…"

"So how does this help us help Dawn?"

"Well, first you should know that deaths—and conceptions, too—are final after three days. It's not that there's anything magical about the number three; it's just an agreement that has been hammered out over the millennia. Seventy-two hours, no more, no less."

"But wait! Death can happen in an instant!"

"True, but for those three days there is always a chance the chain of events will change retroactively. You're not aware of it, of course, although sometimes after the break point you'll have a dream with a flash of what could have been. Sometimes sooner, sometimes later. Sometimes many times, if there was truly a great deal of tension. Your doctors call that 'PTSD.'"

"Okay, but conception? That also happens in an instant!"

"*Fertilization* happens as nearly instantaneously as anything in the biological world," I corrected him, "but *conception* is not final until the fertilized embryo finds a place and implants successfully in the mother's womb. And to know for certain that this has occurred takes, almost exactly, three days."

Mike digested this in stunned silence. I turned to Nathan and his forces. "There are the occasional extended break points, especially if many lives are at stake. Do look up the history of the Cuban Missile Crisis at your leisure. But for day-in, day-out conflicts with the enemy the three-day rule applies in well over ninety-nine percent of cases."

"So where are you going with this?" Nathan asked.

"Isn't it obvious? Someone on the enemy side was willing to allow a holy angel to walk in the human world for three days in order to capture her. That break point is now past; it's Final Reality. What we need to do, if we want to get Dawn back *now,* is to tempt them with something which they will find even more attractive than what they already have. *Before* the next break point becomes final!" And I pointed at Michael.

Jaws dropped amongst all of the Warriors. "We *can't* let them have him back, ever again!" Philip exclaimed.

"I know that. You know that. But do they know that? Wouldn't they give their eye teeth—or loosen their grasp on a holy angel—for the hope of actually breaking a redeemed human loose from us, after so many centuries of trying in vain?"

Mike had finally found his voice. "Look," he said. "I still don't know what, exactly, you're planning. But I'm willing to go along with it if it gives you a real chance of getting Dawn back!"

I gave a thin smile and looked at the clock. "By my reckoning," I said, "we have a little over five hours. Best get busy!"

Chapter Thirty-One

A Plan

Most of the next hour was spent going over dossiers and intelligence. Mike was truly stunned at this glimpse of the infernal activity going on within his very own home town. But there was no time to dwell on it; we identified the Executive Center as the most likely nexus to penetrate and set about to transfer Nathan's team to it without attracting attention. Teleportation was out, as well as flying, of course, and it was much too far to walk. A taxi might do for one or two of us, but too many arriving at once would surely attract scrutiny.

Fortunately, within walking distance of Mike's home are three Metrorail stations on two separate lines as well as two transit centers hosting a baker's dozen of bus lines apiece. We could converge on our target in hundreds of possible ways with no one the wiser. Nathan and his twenty-seven compatriots left Mike's home, on foot, one or two at a time three minutes apart for the best part of an hour. Philip and his shadow Timothy had been the last to do so, some thirty minutes previous. For the most part they were all in disguise; between them were several millennia of experience with many different human cultures. Nathan himself originally served in West Africa before transferring to the North American sector during the waning days of the slave trade. Philip was attached to China nearly as long and came across the Pacific following the laborers who had constructed the transcontinental railway in the nineteenth century. Finally, Mike and I would drive over in his pickup; our routes were planned so that we would all arrive by a quarter past midnight. That left exactly two hours to pull off the miracle of tempting the tempters to bring their hostage back within a combat radius of the Earth plane.

"I can't believe you're doing this," Mike said as he closed the pickup's door. And buckled in, without prompting for a change. Small favors.

I shrugged. "Dawn is my best friend."

"I mean, going in there," he said as he pulled out of the driveway and turned to head towards the freeway. "In that place."

"That's not such a shucks, not for me. Remember the dress code in the Garden of Eden. Men like to admire women. And we girls, for the most part, enjoy being admired. That in and of itself isn't the problem. The sin comes when people twist it and exploit it for money, for power, for advantage and leverage over others… Well. Attraction is normal and healthy and has God's blessing, within reason. But when twisted into lust, then it becomes sin."

"Still…"

"I've made that decision. I'm much more worried about you."

"I thought I just had to be the bait?"

"Yes, and what if they take it? There is no precedent to go on here, none whatsoever even from ancient times. Remember that animated movie of the story of Moses that you liked so much as a youngster? Well, now you truly are 'Playing With the Big Boys.' It's entirely possible that you and I and all of the rest of us could end up in the same predicament that Dawn finds herself in right now."

"You mean…?"

"Look. In normal circumstances, the instant that you shuffle off this mortal coil both you and Dawn would become non-combatants. Officially. Permanently. It's the only way that we were able to get the enemy to agree to grant the both of you safe-conduct under any and all conditions. You can't ever return to the human world—well, at least not until Kingdom Come—you can't communicate, can't influence events, can't even *pray*. Well, not effectively. I mean, you can always share your concerns with the Throne, but once you no longer officially belong to this world you have no standing to persuade Him to act. There is just one Person in Heaven who is qualified to intercede on behalf of those on Earth, and that is the Lord Jesus Christ himself. And that, you should know, is why it is such a great honor and privilege to be able to serve God in the here-and-now— because you won't get another chance like this in the by- and-by."

"So. Prepare me for the worst."

"Well, Michael, keep this in mind: *We won't ever let go of you.* Not for good. Now, since we are acting outside of established scope and precedent there is a chance—and I'm afraid it's a very good chance—that if things go south they will grab you and hold you and all of the rest of us as prisoners. And if that happens, I guarantee that they will lie and try to claim that Heaven has forgotten you, to make you despair of hope. It will be a lie; we will never give you up. Your name is written in the Lamb's Book of Life and we will never quit until those books balance—although unfortunately the recovery process often drags on so long as to make you think we have. But if you do in fact lose hope then don't be ashamed, you're in very good company. Even the Lord Jesus Himself once felt the same way, at least for a moment." I hesitated, and then added. "I'm afraid that from this point on we need to keep our conversations *sub rosa.* We're about to penetrate an enemy perimeter, and we can afford to take no chances. It's time for me to put on my disguise." And I shifted into Dawn's human form.

Michael looked, and then shook his head. "I know it's you, but…"

"From here on out, I'm Dawn. Remember that. *Please* remember that!"

"Okay. Dawn, did you want to stop for a burger or something?"

"I hear they've got a good kitchen where we're going!"

I'm almost as good at imitating Dawn's speaking voice as is Dragora. Mike shook his head again.

*　　*　　*

A Plan

WE FOUND A SPOT AT the back of the parking lot. It was only moderately crowded, but Mike isn't the only one who likes to park his new pickup well away from any other vehicles. As we walked to the main entrance a red and green and white sedan which seemed almost too small to be a taxi pulled up and a very large and loud West African clambered out of the back seat. I recognized Nathan. He clapped the driver on the shoulder, handed him two twenties, and said, "Keeps da change!"

I knew better than to acknowledge him in any open way, but he saw me. He made a motion as if to tip his nonexistent hat and said, "Hey, pretty lady!" I gave a curt nod and then looked away as if embarrassed. But his salutation had drawn attention from those waiting in line at the taxi stand, including…

Oh, no.

It was Rick. Having been released from the hospital and with time off to recuperate but feeling perfectly fine, he had gone out to celebrate. Now he was about three drinks the wrong side of 'jolly'. He saw me, and Michael, did a take and shook his head, then looked at us again. He stepped out of line and came up between us, clapped his arms around both of our shoulders, and said with a rather boozy air, "Dawn! Michael! You sly old salty dog! This is great! Hey, let me show you around!"

Is it too late to dig a hole and pull it in around me?

But Michael responded in the only way he could. "Hey! Buddy! Yeah…I dunno, I've never been here before. But Dawn heard about this place and thought the both of us should pay a visit. Just to see, you know! If you could show us around, that would be great!"

He came off as shy, awkward, country-bumpkin-come-to-town. But that was just about the right note to strike, and it worked in our favor. "Come on!" Rick said. "Follow me!"

Into the demons' lair we stepped, meeting the maître d'. "Jacques!" Rick said. "These are friends of mine, really good friends!" Fortunately he retained enough discretion not to introduce either of us by name, for which I was grateful. "Just put them on my tab, I'll take care of everything!" he said. "Show us to the stage!"

Being just past midnight the place was beginning to empty out; most of the ones remaining were the hard-core patrons. We were shown to a table in the front and center near the stage; a couple of guests who had been hoping to move in on it as it was being cleaned turned away disappointed. I looked around; most of our group was already here but a few faces were still missing. Think of it; my first full evening actually on Earth…and I was here in a strip club.

I supposed that I had time enough to look around. The Executive Center, as seen from the physical realm, was a curious combination of the elegant and the frenetic. In the public spaces around the perimeter of the auditorium, the business center and so forth, two-toned grays predominated with just a hint of royal blue trim. But the stage was an explosion of color and activity; an extravagant red and blue and green laser light show danced its way across the very high ceiling in time with the beat of the music and the gyrations of the performers. The girls themselves, especially that blonde in the black lace panties…God could not possibly have given her that body naturally, could he? I adjusted my vision to look back along the time axis as well as to more clearly see the "fingerprints" of their souls. No, my initial impression was correct...and not just in the obvious places, either. I mused as to whether or not their plastic surgeons deserved a commission on their gratuities.

The music was normally loud, pumping, with a heavy beat...but once in a while they would slip in a gentler tune to allow the patrons to catch a breath. Even I, despite myself, appreciated the occasional respite. It was all well-planned to make the paying customers feel themselves in a special world a cut above that of the uninitiated...and to separate them from their money in the process, of course.

The waitress came by to take our orders; she was topless as were all the others. I remembered whom I was supposed to be pretending to be supposed to be pretending to be Dawn, and looked her over slyly as if I was sizing up the competition. Nothing that a Dragora in Dawn's body would be worried about, of course. As the kitchen was still open until the stroke of one I ordered the "Ring of Fire Nachos". Dawn, with her Texas background, loves spicy food and I have grown rather partial to it myself. It also gave me an excuse to ask for, "Ice water, a big glass...and keep it coming!" in addition to my double shot of 12-year-old single malt Glenlivet. The whiskey was a prop, I did no more than barely taste it, but the water was to drink.

"Good choice!" said Rick. "Hey, make that a double order, Cindi; we'll split!"

The drinks were out in less than two minutes; the nachos a timed five and a half minutes later. *Miss Cindi has earned her gratuity*, I thought to myself. Yes, the kitchen was as good as advertised; I was thankful for the ice water. This was hardly the place to bow my head and ask a blessing on the food publicly, but you had best believe that inside I was praying nonstop for my Master's blessings on the night and what we hoped to accomplish here. And I desperately hoped that Michael, with his standing to intercede in this world, was doing the same. I had 'primed the pump' earlier, but I didn't dare to explicitly ask for such.

It would be so much more effective if it truly came from his own heart.

* * *

"OH, CANDY AND SPICE!" RICK called out as the blonde left the stage and an admittedly striking duo of a brunette and a redhead took her place and began writhing to the strains of, "I Wanna Dance With Somebody." Rick looked on appreciatively for a minute, and then cast a sly look back over at Mike. "So you've never been inside a place like this before in your life? What's it like?"

Mike gave an uneasy look in my direction and I replied with a barely perceptible shrug. But we had both forgotten about Rick's nearly preternatural ability to read body language. "Oh? Oho!" he chortled in triumph. "You *have* been in a place like this! When and where?"

Don't lie. Not now, I attempted to transmit to Mike. Whether it actually got through I'm still unsure, but at least Mike had the wisdom to recognize not to dig a hole any deeper than it already was. "Yeah. In Thailand. In the Navy. First class wanted to treat me to a night on the town. Pop my cherry. I...well, let's just say that I cut it short and left without him. Almost got mugged on the way back to the ship. When I got there, I found something new: they had set up a breathalyzer. I blew an .08 and there were still five hours until morning quarters, so they let me go. When the first class got back—well, he ended up a second class."

"Blindsided!" Rick chortled as he took a sip of beer. Then he looked over at me. "And she brought you here! I knew you were a woman of the world!"

I returned a Dragora-esque smile and purred, "More worlds than you can dream of!"

We were making a dent in the nachos and I was fighting off a rising sense of panic when Philip and Timothy finally walked in through the door. They were only ten minutes late but I must confess that I can be a bit of a worry wart. Philip was disguised as a tall and muscular Chinese graduate student while Timothy, looking very much out of place, came as a rail-thin, rather "nerdy" and lily-white college junior. Both were wearing "University of Houston" red-and-white sweatshirts and blue jeans. *Don't tell me that he forgot to specify that he was twenty-one,* I groaned as the maître d' carefully inspected Timothy's ID. But no, Philip is an artist; according to his quite convincing driver's license Timothy's twenty-first birthday had begun exactly twenty-five minutes ago. Jacques clapped him on the shoulder and said, "Your first one is on us! Happy birthday!" He escorted the two of them to a nearby table; although the unwritten dress code in that establishment frowns upon the excessively casual they do make exceptions, especially after midnight and for first-time customers.

Now the situation was getting serious.

It was "amateur night" at the Executive Center; girls who had been plied with excessive amounts of alcohol by their so-called boyfriends were being encouraged to undress and take their place up with the dancers. I had been scoping out the nearby levels, of course; it was much more intriguing than what was taking place up on the stage. The Warriors had been doing the same; so far none of us had identified any kind of a connection or linkage with certainty. There were several of the enemy spirits with attention fixed upon me and Michael, but no big names which I recognized from our intelligence. Still, although I maintained my poise and nonchalant attitude, I looked in their direction and slipped them a bit of a wink. They responded with chortles.

I should have known better than to attempt any kind of communication with a very perplexed Messenger watching me like a hawk.

*　*　*

AMY WAS FEELING TORN SIX ways from Sunday...and it was still only very early Saturday morning. When it had appeared that Michael was missing and presumed injured—she would have known if he was dead; the Homecoming of a saint is Big News—she was filled with the concern of any close friend and did what she could to help; she in fact was the one who had reminded Rick about the little-used landline telephone number. As earlier recounted, when she first saw Dawn in the human world she was wholly taken with her and did her best to push Dawn and her boy together. Then, in the hospital, when Rick was miraculously healed as Dawn knelt by his bedside fervently praying, she was convinced that Dawn was a saint the likes of those that most of you only read about. She had been stunned beyond measure to see her here at the club, and then to hear from Mike that she had been the instigator of the evening. What did this mean? What could this mean?

And then I winked.

While Amy can be, as she herself cheerfully admits, a bit of a scatterwit, she is by no means stupid. It was a communication, and she recognized it as such instantly. "She's a demon!" Amy cried. Her compatriots confined in the "viewing gallery" just looked at her and shrugged. But Amy wasn't done, not by a long shot. She reached out for me and Dawn. "Ariel! Dawn! This Dawn is a demon!"

I still maintained a connection with Heaven; although perhaps ninety-nine percent of my being was on this side of the Border there was still a vestige of me around the Throne. I was correspondingly more difficult to reach, but a Messenger of Amy's experience was up to the task. But in trying to contact Dawn she encountered that same black hole into nothingness which I had found three mornings ago. There were a few milliseconds of confusion, and then Amy put two and two together and came up with twenty-two. Her eyes narrowed.

Actually she was much closer to the mark than that, of course. I had enough of a connection with her to get an echo of the Message she was composing: *Dawn—our Dawn!—got into the human world, she was captured, and a demon has taken her place!* For an instant I was inclined to just let her hit 'Send'. It was amusing to think of what might happen if the several million Guardians in the region all got that message in the same instant—and Amy had the skill to do so. There would be a search… calls for assistance…Nathan and his key aides would be 'pinged' with no response…surrounding regions would intervene…there would be a titanic struggle…and whatever remained of poor Dawn would be shuffled so deeply into the infernal regions that we might never find her until The Last Japanese Soldier finally surrendered.

I made a split-second decision. Please don't get me wrong; there is definitely a place and a time for subtlety, for shrewdness, for working undercover, for playing a role. At the same time, though, forthright honesty always—*always*—has our Lord's blessing. It is never a bad choice to tell the whole truth. So in a tenth of a second or so I shot Amy, in extremely condensed form, the essentials of what I have spent the last two hundred or so pages telling you. Her eyes went wide and her mouth formed an 'O'. I finished it off with, *Don't spook them!* She indicated assent—but, as a Counselor, one of my own skills is looking much deeper into the hearts and minds of others than most can achieve. And, in Amy's heart of hearts, I could tell she was thinking, *Surely I can tell my friends Hazel and Arianna and….*

I broke off the connection. Now the clock was definitely ticking. I still didn't have a linkage down with certainty but seeing the layout of the facility I could make an educated guess. I yawned and stretched indolently, stroking Michael under the ear in the process, and purred, "I need to visit the little angels' room!"

"It's behind the stage," Rick told me. "Just go through that…."

"I'll find it," I assured him. I stood up and walked away.

Rick watched me leave for a second, and then chuckled. "She's going the wrong way!" he said to Mike.

Chapter Thirty-Two

BREAKTHROUGH, PART IV

THERE WAS A PASSAGE ON either side of the stage. To stage left, or to the right from the audience's perspective, was a corridor which led to the public restrooms, cloak room, and business center. On the other side, to stage right, was another corridor. This one led past the bar to the kitchen and storeroom, the liquor vault, the dressing rooms, and the management office. I entered it.

My guess proved correct. As I approached the enemy's nerve center, through the mists and the various layers I espied a figure which could only be Dravang. He had been watching me like a hawk, of course; it is much much easier to see through the layers into the earthly realm than back out the other way. "Greetings, my prince!" I said with a sly smile and a slight tip of the head.

He seemed surprised but pleased. "You've never once called me that!" he said. "So you managed to get him in here already? Things are going well!"

"I told him he needed to broaden his mind and relax his inhibitions!" I said, widening my smile.

"I must warn you again not to relax them too much," he replied. "It would open a can of worms. We can't risk an Enemy response, not just yet."

Good news. If Dravang was being cautious, it must mean that his superiors were likely not on board at the moment. There would be no general reinforcements. I had to strike while the iron was hot. "Still," I mused aloud, "It would be such a help if I were only able to pump her directly!"

"Not very likely," Dravang sighed. "And there's not that much of her left to connect to. My specialists worked her over very thoroughly. She resisted all the way."

I winced internally at the thought of what this meant for my best friend. But I kept my outward demeanor calm. "Still and all," I said, "can you imagine how you-know-who might respond if she were only able to see her boy here tonight?"

"Oh, that would be rich!" Then he smiled. "And, can you imagine if we only had you up there on stage? That really could break her completely!"

I stifled a sharp inhale, remembering what I knew of Dragora from her reputation and my limited contact with her earlier that evening. I gave a catlike smile and purred, "Oh, wouldn't it though? Let's do it!"

"Yes. Yes! Helspeth?" he called to his newly minted flunky.

"Yes, my prince?" responded a nearby spirit who wasn't in our dossiers. I would have to remember this for Nathan's files.

"Fetch our prisoner. Is she conscious?"

"Not hardly, my prince," said Helspeth.

"Give her a little 'jolt'," Dravang ordered. "Just enough to bring her around. Nothing you can't control. Be very careful!"

"I understand, my prince." Then he slipped away to a level which I could not see...but I could discern the general direction in which he left.

"Go. Get ready!" Dravang ordered me.

"Oh, right away!" *I'm going to Hell, I'm going to Hell.* No, I didn't really believe that. But, if I were, at least it was for a good cause.

*   *   *

I stepped to the door of the dressing room and gave Dawn's name to a bored dancer who was registering the 'amateur night' participants. Then I went inside and shed my clothing. Yes, all of it; in such a situation once you are in for a penny you may as well be in for a pound. I regarded myself in the full-length mirror.

Dawn's human body has no tan lines whatsoever; it's an agreeable fringe benefit of having your own internal lighting source. Nor does my own, although I hold to the opinion that a light dusting of freckles adds a touch of character. Don't you agree? There was rather a bit more up front than I was accustomed to, but this was hardly the time or the place to do something about that. I decided to let matters stand as they were; who knows, perhaps in time they would grow on me.

Wait, that's entirely the wrong thing for a shapeshifter to say.

I stepped over to let the makeup artist give me the once-over. She looked me up and down, and finally opined that I really didn't need much except to touch up a few highlights and spray on a light coat of glitter. I smiled sweetly and was about to tell her to stuff it; if I really want to put on a show I have access to a toolkit of special effects which would make the wizards at Digital Domain and Industrial Light & Magic go green with envy. Just as I was about to open my mouth, however, a much-loved voice in my head suggested that it might be best to keep everything on a purely natural level for the moment. I almost cried with relief; this was the first real sign I'd had that my decidedly daft decisions could just possibly have my Master's blessing. So I held still and allowed the makeup artist to give me the works.

I headed for the open maw of the stage door. I eschewed the furs and the wraps and such which hung nearby as props; using such actually inflames prurient interest by calling extra attention to the bits which you cover up. There was the niggling thought that inflaming prurient interest might be exactly what Dragora would choose to do, but I pushed past it. From this point on, I couldn't let my actions be guided by the thoughts of what Dragora might do. Nor even that of what Dawn would do, in the inconceivable event that she were to find herself in this situation. From here on, I had to be myself.

*　*　*

In a locked and barred crypt there lay a mangled figure which vaguely resembled roadkilled bird. It was

Dawn. Helspeth unlocked the barrier and "Wilbur" and "Orville" roughly dragged the remains out, plunging their claws into her ruined shoulders. Helspeth reached out to touch her neck and gave an infusion of energy. It was more difficult to penetrate through to her soul than even he had realized; the echo was so deep that it was almost lost.

Almost, but not quite. Her desperately wounded body struggled to heal itself as her mind crept towards consciousness. "More…," she pleaded.

"Not a chance!" Helspeth answered roughly. "That's all you get! Now, wake up! You're coming with us!"

* * *

"Music?" the disc jockey asked me as I passed his booth.

I was stumped; I hadn't even considered the question. My mind raced to come up with a suitable number. "Ode to Joy" was unlikely to be in his playlist, and even if it were my own colleagues might consider it to be in poor taste. "'Theme from *Titanic*,'" I finally said. "Instrumental."

He raised an eyebrow; an unusual request. He scanned his playlists, then flipped through his book of CDs. "Got it," he finally said. "You're on in…one minute!"

* * *

"Where did she go?" Mike asked, looking around puzzled.

"I dunno, maybe she took the long way around!" Rick answered. Then, as the music changed to the

"Amateur Night Intro" he said, "Hey, look, another new face!"

The announcer spoke over the sound system, "The Executive Center proudly presents: Dawn!"

This instantly drew the attention of the both of them. The movie theme rose and swelled as I stepped out into the light. "Holy…!" said Rick as his jaw hung open.

"Yeah."

*　　*　　*

ONCE AGAIN, I HAD DECIDED to be myself. While I couldn't help but play into the enemy's plans for the evening by being where I was as I was, I wanted to mitigate my impact upon the audience as much as possible given the circumstances. I was less concerned about my impact upon Michael. He had already seen Dawn emotionally and spiritually naked, there in that airless valley of Taurus-Littrow; from that point physical nudity was an almost trivial step.

So I avoided the customary dance moves designed to inflame lust, although I was ready enough to express my femininity and the beauty of Dawn's body. It's true that 'male' and 'female' are physical concepts, but masculinity and femininity run clear down into the core of the personality…and I am very much a girl. Yes, I could put on a male body if I absolutely had to for some good and sufficient reason, and it would work, but it just wouldn't, well, *fit* right, if that makes any sense at all. So while I was careful to avoid communicating, "I want you" or even, "I'm available," I was willing to use the techniques my good friend Ginger shared with me to say in a kind of graceful solo ballet, "I am beautiful, I know it…and you may look at me." And, in return—

well, as I said to Michael earlier, we girls do enjoy being admired!

Speaking of communication…

What are you doing? Amy pleaded in my head. This was an opportunity that I had secretly hoped for. I did not trust that I had enough skill to communicate what I had learned from Dravang and Helspeth to Nathan and his squad without tipping the enemy off, but Amy did. I shot the information to her, asking her to relay it to all of the Warrior angels in the audience. All twenty-eight of them. They focused their attention upon that sector towards which Helspeth had departed, from the most experienced all the way down to the rawest recruit. Still nothing on the horizon….

*   *   *

HELSPETH AND THE OTHERS ARRIVED in Dravang's inner sanctum with Dawn firmly in tow. The new prince gloated over her. "Well, hello! Welcome to my headquarters. Look around! I do so enjoy beautiful surroundings. Oh, look! There's a friend here to see you!"

Helspeth had given enough energy to restore Dawn's eyesight. She looked around and began to take in her surroundings, and her eyes flared wide as she saw Mike watching—herself. She gave an agonized cry and burst into tears. "No! No! Oh, God, no!"

The surrounding demons burst into taunting laughter. Dravang wasn't finished needling her, of course. "Just think, your little pet human here at home with us. Of course, you should have known that he'd prefer our version of you. What's the saying? 'Good girls go to Heaven—bad girls go *everywhere!*'"

He began laughing triumphantly. He would have been better advised to concentrate on Dawn's face. There was that set look which those of us who know her well have learned to respect—and others who are wise have learned to fear. Inside she was pleading, *God, give me strength!*

*   *   *

THE WARRIORS HAD NOTED THE congregation of demons in the direction of Dravang's lair. They scanned through the mists and the blind alleys amongst the forest of connections, hoping against hope to positively identify their quarry. Success depended upon acting quietly and furtively, without attracting undue attention. If they could only single out Dawn's core personality they could establish a connection to her and, by extension, back to the Throne. Then it would be possible to send in a well-armed penetration team to track her down and finish the task.

Best-laid plans…

Young Timothy—very well, he was as "old" as the rest of us, but he was brand-new on Earth duty—was eager to make a mark. Possibly too eager. He had never actually met Dawn before, but he had studied her file assiduously over this last week. What were those techniques he had studied in training, about sorting through commonly used enemy obfuscations?

*   *   *

THE LAUGHTER WAS REALLY GROWING riotous. Dravang continued on, "He's working so hard for us. And to think, we're just getting started!"

*   *   *

Breakthrough, Part IV

THAT'S HER! TIMOTHY REALIZED.

He reached out to establish a connection. The pain, the anguish, the heartache almost overwhelmed him. Through the midst of it all he heard the clear echo of a prayer, *God, give me strength!*

Without stopping to think Timothy answered that prayer as best he knew how. Through that connection he flooded her soul with all of the energy he could spare— and then some. As he did, he remembered that he had to get the word out. "I see her! I see her!" he cried.

Out loud. At full voice. Up on stage, I heard him. *Uh-oh!*

Nathan heard him. *Oh, no!*

The surrounding humans heard him. *Huh?*

Philip heard him and looked as if he wanted to crawl inside a hole.

Finally, the demons heard him. *What's that?*

They looked around for the source of the disruption. But it took their attention off of Dawn for an instant. Long enough. With an enraged cry, she tore herself away from her captors.

"NOOOOOOOOOOOOOOOOOOO!!!!!!!!!!!!!!!!!"

Samson in the Temple, may I introduce Dawn in the Nightclub?

* * *

AT THE VERY LEAST WE had the advantage of the element of surprise. Not that much of an advantage, however, because we were surprised ourselves. Still, Nathan and his team reacted a split instant before the enemy. *"Cross-rip! NOW!"* Nathan cried out.

This is a technique which is used in spiritual combat where you tear through a number of layers and collapse them together as one, but Nathan had never before used it upon Earth. Matter of fact, I don't know of anyone who ever has. He had no idea if it would even work on this level.

It did.

As when Samson of old collapsed the pillars in the temple of Dagon, Nathan and his team reached out and collapsed all of the layers between us here in the Earth-plane and that where Dawn was lashing out in fury. Dravang and his forces were so intent upon restraining and subduing her that they didn't even notice, for a few seconds.

But the humans certainly did, as the dozens of layers tore away and their shredded remnants manifested as a coruscating display of colors, while spiritual beings representing both the finest of heaven and the worst of hell now visibly filled the cavernous high ceiling. At first some of the patrons thought that it was some spectacular new special effect and applauded. But the waitresses and the dancers waiting in the wings knew better; they screamed and, heedless of their *déshabillé*, many of them ran for the exits.

Only to find them blocked. The cross-rip had succeeded in sealing off the perimeter of the space on all levels. No one inside could get out and, more importantly, no one outside could get in. It was a cage match, now. Best to keep it that way! I reached out again to Amy. *Get the word out! Get the word out, now!*

By this time the enemy was reacting; forces from outside were attempting to penetrate Nathan's perimeter. At the same time, though, angels from all over the region—and even from surrounding regions—were flooding in to reinforce the barrier and keep it tight. With some satisfaction I realized that it would be a fair fight.

Then my face fell and I realized that, within the "cage", our forces were outnumbered by some fifteen to one.

* * *

NATHAN RECOGNIZED THAT EVEN BEFORE I did. With a sigh, he vowed that his team would sell themselves dearly. He called them into formations and began to execute maneuvers intended to keep them together while dividing the enemy and inflicting maximum damage.

Nobody was watching the stage any longer. With good reason; the cross-rip had wrought physical as well as spiritual damage. Several walls had collapsed and the downstage right section was tilted at a crazy angle. There was no reason why I had to remain as a distraction any longer. I shifted into my proper body, fully dressed in combat gear, and prepared to strike whatever kind of blow I could for the right side. I may not be a Warrior, but I would hate to waste Dawn's coaching.

* * *

THE TWO POLICE OFFICERS IN the front row of the audience—actually, there were three more at a table in the back corner—reacted as well. Rick's eyes popped and he reached for his holdout gun…and then he remembered. While Rick may play fast and loose with department policy when it comes to accepting gratuities from companies who have made it abundantly clear that they wish to offer them, he goes by the book in all other respects. Well, most other respects. Some other respects? In any event, having planned an evening of inebriating he had left his Corvette in the garage and his sidearm in the gun safe. He felt naked.

Michael, not so much. While his company policy likewise prohibits the possession of a weapon while consuming alcohol off duty, he like me had used his Genuine Draft as a prop and had only taken the barest sip of it. Besides, he had gone into this expecting trouble and, as at the roundhouse, was fully prepared to face the music and look for a new career if things went south. And so he was armed with his Colt Defender 1911 ACP, little brother to his great-grandfather's M1911A1. Shorter barrel and one less round per magazine, but it was easy to conceal—it was in fact the same weapon he had carried that day he and Dawn went to the beach. And it would accommodate the full-size 1911 magazines in a pinch, if you didn't mind them sticking out the bottom of the receiver by an inch or so—Mike had two of them in a leg pocket of his cargo pants. He pulled the pistol from his concealed waistband holster and stood there a second, wondering what to do.

The enemy demons, however, were showing a decided lack of military discipline. Many of them were reveling in this opportunity to terrorize humans face to face. Screams and shrieks filled the floor of the nightclub. One saw Michael standing there, pistol in hand, and flew up to him, pointing and laughing at the useless weapon. But, as Mike stood there wondering what to do, Nathan came up behind the demon and cleaved him nearly in two with a blow from his sword.

"What do I do?" Michael cried.

"Get them back!" Nathan answered. "Back, in the corner!" indicating an area near the main entrance which had received less damage than most of the room. "Where we can cover them!"

"Gotcha!" Mike said. Nathan turned away. Mike called out to the civilians surrounding him, "Police officer! Get back! Back in the corner! Stick together! Move it!"

Rick, who was sobering up much quicker than planned, also took up the call. "Houston Police!" he called, flashing his badge. "Move back! Move back!"

The three other officers in the back corner, not having any clue of what else to do, followed their lead. In fairly short order the human civilians were all back in the far corner, with Mike and the four Houston Police officers standing guard at their leading edge. One of the three other officers had also neglected to fully comply with department policy and had his weapon at hand; neither Mike nor Rick were inclined to report him.

Doing my best—and a little bit more—to fight for our side, I looked around the scene. We were far more disciplined and unified, but we were still hopelessly outnumbered. I had by now lost sight of Dawn; I could only hope that the perimeter of the cage was holding. I landed next to Michael, sword in hand. "See you on the other side," I muttered to him as I advanced upon the enemy with Nathan's forces at my side. *Alamo it is…*

But there was one factor which I, not being of a military background, had overlooked. Nathan had not, but being a wise general he had not relied upon it. But it made the difference. *Esprit de corps*—fighting spirit. Dravang's forces were a hodgepodge of conscripts, mercenaries, blackmailed rivals, and the few who weren't were only looking for personal advantage, à la Helspeth. Nathan's team, on the other hand, would have followed him directly into the gates of Hell; had he in fact ordered them to assault the Lake of Fire itself their only noticeable hesitation would have been for to pick up a few packages of wieners and marshmallows. As the enemy forces saw that they were cut off, without escape—and, moreover, that there was nothing which their putative leader could do about that—they surrendered in droves. It was when I saw "Orville" and "Wilbur" raising their hands in surrender that I began to believe that we had a chance.

More than a chance, as it turned out. Nathan was able to open a hole in his cross-rip and funnel the captives out to our forces waiting on the other side. Now the tide of battle had clearly turned, and as the enemy realized that they abandoned their malevolent pipsqueak "prince" right and left. Our phalanx converged upon the offices and storerooms....

The last to surrender—actually, to be dragged away kicking and screaming—was Dravang himself.

Chapter Thirty-Three

Parting...For Now

Philip appeared at Michael's side. "We found her," he muttered to Mike privately. He placed a hand around Mike's shoulder and teleported him to…

…the still-intact wine cellar and liquor vault. The other angels, those who had not accompanied the prisoners to their new extended-stay homes, were all clustered around the sommelier's table, where lay a broken figure which vaguely resembled Dawn. Some of them, those with advanced Healer training, were reaching out to her, attempting to restore her shattered body and psyche. Her eyelids fluttered and she was mumbling disjointed, incomprehensible sentences.

Mike saw her and pushed his way through the crowd, kneeling by her side. "Dawn? Dawn!"

Suddenly her eyes opened and focused. She spoke weakly, but clearly. "Michael?"

Her eyes met his and the expression on her face implied that there was nothing in the world which she would have rather seen at that moment. But then she slowly became aware of the ruined condition of her mutilated body. "No!" she cried. "Not like this. Not… like…THIS…!"

She closed her eyes, clenched her fists, and began to writhe in agonizing struggle, willing her body to heal itself. The Healers nearby supported her as best they could but they knew that she was attempting too much, too fast.

I took her hand, vainly trying to calm her down. "Dawn! No!" I said. "Don't do this! You haven't the strength!"

She was trying to shift back into her normal, glorified body. But there was no easy and confident surge of power this time. Waves of black and white washed over her figure, and it appeared that she was in danger of fading out completely.

"Dawn! Stop it!" I cried. "Dawn!"

Her shifting completed, the waves of black slowly faded away. She lay there, ghost-white pale and still, but whole. You could have heard a pin drop. Her eyes weakly fluttered open and she mumbled in a slurred voice, "M'alright."

I was still holding her hand. She used it to pull herself up into a sitting position. "Dawn…" I said with hesitation.

"M'alright."

She willed herself to stand up, took an experimental step—then faded. Losing her balance, she began to fall.

Mike caught her left arm, I caught her right. I began to scold, more out of relief than anything else.

"You are *not* all right, you're as weak as a newborn kitten! We have to get you Home, let you rest, recharge…"

"I'm all right," she said, a little more clearly if still unconvincingly.

Mike found his voice. "Dawn…I'm sorry!"

She turned an expression of pure love upon him. Gently she reached her free hand up to stroke his cheek. "S'not your fault! Don't blame yourself!"

"Yes, but… You didn't have to stay… I mean, I could have… Oh, you never had to be here in the first place! If I had just…"

She gently placed her hand on his lips, silencing him. She looked him in the eye and quietly spoke from the very depths of her soul. "It was worth it."

I finally broke the ensuing silence. "Yes. Well, it may have been worth it, but we still have to get you back Home. It's not safe to wait around here any longer. And, after an experience like that, I know you're going to need therapy…"

She held up a hand, motioning me to stop. "Just… fifteen minutes."

I turned away, shaking my head. *Why do I even try?*

One of Nathan's troops spoke up. "Boss? We haven't got fifteen minutes. We can't hold them out much longer, not much longer at all!"

Dawn turned back to Mike. "She's right, you know," indicating me. "I do have to get back. But I don't want you to worry about me. I'll be right back on the job before you know it!"

"Will I ever see you again?" Mike asked.

Dawn snorted as if insulted. "Of course!"

Mike hastily remembered. "I mean, before…?"

"Probably not," Dawn sighed. "But you never know!"

She smiled and reached out to touch his cheek one more time, then started to step away towards me. I nodded to Nathan and he opened a large portal into a realm of unimaginable brightness. My compatriots began to leave through it.

Mike was struggling with himself, wanting to say something. Almost without realizing it, he followed Dawn towards the portal. Just before she stepped into it, he spoke. "Dawn?"

She stopped and turned back towards him. I rolled my eyes; I said nothing but I thought, *Any day now…*

"Yes?" Dawn asked.

"I, uh, hope this isn't the wrong thing to say," Mike said. "But I just wanted to tell you, of all the people I've ever met—even without the, uh, you know, the angel thing—I still can't think of anyone I'd rather spend the rest of forever with!"

Do I really have to spell out the next few minutes? Eventually, despite myself, I smiled and leaned over. "Chief, don't forget—*he* has to breathe!"

Dawn eased off, a little, and uncurled the wing she had wrapped around him from head to foot. They looked into each other's eyes from a distance of perhaps

316

two inches. "Someday," she said, "we'll never have to let go."

She released him and slowly began to move away. "Goodbye," he called.

She turned her head to reply as she stepped into the portal along with Nathan and myself. A hint of the old fire re-entered her eyes. "See you later!"

With an ache in his heart, Michael watched the portal close behind her. He closed his eyes for a moment, remembering, and sighed. Then he opened his eyes again.

"Hey… how do I get out of here?"

Guardian Angel

Chapter Thirty-Four

EPILOGUE

"So how in the hell did you ever manage to get locked in the liquor vault without a key?" the responding officer asked incredulously.

"Long story," Mike sighed. "Long story. At least I had my cell phone!"

"I'm not sure whether I'd believe it or not," the other said. "Looks like you're just about the last of the missing. Come talk to the captain; he's trying to put together a report."

*　*　*

The fire department had two trucks out in front of the ruined structure, although there was no fire. There were a half-dozen ambulances; several of the patrons had been injured both by falling debris and by malevolent demons. The paramedics treating them and the officers collecting evidence weren't sure whether to believe them or to believe that everyone inside had been on drugs.

When interviewed by the police, Mike clammed up. Oh, he spoke freely about what he had seen inside the auditorium; there had been numerous witnesses. But what came before and what happened after never passed his lips. Knowing no better, they soon let him go.

Rick finished his grilling at almost exactly the same time. He intercepted Mike. "Mike?" he asked. "How are you, buddy? Where's Dawn? I asked them to look for her; they found a set of women's clothes in the dressing room, but no purse, no ID. What happened to her?"

"Last I saw her she was being taken away for treatment. I don't know anything more than that. Come on, let me give you a ride home."

*   *   *

THE INCIDENT IN THE EXECUTIVE Center headlined the news on the telly and the front page of the local birdcage liner the next morning. It was even briefly discussed on the national television news that evening. By then, of course, the enemy had found some would-be "expert" who propounded the bollocks theory that a gas explosion had ignited a stash of hallucinogenic drugs, resulting in the illusion of supernatural beings in conflict. Those who were inclined to believe materialistic explanations first, last and always, no matter how unlikely, did so of course, but practically nobody else did.

News reporters eagerly tore into the lives of the patrons and employees who had been in the club that night; most had their requisite fifteen minutes of fame. Rick, especially; the dancers had fingered him as a regular and by the time that the reporters had a field day about a police lieutenant hanging out in a strip joint Rick had some serious 'splainin to do to Internal Affairs. He ended up retaining his position—Amy was able to help him that much—but he knew full well that his next several annual reviews would be conducted under a microscope.

But one man who never was identified as a patron or visitor was Michael. Oh, he could have had nationwide publicity on network television, had he chosen to share what he knew—but he just faded off into the woodwork. No one in that club had ever seen him there before, nor would anyone ever see him in such an establishment again. Rick knew who he was, of course, but Mike begged him to keep the matter quiet. K. P. & G. would never understand, he had said. And Rick, busy with his own problems, was able to empathize and never said a word. He really is a true friend.

Back Home, our senior commanders were thinking long and hard about the problem of what to do with the ticking time bomb of several hundred enemy spirits now held in our midst, some of whom still had a most uncooperative and reluctant attitude. Yes, Dravang, I'm talking about you. But in the meantime Dawn began her therapy and recovery as Mike resumed his patrols on the night shift. I kept good watch on the both of them; between the two of us Dawn never missed a single day of her nightly missives. That wistful look never left Dawn's face; for his part Michael prayed about her and for her daily. But he never said a word about her to another human soul; giving only a quizzical shrug when Rick asked about her whereabouts and well-being. It did strain their friendship a bit; Rick thought that Mike had judged him as unworthy of her and was protecting her from any further contact. Well, yes, he was protecting her—protecting her human alias, against the remote chance that someday she might be able to use it again.

But more on that later.

ᴀCKNOWLEDGMENTS

For her most helpful critique and review of the manuscript, my editor Imogen Howson, author of the *Linked* series of young adult fiction.

For suggestions to improve realism in the portrayal of police work, the members of the "Officer.com" forums, notably "Rick Shaw," "CCCSD," "Retired1995," "Kraut0783" and "Ratatatat."

A special thanks to my Down Under correspondent Ray W. for his helpful comments on an earlier version of the manuscript. G'day, mate!

The Spencer Ogden company, for bringing me on as a temporary employee at the Atlantic Coffee Solutions (former "Maywell House"...thank you, lawyers!) plant during its last two months of operation as a producing coffee facility...barring divine intervention, of course!

Mr. George Harris, professional civil engineer specializing in high-speed rail, for the curves of locomotive acceleration and braking provided to assist in fleshing out Chapter 15.

Frankie Valli and the Four Seasons, for performing the song which came on the radio at exactly the perfect time when I was struggling with the question of a suitable name for my angelic protagonist...and to the

Walt Disney Company for the name of her redheaded assistant.

To all of the employees of power plants, railroad yards, skyscrapers, drawbridges, freighter ships, locomotive terminals, airport control towers and more who turned blind eyes to a certain curious youth who wandered in and through their facilities going places where he really never should have gone. I readily admit that it's not believable that two kids could walk through a facility like the old, ahem, "Maywell House" coffee plant during the heyday of "access control" in the mid-2000s as I've postulated here...but twenty to thirty years or so previously, one could get away with quite a lot.

Finally, I have to acknowledge one lady with whom I've never conversed...well, not while I was awake; not knowingly, at least. But when I was seven years old, I had a very vivid dream of three young women. "We'll always be together," they said. I had flashes of them here and there for several years, but nothing definite...until I was twenty-five years old and out of the Navy. I had an unsettling dream, almost a nightmare, actually, until I recognized a personality inside it with me, protecting me. Right or wrong, I identified her with one of the girls from eighteen years earlier. "What's your name?" I asked. "What do I call you?" She didn't answer at first; it almost seemed as if she was asking for permission. But finally she looked at me, and answered… and then I woke up. So I would like to end this story by saying, "Thanks, Delle, for all the help!"

A Preview of Coming Attractions

Have you ever suddenly been awakened right when you didn't want to be? *And that was such a good dream, too.*

"...one of our famous ten-dollar ribeyes! Friday nights are amateur night at the Executive Center; bring your girlfriends and let them show their stuff! Ladies always drink free on Fridays! So come on down to the Executive Center, Houston's premier entertainment destination for gentlemen...and ladies!"

What? Did that place open back up? I hadn't even known it was being rebuilt! Mike muttered to himself. He stretched, and yawned, and reached for the snooze button. It was eight o'clock; already dark outside. He generally set the alarm two hours before his scheduled time to clock in. Plenty of time for a few more Zzzs...but then the next commercial came on.

"This weekend in concert at RodeoHouston! Featuring...."

Mike shot bolt upright. The Rodeo was held every March...he had taken Dawn there six months ago! What was going on here? He looked at his bedroom door, hoping against hope to see light pouring through underneath it...no. But wait! The room was neat and tidy again! During the last six months, despite his sincere resolution to maintain it as Dawn had left it, his slovenly bachelor habits had reasserted themselves and the room had come to resemble nothing so much as the set of *Sanford and Son*. He jumped out of bed and sprang for the door. As he placed his hand on the doorknob I called out from the next room, "Put some clothes on, Michael! You'll feel much more comfortable!"

Ariel?!?!

Still...if I was here, could Dawn be far away? It was true; he would be more comfortable in something more decent than the underwear which was the only thing now covering his nakedness. But it would take too long and be too much trouble to put on his uniform. And there was a chill in the air, as well. In Houston? In September? It had been ninety degrees when he had gone to sleep that afternoon! He opened the closet door. His sweats were right there at hand.

Seconds later, with some hesitation, he pulled on the door. There we were...a saucy redhead and the spunky blonde he had missed so much. Both of us were in a normal, even ordinary human appearance. The blonde spoke. "Hello, Michael."

"Dawn! You look beautiful!"

To an outside observer he was being kind. When he had last seen her, Dawn's body had redefined 'beauty' in every regard...even when she wasn't in glorified form. She could have caused multiple traffic accidents simply by crossing the street. Now she was...well, still good-looking, but much more ordinary. She wouldn't attract more than a second glance if walking through a crowded airport or shopping mall. Even so, there is a beauty beyond the senses and it shone from her face in a way which was palpable to Mike. He loved her for whom she was...not simply for what she was. "I thought I might never see you again!"

"Hey! I told you I would be back for you! I just didn't expect it to be this soon!"

He drew up sharply. "Wait...you mean it's my time?"

"Not exactly," I interrupted. "Allow me to explain."

"Please do. What's going on here? What's with the weather, and those commercials on the radio?"

"Easy enough. It's often cool in these parts in March."

"But it's September!"

"It *was* September. At least for you. Now it's March. Again. Attend me. After that little altercation in the topless club which made the national news, the enemy attempted to damp it down and hush it up. They failed."

"Yeah, I know. It's been in the headlines almost every week since. Rick has been on TV at least a half-dozen times. He's got another interview...uh-oh!"

"Go on."

"I told him about you! Well, about her," he said, indicating Dawn. "I tried to keep quiet about it, but he did too much research! He even got my phone records! He knew there was no way she could be my cousin... my aunt and uncle in Montana both died childless! I couldn't...you didn't want me to lie to my best friend, did you?"

"No, we didn't want you to lie," I reassured him. "Although sometimes it is best for all concerned for one to play a role. You did the right thing by keeping a low profile...but the truth will out. Eventually."

"So how come it's *March*? Did that happen because I spilled the beans?"

"Indirectly, yes. When Rick went on that TV interview, a police lieutenant armed with his research and what you had told him and the news reports from the last six months, not to mention his medical records, he was able to make a convincing case that there is a God and that there are angels active in this world. Convincing enough that people believed him. Including some key non-human people."

"Say what?"

"Mike, you don't know this, but there are a number of the enemy who want out. They want out *badly*. But as long as it appeared that there was no hope they went along with Old Scratch and his lackeys. No other choice. Six months ago we demonstrated that there might yet be another choice. Many of them wanted to take it."

"Still..."

"When the enemy gets desperate, strange things can happen. Very strange things. Including resetting the clock. It doesn't happen very often...the last time I'm aware of was two thousand years ago. But when it does, opportunities open up. For both sides. This is ours."

"So what does that mean to me?"

"Well, for one thing, it means you don't have to go in to work tonight! You're back on your old schedule... three days on, three days off, three days on, five days off. It's Thursday; your five-day weekend is just ending so both you and Dawn have the evening off. You have to be

328

back at work tomorrow night…she has to report to work Monday morning."

"What?" He turned to Dawn, who had been uncharacteristically quiet. "You're working? Where?"

"Room 615!" she answered.

"Room 615…wait! That's my office!"

"Well, the one we share. I'm your new investigator!"

"What? The boss tells me we've been trying to get a full-time investigator in our office for seven years!"

"Looks like your prayers have been answered."

"Yes, but…how?"

"When the clock gets reset, a lot of threads can change," I said. "Here's her portfolio. Birth certificate, high school diploma, Associate's degree in criminal justice from Flathead Valley Community College, Bachelor's degree from Montana State, Montana Law Enforcement Academy certificate of completion, service letters from five years on the force in Billings…we were most thorough."

"So we'll be working together? I don't believe this!"

"I know," Dawn said. "It seems almost too good to be true!"

"Almost," I cautioned. "There are a few Easter Eggs which we had to swallow in order to get the enemy to buy into this timeline. The first one is…well, she does not have the same level of power you knew before. Not even close. As a matter of fact, she's as weak as that night we got her back from the enemy. She had been in therapy; almost back to her full strength. Now she has to do it all over again...and on this side. She will recover, but it will take much longer here than it would back Home."

"Okay, that's one. What else?"

"Mmm...this gets technical. You need to know that while we angels are not omnipresent, we do have the capability to be multipresent. We normally maintain a link to the Throne at all times. When she was here last, Dawn had gone 'all-in'...she didn't have that link. Which is why you and I and the others had to resort to such daft measures to rescue her. Now she does...and that's a good thing. A very good thing. But in order to conceal it in a way that the enemy could not uncover, we had to tether it to run through this physical location. This property you personally own, where our breakthrough was made in the original timeline. Don't get me wrong; as long as this remains your home and base of operations the both of you can travel anywhere in this world you like. But neither of you can move away from this property permanently, or her link will be broken."

"You mean she's living *here*? With me?!"

"Yes, in your garage apartment."

"But I don't have a garage apartment!"

"Yes, you do. It's been here since the house was built a century ago. It was just all full of rubbish when you bought the place five years back and you never used it."

"What? I would know if my own house had a garage apartment!"

"Look and see."

With a gesture, I telekinetically drew the blinds for a moment. There, behind his garage, was an addition perhaps twenty-five feet by twelve feet. The lights were on in the windows. Mike was stunned. "How?"

"You and Dawn spent the last four days cleaning out the crap and getting the place livable. Had to buy new appliances, too. Do you realize how hard it is to find a twenty-one inch gas range in good used condition on short notice?"

"Don't worry," Dawn interjected. "I'll pay rent!"

"Well, at least it's fair to share utilities," I said. "Go easy on her, please; in order to get the enemy to accept her cover story we had to saddle her with forty thousand in student loans. Plus a very well-used credit card. Now, listen. I'm running short of time. Right now we've got you in stasis, in a parallel timeline, but it's only good for one hour. By nine o'clock I have to be out of here and well away. I may be able to see the two of you again in person...but not here. It's too risky. These are the basics you need to know. Much is different from the way you remember it. For starters, there's an entirely different administration in the White House. The last elections went the other way. But that's trivial. Here are the events which matter to you: That cocaine bust? It never happened. The old coffee plant is *gone*; it was torn down two years ago and the first block of condos on its site is now on the market. And that means that Rick was never shot, and so was never miraculously healed...he doesn't remember a thing. In fact, nobody in this world remembers a thing. Except Dawn...and you, and I, and Nathan and the other angels who were here in this your home that night we all broke through. We remember the details. Nobody else does."

"What about that...you know, that fake angel?"

"Dragora? Yes, she remembers something. But if you'll recall we hustled her out of here to a holding cell in territory we control not five minutes after we broke through. All of those tens of thousands of variations of events, stretching back a full century and more, which we cycled through before we arrived at a reality which both we and the enemy could accept...they're all jumbled up in her mind. She has no idea of which one is really real. It's those of us who were here for the entire drama who remember it all. But, yes, she is the second biggest threat which you and Dawn will have to deal with."

"Okay, what's the first biggest threat?"

"In a moment. I want to make certain that you understand the gravity of the situation. I told you, the last time there was a reset like this was two thousand years ago. We may never get such a chance again. You must not spill the beans this time. Not to your best friend, not to your mother, not to anyone. I don't want you to lie; we truly hate that...but if you're put under oath, take the Fifth. Or stand mute. If the judge throws you in prison for contempt, you'll be in good company. I tell you the truth: If the enemy knew for certain that Dawn was somewhere in this neighborhood and that she was sleeping here tonight, a nuclear bomb would be dropped on this city before morning."

"Now that's a little over the top. Aren't you kinda, you know, stretching it a bit?"

"The word you're searching for is 'hyperbole'. And the word I'm searching for is 'no.' If you don't believe me, ask the mothers and baby boys of Bethlehem. Or ancient Egypt."

This was sobering, as I intended. I continued. "Finally, the both of you must be on your best behavior. *Must.* You mustn't give the other side a chance to accuse you. Of *anything.*"

"But I thought that they wouldn't know I was here!" Dawn objected.

"No, they don't know...right *now*. But someday they will know. Keep that in mind. I don't know whether it will be a year from now, or five years from now, or five thousand years from now...but, someday, they will know. Someday everything hidden will be brought to light. And that includes the two of you. When that day comes, I guarantee that the enemy will be crawling up both your bums with a proctoscope, looking for any possible excuse to call for a 'do-over'. You must not give them that excuse!"

I paused, making sure that both Mike and Dawn understood me. Then I continued. "Now, for the greatest threat you face." I handed Mike his smart phone.

He stared at it stupidly, and then at me. "What, you want me to call someone?"

"No. I'd prefer that you not have it at all. But it's company-issued. You're required to carry it. And Dawn will be issued one just like it on Monday."

"Okay, so?"

"So? Mike, you really have no clue, do you? This phone is always on. It's always beaming your location. It's always transmitting your conversations. That's all being recorded...by entities which you have absolutely no control over or even knowledge of. Right now the stasis is protecting us; all it hears is you hitting the snooze button over and over again in the next room.

But as soon as I leave, you must consider it 'hot'. And dangerous."

"What is a phone going to do to me?"

"Let's say that Dawn gets her strength back. She teleports to the other side of town. You remember that 'glitch' that Rick asked you about, when your phone's location suddenly changed to a tower two miles away in an instant on that night you were attacked? That was only two miles, and it was to your home location, and it was just a one-time thing so you were able to explain it away successfully. And it has been erased now. But if it ever happens again, and if the enemy ever decides to sort through phone logs to look for such 'glitches', well... do you have any two million sunblock handy?"

"Oh."

"And that's not the half of it. You can't even talk to her about, ahem, confidential matters if you're in the same room as that phone."

"Suppose I change the permissions? Turn off the microphone?"

"Better read the very very fine print in your company's Terms of Service. But even that doesn't mean a thing. When the day comes that you see the officers and directors of a major technology firm marched off to prison for mishandling customer data, then maybe, just maybe, you can suppose that your carrier and the other companies involved will play by the rules. Until then...well, I must say that I'm fresh out of two million sunblock. How about you?"

"In that case, what about...?"

"Your smart speaker? I've already taken care of that. Funny how even a touch of static electricity can utterly fry a very-large-scale integrated circuit. Don't buy another one. I mean that. Oh, and your truck? Both your personal truck and your company Jeep are reporting your location to Chrysler constantly, everywhere you go. And hackers can take control of your antilock brakes by remote control; that's been proved. Bad news if the enemy ever positively identifies the two of you, and much easier to explain away than a nuclear war. Too bad we can't have your grandfather's '69 Charger; his estate sold it off to the producers of *The Dukes of Hazzard*. And your computer, too; it's almost as bad as your phone. But no one will get suspicious if you leave your computer behind for a while. Ditch your phone for more than an hour or so on a regular basis and you establish a pattern which someone could possibly key into. Especially when your company wants you to have it with you night and day."

"So what do we do?" he asked.

"Well, for starters, the electrical in Dawn's apartment was never upgraded. Very few outlets, and they're all ungrounded. Obviously the thing to do is for her to set up her laptop in your spare bedroom. She can charge her phone there, too."

"Oh…."

"If you need to talk, privately, just go over to her place. Leave your phone here. After all, it needs to be charged too, right?" I gave him a wink.

"Gotcha."

"Good. I need to be leaving now. It's a little late for a nice girl to be walking the streets alone in this neighborhood, don't you agree? But if I can make it the few blocks to the Metrorail station I can get clear of here and then disappear without anyone noticing. On either side. Cheerio...and all the best to the both of you." I gave each of them a friendly kiss, then turned for the door. "Good luck, and God bless!"

As soon as the door closed Dawn and Mike looked squarely at each other. They embraced as though neither had seen the other for six months...or six thousand years, for that matter. Both their eyes were wet.

The larger portion of my awareness, safely watching them from behind the scenes, smiled. But my human facet hustled towards the Metrorail station by the old Coffee Plant site. If I caught the 8:55 bus I could transfer downtown and make it to the hotel and get to sleep a full half-hour earlier than if I waited for the train. After all, my flight left at four in the afternoon of the next day, and British Airways would be most upset if I was not suitably chipper and perky at departure time....

* * *

*The Story of Dawn & Mike
Will Continue in:*

UNDERCOVER ANGEL

Coming soon!

See https://www.celestapress.com for latest details!

$\mathcal{A}$BOUT THE $\mathcal{A}$UTHOR

ERIC WASN'T BORN A TEXAN—BUT he got here as quick as he could! A resident of the Houston area since his father Ken took a job as an Apollo program simulation engineer in 1967, Eric is one of the few surviving people to have experienced an actual training run in the Lunar Module simulator. A rail fan since early days, he has traveled by Amtrak extensively and maintains the web site Streamliner Schedules. Still active in the space enthusiast community, Eric has served as the local (Clear Lake Area) chapter president for the National Space Society for more than a decade.

Eric served in the U. S. Navy for six years, three of them aboard the battleship *USS Missouri* (BB-63) including the last circumnavigation (around-the-world cruise) of a battleship in 1986 and duty in the Persian Gulf for Operation Earnest Will in 1987. He also worked as a merchant sailor for two years, and then transitioned to shore-side engineering in commercial and industrial mechanical plants.

Along the way Eric learned to fly aerobatics, soloing in a Super Decathlon, and volunteered for Project 1225 in Michigan. He has been an active member of conservative Southern Baptist and Independent Fundamental Baptist churches for over 50 years and is currently active in Airway Baptist Church Houston. He lives nearby with (currently) three cats and two dogs...and is still Waiting For The Right Girl.